THE INTREPID
MISS HAYDON

Alice Chetwynd Ley

SAPERE
BOOKS

THE INTREPID
MISS HAYDON

Published by Sapere Books.

20 Windermere Drive, Leeds, England, LS17 7UZ,
United Kingdom

saperebooks.com

ISBN: 978-1-80055-145-9

For Ken and Graham,
in memory of an excellent bottle of Saumur wine shared at the Relais
des Pins.

CHAPTER ONE

Mrs Haydon's elegant house in the classical style was situated in the exclusive road known as Mount Ephraim in the Kentish spa of Tunbridge Wells. It was set well back from the broad thoroughfare amid trees, and the windows of its upper rooms looked out over the green common which sloped down to the main part of the town.

On an afternoon in early March 1803, Mrs Haydon was sitting in the drawing room, which was tastefully decorated in green and gold, with her four daughters. They presented a charming picture as they sat with heads dutifully bent over their embroidery, although their tongues worked rather faster than their needles. Lydia, the eldest, a slim young matron of two and twenty not long married to Lieutenant John Beresford of the Royal Navy, had hair of a rich corn colour and clear blue eyes. Her sister Corinna, two years younger, had once been dubbed 'the golden maid' by one of her more poetic admirers, because of her unusual golden eyes, which almost matched her gold-brown curls. Corinna was of a romantic disposition, but this had proved too much for her sense of humour, and she had later shared the joke with her sisters.

Irene and Anthea were still in the schoolroom at sixteen and fourteen respectively, but already they bid fair to be as attractive as their elders. Irene was of the same colouring as Lydia, but Anthea's hair was dark brown and she had not yet lost her puppy fat.

A remark just made by Lydia had caused Corinna to allow her embroidery to fall unheeded into her lap. Needlework never prospered with Corinna. It was not a form of employment which appealed to her volatile temperament; and when, as now, she was persuaded to embark on a piece of work, it was most likely to end in the rag bag.

"A visit to Paris!" she exclaimed in ecstasy, repeating Lydia's words. "Oh, what a famous notion, Lyddy. How I envy you!"

Mrs Haydon did not share her enthusiasm.

"Are you sure that's wise, my dear?" she asked dubiously. "I confess it makes me uneasy to think of your going to France. To be sure, we're no longer at war with the French, but it's only a year since peace was declared, and when one thinks of the dreadful things that occurred there during the Reign of Terror…"

"But all that was ten years since, Mama," replied Lydia, in the reasoning tone one uses to a child. "Law and order is completely restored there now. Indeed, they say Napoleon Bonaparte is an altogether admirable administrator. John is quite set on the scheme, I assure you, for he's a trifle restless after so many months ashore."

"Restless?" Corinna looked shocked. "When you have been married less than a twelve-month? Upon my word, that's prodigiously unromantic, Lyddy — I should have supposed that he would wish for nothing more than to be at your side."

Lydia laughed, but not unkindly.

"My dear sister, even the most devoted couple cannot spend the rest of their lives in gazing into each other's eyes! If one marries an officer in the Royal Navy, one must accept the fact that one's husband will never be entirely content to be ashore for long."

"I don't see why not," persisted Corinna. "His brother seems content enough."

"But Richard, being the elder, has the estate to manage, and that occupies all his energies. I dare say if John is not recalled soon to active service we may perhaps purchase a small estate of our own, later on. But at present he's still hopeful of a recall, and we do very well in the property Richard found for us a few miles from Chyngton Manor. It's high time you all paid us a visit there, Mama. We're not so far from the gaieties of Brighton, and the girls would welcome the change, I know."

This suggestion found instant favour with Irene and Anthea, who at once began persuading their Mama to agree to it.

"Well, we shall see," temporized Mrs Haydon, never one to embark hastily on a project. "But if your sister is to visit France, it cannot be for some time, in any event. I suppose, Lydia, that it will mean an absence of several months? Naturally, since your husband wishes it, I must not try to set you against the scheme. I trust I've inculcated in all my daughters the principles of duty and submission to a husband which every right-thinking female must observe."

Lydia and Corinna exchanged speaking glances at this, while the two younger girls hastily stifled giggles.

"Don't depend upon that, Mama!" laughed Corinna. "I can't speak for the others, of course, but I doubt I'd make a submissive wife!"

Her golden brown eyes sparkled with mischief.

"I sometimes have grave misgivings as to whether I shall ever see you a wife at all!" retorted her Mama tartly. "At the age of twenty, one might surely expect your thoughts to be turning towards matrimony, and goodness knows you don't lack for admirers! But I've yet to see you give any one of them the smallest encouragement!"

Corinna shrugged, but her look was wary. "Oh, they are all such dead bores, Mama."

"You're a deal too fastidious, is all I can say. You should have a care, lest you're quite left on the shelf! But I fancy I know the reason of it," she went on, in a gentler tone, "and I do implore you, my dear child—"

"Pray excuse me, Mama." Corinna rose hastily, casting her needlework aside. "I feel the need of some air — I'll take a turn or two in the shrubbery."

The door closed behind her. Lydia shook her head reprovingly at her mother.

"You shouldn't, Mama. You know it does no good at all."

Mrs Haydon's cheeks showed a slight flush.

"It puts me out of all patience!" Then, turning to the younger girls, whose ears were alert: "Irene and Anthea, pray take your needlework into the schoolroom! I wish to speak to your sister alone."

They rose obediently, but their expressions registered keen disappointment. The conversation was evidently about to take an interesting turn, and they felt a natural disinclination to be excluded from it. Mrs Haydon kept her lips firmly closed until the door had shut behind her two youngest offspring and then said, bitterly, "Of course she's still hankering after that young gentleman Fabian Grenville, I know that well enough. But it's a prodigious waste of time, as she must realise herself that nothing will ever come of it! Oh, why did he have to take it into his head to visit Tunbridge Wells last summer? I'm sure there is ample choice for a gentleman like himself, with no ties of any kind!"

"But you must know all about that, Mama, because Richard explained it to you at the time. Fabian Grenville was seeking a wealthy marriage to mend his fortunes, and he'd already cast his net without success in London and Brighton before deciding to try his luck in the Wells. Old Grenville was as hardened a gambler as his son, besides bringing his mistresses into the house. It's no wonder that the Beresfords were never on intimate terms with that family, in spite of being near neighbours!"

"No, indeed. Dear Sir William and his wife, Lottie, could have nothing to do with such a man! But have you any notion, my dear, where that young man is at present? Not for worlds would I have Corinna fall into his way again!"

Lydia shook her head. "No, Mama, I haven't. But I would hazard a guess that he is still trying elsewhere for an heiress — that is, if he hasn't succeeded already in capturing one. It was a close run thing with the Pemberton girl when he was here last summer, was it not?"

Mrs Haydon nodded grimly.

"Indeed it was. She was whisked off by her relatives in the nick of time once they had learned from connections in London that he was a gazetted fortune hunter. But Corinna is quite well aware of his situation and knows that her fortune is not large enough to tempt him — that was made abundantly clear when he transferred his attentions from her to Miss Pemberton!

"How long do you suppose this nonsense will continue? It's seven months or so since he quitted the town, and Corinna must know very well that he will never return on her account. Any right-minded girl would have taken him in disgust when he so blatantly transferred his attentions from herself to another female!"

"Oh, she'll get over it in time, never fear," replied Lydia bracingly. "I don't think, Mama, you allow sufficiently for Corinna's romantic disposition. After all, she was only nineteen and it was the first time that any gentleman had ever taken her fancy. I dare say," she added shrewdly, "that she may secretly be feeding her infatuation, thinking it a romantic situation to be crossed in love! I fail to detect any signs of genuine suffering in her."

"Then you think there's nothing to be done — about your sister, I mean? Nothing but wait for her to come to her senses? You don't feel it might perhaps help if you were to talk to her?"

"I might as well address myself to the moon, Mama! No, I have a better notion altogether. Why do you not let her come with us to France? A change of scene will give her thoughts a new direction, and she may well meet some eligible young men among the English visitors. I am positive she'd like the scheme vastly!"

Mrs Haydon appeared much struck by the wisdom of this suggestion, and she urged Lydia to follow Corinna into the garden and put it to her.

Corinna had left the house feeling decidedly ruffled, and it had taken quite ten minutes of brisk walking in the shrubbery to calm her. Why could not Mama let her alone? It was surely her own concern whether or not she chose to marry, and whom. As if any of those young men who dangled after her could stir any of those tumultuous emotions which had started to life when first Fabian Grenville had taken her hand to lead her into the dance. She could never forget him — never!

There could be no shame, she reflected defiantly, in his need to marry for money. Many gentlemen were in a similar situation, especially when — like Mr Grenville — their fathers had wasted the inheritance which should have come to them. No wonder if he were a gambler, with such an example; the love of a good woman — here she paused doubtfully in her high flights, unable *quite* to recognise herself in this guise — must surely redeem him from his youthful follies. That he had been in love with her, she refused to doubt. She hoped she was not conceited; but surely no man could possibly prefer the plain, gushing Miss Pemberton to herself? She was convinced that, had she been in possession of a fortune equal to Miss Pemberton's, the issue could never have been in doubt. He had given her ample proof of his attachment, and most likely was now nursing a broken heart to match her own.

At this stage in her reverie an unwelcome interruption occurred with the appearance of Lydia's brother-in-law on the path she was following. Sir Richard Beresford was a man in his late twenties, taller than average and of slim build, though with a suggestion of muscular strength due, no doubt, to his interest in sporting activities. His fair hair was at present rather more windswept than the dictates of fashion decreed, while his usually immaculate top boots and breeches were dusty.

He apologised for this with a rueful gesture; but before he could speak, Corinna greeted him, frowning.

"Oh — so you're back," she said, in a flat tone.

He raised his brows. "No, really?" His pleasant voice held the hint of a drawl. "Deuced perceptive of you to notice."

She shrugged impatiently. "I'm not in the mood for funning."

"In a miff, are you?" He looked amused.

"No, I'm not!"

"I apologise for putting that badly," he said in mock humility. "I should have said instead that something must have occurred to put you out."

"Well, yes, it has," she admitted reluctantly.

He fell into step beside her, moderating his long, easy stride to her shorter one.

"If you wish me at the devil, don't hesitate to say so," he invited. "Otherwise, perhaps you may like to tell me about it?"

"Oh, it's Mama and Lydia," she complained. "They *will* keep nagging about my being married!"

He checked in his stride, a frown on his brows.

"Being married?" he repeated, and there was no drawl in his voice now. "Why, what is this? Lydia has said nothing of it. Are you betrothed? Who is the lucky man?"

She laughed, and at that some of the tension went out of him.

"Oh, no, stupid! The boot's quite on the other foot — they wish I were! Mama keeps *on* and *on* about it — she says I shall be left on the shelf, if I don't take care!"

"I don't think that at all likely," he remarked calmly as they resumed their pacing towards the house.

"Yes, well, I'd rather be left on the shelf than marry some of the gentlemen whom Mama thinks suitable," she said without heat, having now almost recovered her temper. "I've known them all my life — as is natural, since they reside in and around Tunbridge Wells — and nothing could be more odiously boring!"

"You think it a disadvantage to have known a suitor all your life? Then you can't possibly approve of your sister's marriage to my brother, I collect?"

She coloured a little. "Oh, no, I don't say that! It's very well for Lydia, and I'm sure she never even *considered* anyone else. But then, you see, she's not like me — she is not — not—"

He gave her a quizzical smile.

"Can the word be — romantic?"

"Perhaps so, and what is wrong with that, pray?" she flashed at him. "Can't a girl have dreams of something more exciting than being married to a man she's known since she was in leading strings?"

He nodded. "Certainly. But perhaps she should be wary, too. There's a saying you must have heard: 'Better the devil you know.' Dreams, my Sleeping Beauty, can sometimes lead to a rude awakening."

"Oh, if that isn't just like you — you must always be cynical!" she exclaimed in disgust. "I declare, you put me out of all patience!"

"I'm sorry for it. Perhaps it's just as well that your sister is here."

Looking up, Corinna saw Lydia standing at the end of the path, gesticulating excitedly.

"Come along, you two, it's time to change for dinner," she commanded, as she ran impulsively forward to meet them. "Corinna, I've a scheme to suggest to you, and for once Mama is in full agreement with it!"

She paused tantalizingly, seeing with satisfaction that she had their full attention.

"Well, out with it, then! Why must you be such a tease, Lyddy?"

Corinna's face was alight with curiosity.

"It is this," went on Lydia, as they all took the path back to the house. "How would you like to come with us to France?"

For answer, Corinna flung her arms about her sister in an ecstasy of delight, stammering incoherent expressions of gratitude.

"Well, I thought you'd like it," said Lydia complacently. "And we shall take you back with us to Sussex in a day or two, for we mean to set out for the Continent without undue delay. That's to say," she added, turning to Sir Richard, "if Richard does not object to offering you a seat in his carriage?"

Sir Richard bowed. "My poor equipage will be honoured by your presence, ma'am."

Lydia chortled. "Poor equipage, indeed! That's doing it too brown. Why, it's the best sprung I was ever in, not to mention the handsome blue velour upholstery! But you'll say I am toad-eating, you detestable creature, though it's no such thing! He is so — so — *contrary*, is he not, Corinna?"

"To be sure," agreed Corinna, her golden brown eyes twinkling. "I've come to cuffs with him once already on that account. But I must say," she added, relenting as he assumed a suitably chastened air, "I was in a mood to quarrel with a saint. However, that's all forgotten now."

She took his arm with a pretty gesture of confidence, and Sir Richard smiled down at her, though the expression in his eyes was guarded.

"Does Richard go with you to France?" she asked Lydia.

"Oh, no! He thinks the peace uneasy, and tried to persuade us against the venture at first, but John pooh-poohed the notion. There was something said in Parliament a few weeks back about hostile preparations being made in the French and Dutch ports."

"But surely no one can wish to go to war again!" exclaimed Corinna incredulously. "Besides, if one took heed of every alarm, one would scarce dare to venture outside one's own door!"

"Exactly what John feels," agreed Lydia. "So we are to go, despite the douche of cold water with which Richard greeted our scheme. I'm sure he'll wish later that he'd decided to accompany us, aren't you, Corinna? We shall have famous fun!"

Corinna agreed, looking up challengingly into Sir Richard's face.

"Perhaps I may," he said, yielding to an impulse. "Very well, Lydia, I'll make one of your party, after all."

CHAPTER TWO

It had not been Sir Richard Beresford's wish to adopt the role of mentor to the Haydon family, but circumstances had forced him into it. Like most females of genteel birth, Mrs Haydon could never be entirely comfortable without the support and advice of a gentleman in regulating her affairs. When her husband had died some eight years previously, her only son had been a boy of ten years, and she had no other close male kin. It had seemed natural, therefore, to turn to the man who had been her husband's lifelong friend, Sir William Beresford.

The death of his childhood friend, George Haydon, was deeply felt by Sir William, so that he was only too willing to render any service he could to the widow. She had been left in extremely comfortable circumstances and had no material wants; it was simply a matter of advice and reassurance on his part. He therefore continued to visit her with his family as frequently as before, and to make the Haydons welcome at Chyngton Manor. This happy intercourse had continued until three years ago, when Sir William and his wife had been tragically killed in a carriage accident.

At that time, John Beresford, the younger son, was a second lieutenant in the Royal Navy and frequently away at sea. Richard, the elder by two years, inherited Chyngton Manor and the title. He soon discovered that he had also stepped into his father's role of counsellor to Mrs Haydon. His nature being amiable, he cheerfully took on the charge; becoming a frequent visitor to the house in Tunbridge Wells and dispensing advice and giving support whenever Mrs Haydon fancied herself in need of either or both. If at times he could have wished to appear in another, less prosy light, to one member at least of the family, he did his best to suppress the feeling.

There had been only one point on which Mrs Haydon had not accepted Sir Richard's advice, and that concerned her son. Laurence Haydon was at present a high-spirited youth of eighteen with nothing to occupy him but whatever sporting activities offered locally, or else protracted visits to former schoolfellows who lived elsewhere. What he most ardently desired was to take up a commission in the army, and Sir Richard thought this the very thing for him.

But the mere mention of such a scheme had thrown Mrs Haydon into a spasm.

"The *army!*" she moaned, when frequent applications of sal volatile had restored her powers of speech. "Oh, no, no, it's not to be thought of! My only son — the head of my little family! And with this dreadful war — yes, I know there's a peace at present, but who can tell if that will last? No, pray, dear Richard, don't expect me to consider such a thing for one moment, I implore you!"

Laurence, a sturdy youth obviously built for an active life, made a gesture of disgust.

"Good God, Mama, what a piece of work over nothing! Why, I might just as easily come to grief in the hunting field, or out on a day's shooting!"

"Oh, dear, what is to be done with him? He lacks a father's guidance, alas! You are so good, dear Richard — go and reason with him, and tell him I think only of his welfare."

Sir Richard hesitated.

"I'll do my best, ma'am," he said, at last. "But I feel impelled to point out that the welfare of a young man extends to more than his physical well-being. A high-couraged lad like Laurence needs to prove his manhood by engaging in exploits which may seem dangerous to a woman, but when you stop to consider that all his friends are permitted this necessary freedom, I'm sure you wouldn't wish to throw the least rub in his way."

"Oh, no, true, very true! He must take part in all the usual *sporting* activities of gentlemen, I do see that. But as to purchasing a commission for him — no, I cannot bring myself to agree to *that*, at present. Perhaps when he's older — after all, he is only just eighteen and the merest boy, though he doesn't like to think so, of course. Pray, say no more about it, for it quite distresses me!"

Seeing the futility of further argument at that time, Sir Richard desisted, later consoling the disgruntled Laurence with the thought that his mother might gradually be won over when she had been given time to accustom herself to the notion.

This discussion had taken place a few months since; and during the present visit of the Beresfords, Laurence once more urged Sir Richard to have another touch at Mama, as he phrased it.

The three gentlemen were standing about in the parlour which led off the dining room, awaiting the appearance of the ladies before going in to dinner.

"It's no use my trying to persuade her," Laurence continued disgustedly. "I'm sure I've nagged at her until I'm blue in the face — Corinna, too, for she's a rare sport and does her utmost to back me up. But when m' mother gets out that cursed smelling bottle of hers and asks me if I want to bring her down in sorrow to the grave, and such like gammon — well, I ask you, what can a fellow do?"

"Take a glass of sherry," advised Sir Richard promptly, as a footman appeared with a tray of glasses.

Laurence laughed reluctantly as he accepted a glass.

"If that ain't just like you, Richard, turning everything off with a jest! But it's no jesting matter as far as I'm concerned, y' know."

Sir Richard sipped his sherry. "Believe me, I do know, Laurie, and I'll try again when I think the time's ripe. One cannot rush your mother, as I'm sure you've realised by now for yourself."

"No, but I don't think you quite understand how blue-devilled I feel sometimes, kicking my heels here at home with a parcel of females! I wish I'd had a brother — you two can't begin to know how lucky you are!"

Sir Richard and John exchanged grins. "Well, as to that—" began John.

"No need to tell me you've come to cuffs now and then," interrupted Laurence with a laugh. "Corinna and I do, too, though for the most part we deal famously — she's a right one, for a girl," he added, a shade patronizingly. "I needn't tell you she's no bread-and-butter miss."

"And they say eavesdroppers never hear any good of themselves," put in Corinna, who had that moment entered the room with Lydia. "No, I don't think you need to explain my character to these two, Laurie, since we've known each other forever."

Sir Richard turned to look at her. She appeared at her most demure in a gown of white sprigged muslin, but the effect was belied by the mischief in her eyes.

"Gad, no, for they've had a taste of your tongue often enough, my girl!" chuckled Laurence. "Still, there's no harm in you, I'll say that."

Corinna swept him a mocking curtsey. "Oh, la, sir! You are too good!"

"Foolish children," chided Lydia, as she moved closer to her husband. "John, I suppose Richard will have told you that Corinna is to come with us to France?"

"Is she, by Jove?" asked Laurence, unable to keep a note of envy out of his voice.

"Yes, I'm delighted to hear it," said John, as he placed an arm about Lydia's slender waist. "Tell you what, Laurie" — turning to the youth — "why don't you come along, too? Give you something to do for a few months, and the more, the merrier, eh? What d'you say? Would you like it?"

Laurence lost no time in expressing his thanks, rendered almost incoherent by excitement.

They discussed the proposed expedition at some length during the course of the meal.

"Tell you what, Richard," said John presently, "how would it be if we went by way of Rouen and looked up Patrice Landier? I told you I had a letter from him some months back in which he said that he hoped we might meet again now that our countries are at peace. He's a good chap, even though he did belong to the wrong side."

"Yes, a capital notion," agreed Sir Richard.

"Landier?" asked Mrs Haydon. "Do I know him?"

"He was a lieutenant in the French navy," explained Sir Richard, "and John fished him out of the sea after a naval engagement — saved his life in fact, for he'd been knocked senseless by a falling timber. He was brought to England as a prisoner on John's ship, and the two struck up a friendship on the voyage. Afterwards he was detained in Lewes for a time, and we both visited him until he was later returned to France."

"Is he still in the French navy?" Laurie asked.

John shook his head. "His father owned a banking business in Rouen and Landier has now resigned his commission to assist in it."

Laurence's expression showed that he could not think highly of a man who preferred commerce to active service; but a warning look from Corinna prevented him in time from expressing this opinion. Sir Richard intercepted the exchange of glances, and his lips twitched in amusement.

"I wonder what the ladies at the French court are wearing?" asked Mrs Haydon. "We were always used to consider French fashions as being the latest in modality when I was young, but perhaps that is no longer so, with that dreadful creature Napoleon ruling the court. It is all very sad, to be sure."

She sighed.

"Why, Mama, that's one reason why I wish to go," explained Lydia. "I've heard all kinds of rumours, such as that they dampen their muslins in order to make them cling to the figure! I can't rest until I know the truth of this!"

"Good heavens, I trust you and Corinna won't follow their example!" exclaimed Mrs Haydon, quite shocked. "Apart from the immodesty of such a proceeding, only think of the hazard to your health! It would surely bring on an attack of the rheumatics!"

"Oh, Mama!"

Both girls collapsed with laughter in which their two younger sisters joined.

"You may laugh," said their mother ominously, "but I can assure you that it's no laughing matter to be crippled with the rheumatics. John" — turning to him in appeal — "you surely would not permit Lydia to indulge in any such foolishness?"

"As to that, ma'am, I dare say she'll go her own way," he replied, smiling at his wife, who was still laughing.

"Never fear, Mama," said Lydia reassuringly. "I've no intention of carrying modality to such lengths. I imagine it would be vastly uncomfortable to go about in wet garments, in any event.

"I have an idea," she continued, changing the subject. "Would you like me to bring you back a bottle of French perfume?"

It was not to be expected that any female could resist this offer; and it succeeded in diverting Mrs Haydon's thoughts away from the possible hazards of the proposed expedition.

CHAPTER THREE

The pale sunlight had been warm on her back as she walked through the village, her basket on her arm; but now, as the door of the house closed behind her, the air struck chill and she shivered.

"He's been asking for you," said the elderly woman dressed in peasant black who admitted her. "Give me the shopping. You'd best go straight up."

The girl handed over the basket. She was slight but shapely, with dark, glossy hair and eyes that were almost black in an oval, fine-boned face that wore a deceptive air of serenity. She mounted the stairs and softly entered a room where the door was ajar. As softly, she moved over to the bed and stood looking down at the man lying there.

His sparse white hair clung damply to his high, domed forehead and his eyes seemed deeply sunk into a face lined with suffering. Yet now he lay quietly in the bed as if in slumber.

After a moment he stirred, looking up at her with clouded eyes which cleared momentarily as they rested on her beloved face.

"You are there, *ma petite*."

His voice was a mere thread of sound.

She placed her firm young hand over his wrinkled one as it lay inert on the coverlet.

"Yes, *mon oncle*, I am here. I shall stay with you now, so do not distress yourself. Try to sleep."

He gave a faint motion of dissent.

"Soon there will be sleep everlasting," he breathed. "But now we must talk, you and I."

She was about to forbid this, but changed her mind, reading the trouble in his countenance.

"I must tell you what to do when I am gone," he continued, speaking in a slightly stronger tone.

She shook her head as tears filled her dark eyes.

"No, no! You will be well again — the doctor is on his way, and he will give you another draught—"

"His draughts no longer have the power to draw me back from my eternal home. Save for you, dearest child, I have no wish to stay." He paused to draw in a laboured breath. "Dry your eyes, little one, and listen well to what I tell you now. You see my writing desk over there?"

The girl nodded, for his sake making a strong effort to master her emotion.

"Open it, and press your thumb upon the carving in the panel between the small drawers."

He watched as she rose, having first dried her cheeks, and followed his instructions. There was a click as a small door flew open, revealing a space behind.

"There is a box. Bring it to me."

She obeyed, reaching into the cavity to produce a black wooden box; though small, it was quite heavy. She lifted it carefully, carrying it over to the invalid. He opened it with trembling fingers.

At sight of its contents, she gasped, for a moment diverted from her grief.

"So much money, uncle! Is it — is it—?"

She faltered, the tears starting again.

He shook his head feebly.

"No, my child, not for my obsequies. That's provided for elsewhere." Again he took a deep breath. "I've been saving this for you ever since the war between our country and England ceased. It is to reunite you with your own kin."

"I won't go!" she said in a passionate undertone. "I won't leave you!"

"It is I who must leave you, *chérie*," he whispered. "Now listen carefully, for I've little strength left, and there is more for you to do. You will go to Paris — Sister Thérèsè will accompany you, and she knows my plan. She will explain all. In that box there is also a letter giving your aunt's direction. You will take that and the money with you."

He stopped suddenly, fighting for breath.

"You mustn't speak anymore!" she exclaimed in a frantic whisper. "Oh, why does not the doctor come! I will send Marthe for him at once!"

She turned impetuously to go and summon the housekeeper, but stopped as his voice weakly called her back. She returned irresolutely to the bed, and stood waiting while he made an effort for further speech. It was several minutes in coming.

"I want your promise," he said at last, meeting her eyes with something of the force that had once lain in his own, "that you will carry out my wishes, and let nothing stand in the way of a reunion with your kin. Nothing, do you understand? Not even that young man from Rouen who has been showing so much interest in you these last few months."

He paused, regarding compassionately the mounting colour in her cheeks.

"You're young, *chérie*, and the good God has decreed that lovers will come for young girls. That is right and natural. But though this one is, I am sure, an upright and worthy man, he is not for you. You must wed with one of your own station —

that will be arranged when you are safely in your aunt's charge."

The girl bowed her head in submission. In a quiet voice, she gave her promise.

The invalid raised his trembling hand in blessing. Weeping, she crossed herself.

After a somewhat stormy sea passage, Lydia and Corinna were in no mood to be diverted by the sights and sounds, not to say odours, of Dieppe. There was a pervading smell of fish mixed with the sharp tang of the sea, no doubt due in part to the sellers of shrimps, mussels, and other *fruits de mer*, who wheeled their barrows about the streets plying for trade.

Corinna wrinkled her nose fastidiously as Sir Richard helped her into the hired carriage that was to take them to their hotel.

"You don't care for fish?" he asked with a teasing smile. "A pity, for I fancy it will figure largely in the menu here."

"It's the odour," she complained. "It's so powerful — I had no notion!"

"That comes of leading a sheltered life in an inland town."

"Well, at least your fish will be fresh here," John consoled her, as he took his seat beside Lydia.

"By Jove, yes!" exclaimed Laurence, who had been eagerly surveying the scene around him. "Only look at those lobsters, Corinna — they'll have crawled right off the barrow in a moment! Famous fun if the man has to chase them along the street! I've a good mind to buy a couple and have a race with odds on! What d'you say, Richard?"

Sir Richard grinned, but shook his head. "I fear it wouldn't amuse the ladies. Jump in, Laurie."

Laurence obeyed, mumbling that it seemed a shame to miss the chance of what would have been a capital bit of sport, and the vehicle moved off at as brisk a pace as the crowded street permitted.

Once installed in their comfortable hotel, at some distance removed from the quais, however, the ladies soon recovered their spirits. They were partaking of some excellent coffee in company with Sir Richard and his brother, Laurence being missing for the moment, when they heard a commotion going on in the passage outside the door of their private downstairs parlour. Excited French voices, some raised in laughter, others in protest, mingled with English ones; through the hubbub, they managed to identify Laurence's tones.

"No, damme, I say, give them room!" they heard him cry.

"What the deuce—!" exclaimed Sir Richard, striding to the door and flinging it open.

The others followed him, then gasped at the scene which met their eyes.

About a dozen people were gathered in the passage standing about in varying attitudes of wonder, mirth, or disgust. Some were guests, others kitchen staff and waiters; the most voluble of all was the landlord of the inn, who was advancing on Laurence in a threatening attitude.

"I tell you I won't have such a thing in my house!" he shouted, red in the face. "It is *incroyable, voyez-vous!* Pierre — Louis" — gesturing to two men in white aprons — "remove these creatures at once — at once, I say, if you value your places in my hotel!"

"Yes, Monsieur Panton, of course," replied one of the men, advancing nervously towards Laurence, who was crouching on the floor over something which was hidden from Sir Richard's view. "But the English milord—"

"No, no, my good fellow," put in a drawling English voice. "You wouldn't spoil sport, would you?" An impeccably attired young man bearing the hallmark of English quality stepped forward and gently took the landlord by the arm. "Tell you what, sir," he went on, addressing Laurence, "I haven't the honour of your acquaintance, but trust you'll accept my wager of twenty guineas on the creature nearest me. My name's Cheveley, by the way."

"Done!" returned Laurence, glancing up briefly from what was occupying him on the floor. "Mine's Haydon — forgive my not rising, but you see how it is, sir — oh, devil take it! Now they're grappling with each other, and there's an end of the race!"

By this time, Sir Richard and John had moved forward so that they could have a full view of what was occupying everyone's attention.

Two large lobsters had been placed side by side on the carpet; and Laurence, with the aid of a wooden spoon, had been trying to urge them into a race.

John gave a loud crack of laughter. His brother's mouth twitched, and when he spoke there was a tremor in his voice.

"For God's sake, Laurie, you can't do that here! The landlord will go off into an apoplexy, and most likely turn us out of doors."

Laurence stood up, throwing down the spoon.

"Oh, well, the sport's over now, anyway. You may as well take them off to the kitchen," he said to the hovering kitchen hands. "Oh, and here's for your pains."

Thrusting a hand into his pocket, he produced some money. They took it hastily, then scooping the lobsters up by means of the spoon into a large cooking pot, scuttled off to the kitchen.

This was the signal for the spectators to drift away, most of them still laughing.

"Sorry for that, sir," said Laurence to his newly found acquaintance. "They were doing famously to begin with, too."

"Think nothing of it," returned Mr Cheveley handsomely. "Perhaps some other time. Do you stay long in Dieppe, sir?"

"Only overnight. We're bound for Paris. Oh, permit me to make you known to the rest of my party."

As Corinna and Lydia had now emerged from the parlour, he was able to include them in the introductions that followed. Mr Cheveley murmured that he was delighted and bowed gracefully. The ladies were favourably impressed.

Meantime, the innkeeper had been fulminating in the background, and now he burst into impassioned speech, addressing himself principally to Sir Richard.

"I hope I'm a reasonable man, milor', but what about my carpet? It is ruined, quite ruined! I'm not accustomed to such an affair, no, *mon Dieu!* Always I keep a house of the most respectable, where the English milords and their ladies come knowing they will find all to their liking! Such a brouhaha as this—"

Sir Richard raised his quizzing glass and surveyed the man through it, effectively putting an end to the tirade.

"My good fellow," he said quietly in his excellent French, "it is you who are making the brouhaha. As to the carpet, I admit you have cause for complaint. Let us draw apart where we shall not incommode these ladies and gentlemen further, and I will endeavour to arrange that matter to your satisfaction."

"Oh, Laurie," exclaimed Corinna, laughing, "you are the most complete hand! What a mad trick!"

"Where in the world did you find those creatures?" demanded Lydia with a chuckle.

"I stepped round to the stables and saw one of the vendors delivering a barrow load of the things to the back door, so I bought a couple," explained Laurence airily. "The notion came to me on the quai, you know, and it seemed a pity to waste it."

"Quite right," approved Mr Cheveley. "It was a novel notion, and worthy of a more successful outcome. Perhaps I may have the pleasure of seeing you again in Paris," he concluded, bowing slightly again to the whole party. "I am going there myself to join the rest of my family, who've already been some months in the capital."

They replied suitably and the young man took his leave.

Early on the following morning the party set off for Rouen, the men electing to ride for the first stage of the journey rather than being obliged to sit for so many hours in what Laurence described as a stuffy carriage.

It was shortly after midday when they arrived at their hotel in Rouen, by which time no one was sorry to have a respite from travelling. Bedchambers and a private parlour had been reserved for them in advance and proved highly satisfactory. Scarcely had they settled themselves in and removed the marks of travel when a waiter tapped on the door of the parlour to present a visiting card.

"It'll be Landier, without a doubt," said John, taking up the card and scanning it. "Yes — presents his compliments and will wait on us later, if not convenient at present. What d'you say? Shall we have him up?"

The others agreed. The waiter departed, and a few minutes later returned to usher a gentleman into the room. He was fashionably attired in a brown coat, buff waistcoat, yellow pantaloons, and Hessian boots, and he carried a walking cane. On entering, he swept off his hat, bowing deeply to the ladies, then tossed hat and cane aside to stride forward and grip John Beresford warmly by the hand.

"Good God!" whispered Laurence to Corinna. "I hope he don't take it into his head to embrace the poor fellow!"

The remark must have been overheard by Landier, for he grinned at Laurence. He was of medium height and dark complexion, with an aquiline nose and lively grey eyes.

"At last we meet again, *mon vieux!* And Sir Richard, too — it is a felicity to see you both!"

"Indeed, we're delighted to see you again," returned John cordially. "Permit me, my dear" — turning to Lydia — "to present to you Monsieur Patrice Landier, of whom I've often spoken. Landier, this is my wife."

Landier bowed again. "Charmed, madame. My friend is fortunate indeed."

"And this is her sister, Miss Haydon, and her brother."

There was another bow and a glance of admiration for Corinna.

"I bring you an invitation from my parents," said Landier. "It will give them inestimable pleasure if you will dine at our house this evening. Indeed, they are desolated that you are not to stay with us."

"We couldn't put you to so much trouble for one night only, my dear chap."

"Then make it three — four — a week — what you will," replied Landier, with an expansive gesture.

"You are very good, but unfortunately our reservations in Paris are already made."

"Ah, of course. Then you must honour us with a sojourn on your return trip. My mother in particular is all eagerness to receive you, knowing the extent of my indebtedness to you."

John replied suitably, protesting that there need be no talk of indebtedness, and Landier was invited to stay and partake of a nuncheon with them at the hotel. This he was most ready to do; and soon they were all seated at table, laughing and chatting together in the easiest possible way. Afterwards, he offered to show them around the town if the ladies should not feel too weary from travelling.

"I think I may fairly claim that it is a fine town," remarked Landier, with a creditable attempt at modesty, "even though we do suffer here from the — how do you say? — the thick mist that sometimes you have to endure in London—"

"Fog?" suggested Corinna with a smile.

"Ah, yes, that is it, mademoiselle. I see that you will soon effect an improvement in my English."

He smiled back at her, and Lydia cast a meaningful look at her husband which was intercepted by Sir Richard.

"Yes, some visitors have been known to complain of our fogs," he continued. "However, today it is clear, so I will be able to show the town to advantage."

He proceeded to do so, taking them first to the magnificent cathedral by way of the rue de la Grosse Horloge, which took its name from a large clock of Italian sixteenth-century workmanship set high above the street in a spanning archway. It was in this street that the Landiers resided; but by common consent they agreed to defer their meeting with Monsieur and Madame Landier until the evening.

"We have the marketplace at one end and the cathedral at the other, you observe," he said with a laugh. "God and Mammon, *n'est-ce pas?*"

"And a banker in between," riposted Sir Richard.

Corinna glanced quickly at Landier, wondering if this remark might possibly give offense. But she had forgotten how well these three knew each other from the past; Landier laughed heartily.

"You may well say so," he remarked, sobering a little. "Too often we men of commerce find ourselves between two extremes. In politics, for example — but, bah! I mustn't weary the ladies with such matters! We will talk later, *mon vieux*, over our wine, as your English custom is."

By the time they had visited the cathedral, the churches of St Ouen and St Maclou and one or two other buildings of interest, both their energies and the daylight were fading. Accordingly, Landier parted from them outside their hotel in the pleasurable expectation of seeing them later.

Nothing was lacking in the cordiality of their reception by Patrice Landier's family that evening. Madame Landier, a short, plump lady with sloe-black eyes set in a somewhat austere face, took John's hand in both of hers and seemed reluctant to release it. Monsieur, who was an older edition of his son with the same aquiline nose and shrewd grey eyes, ventured a word or two of welcome in halting English.

"And that entailed a great effort, *voyez-vous*," said his son to the visitors, "for Papa has very little English and has been rehearsing his speech all day! As for Maman, she does not speak your language at all, alas."

Presently they were all gathered round the dining table to do justice to a meal which combined all the best in French cuisine, accompanied by a wine which caused Sir Richard to raise his eyebrows in approval.

When the ladies retired to the salon, Corinna found herself taking the lead in conversation with Madame Landier. After a few polite exchanges about their travels, she steered the talk round to Madame Landier's family, guessing that the older woman would be tolerably at ease on that subject.

She learned that madame had three daughters, all of whom were married with young families and lived not very far distant.

"And you have only the one son, madame?"

"Ah, yes. And that is why I can never be sufficiently grateful to the good Lieutenant Beresford, who preserved his life. If there were anything I could do — anything in the world, at any time — to repay that debt, mademoiselle, be sure I should be ready, no matter at what cost to myself!"

"I understand your feelings perfectly, madame. Your son is not married, I collect?"

"Ah, no." Madame looked doubtful. "But I have sometimes wondered of late — in short, I believe there is someone. But I think the affair does not go well, for he says nothing to us about it, and I am sure he would do so, if matters were favourable." She sighed, then recollected herself. "But I must not weary you with so much talk of my family. Tell me of yourself, mademoiselle. You are affianced, perhaps?"

Corinna shook her head, smiling. "No. I am what we call on the shelf."

"Never! That's impossible, an attractive young lady like you! You jest, I think."

At this point the gentlemen entered the room, Patrice Landier promptly taking a seat beside Corinna.

"What do you think, mademoiselle?" he asked, his grey eyes twinkling. "I am to come with you all to Paris — that is, if you and Madame Beresford do not object. I have some business which I must attend to in the capital at some time or another, and now will be an ideal time, when I may combine business with pleasure."

Caught by the happy camaraderie of his manner, Corinna reflected that such a pleasing gentleman could not be other than a welcome addition to their party. She allowed Lydia to express their approval, however, contenting herself with a look of smiling acquiescence.

The rest of the evening was whiled away agreeably in conversation, the party breaking up early because of the long day's travel ahead of them on the morrow.

Later, in the seclusion of their bedchamber at the hotel, Lydia lay pensively beside her husband for a few moments after the candle was extinguished.

"Do you know what, John?" she asked.

"No — what, my love?"

He placed an arm about her, drawing her close.

"Well, I'm just speculating about your friend Monsieur Landier," she said slowly, stroking his cheek.

"The devil you are! I'll thank you, Mrs Beresford, to keep your thoughts away from other men," he replied with mock severity.

She chuckled. "Oh, nothing of that kind! Only I was wondering if perhaps Corinna—" She paused, then went on. "He seems to admire her."

"Any Frenchman worth his salt admires a pretty female — any man at all, come to that."

She drew away a little. "Oh, indeed, sir? Just let me catch you at it!"

"Ninnyhammer," he whispered, his lips close to her neck. "As though any female in the world can compare to you."

"I'm relieved to hear it. But do you think that possibly Corinna may come to like Monsieur Landier — a great deal, I mean?"

"Well, if females ain't the limit for matchmaking! I thought you said she was still sweet on that good-for-nothing fellow Grenville?"

"Oh, that's just her nonsense — I doubt she was ever truly in love with him. It was just one of those heady fascinations that sometimes afflict young girls," said Lydia, from the greater maturity of her two and twenty years. "She positively *enjoys* prolonging it, because she thinks it romantic to be crossed in love. I know my sister."

"Well, what I say is, fiend seize her!" exclaimed John, exasperated. "If you think I wish to talk all night about your sister, when I'm holding my wife in my arms, you're faint and far off, my dearest!"

CHAPTER FOUR

Corinna found that Paris lived up to all her eager anticipations. Napoleon's efficient administration had removed much of the dirt and squalor which had marred the city's beauty during the Reign of Terror: and if the present court lacked the elegance of the old, there were entertainments enough to satisfy a young lady from Tunbridge Wells.

The two sisters lost no time in visiting the fashionable shops in the Palais Royal to view the latest modes. Lydia purchased one of the new square shawls fringed with gold tassels; while Corinna ordered a gown to be made for her in one of the latest shades, curiously, as she thought, named Fumée de Londres.

"Well, I do not call it smoke coloured — or, at least, only a very pale, misty shade. Don't you think it pretty, Lyddy?"

"Oh, vastly," agreed her sister, fingering the fine muslin. "But I hope you may not catch your death of cold in it," she added, twinkling. "Remember what Mama had to say about that!"

"Goose, of course I shall wear a petticoat beneath it — I've no desire to be considered fast! Though if only one dared, you know, it might be famous fun to set people staring! Only imagine Richard's face, for example!"

She went off into peals of laughter, in which Lydia joined.

"I declare you're almost as bad as Laurie, though thank heavens you have a little more discretion! What a fortunate thing that he should have met that young man Cheveley yesterday, for they are two of a kind, and being much of an age will be excellent company for each other. Besides, it will give us a respite now and then from Laurie's nonsense."

They had met Mr Cheveley with his family on the previous day while strolling in the Palais gardens, and the two young men had greeted each other with enthusiasm. His parents, Sir George and Lady Cheveley, and his sister Frances having been presented to the new acquaintances, they had all walked about the gardens together for a while. The Cheveleys owned a property not far from Brighton, and they had hired a house in Paris for the duration of their stay.

Explaining this to Lydia and Corinna, Lady Cheveley had concluded by issuing an invitation to dine there on the following evening.

"I shall be pleased to see your whole party," she said graciously. "There will be a few other English visitors present, too. Perhaps you may be acquainted with some of them?"

She proceeded to mention a short list of names, one of which was quickly repeated by Sir Richard.

"Did you say Mr Langham, ma'am? Would that be Edmund Langham, a man of about my own years?"

"Yes, indeed it is. Mr Langham is attached to the British embassy here. An excellent young man," she pronounced approvingly. "Are you acquainted with him and his wife, Sir Richard?"

"With his wife not at all, but Langham and I were friends in our Oxford days. Since then we've lost touch, and I had no notion that he was in the diplomatic service. It will be a pleasure to meet him again."

After their shopping expedition, therefore, Lydia and Corinna returned to the hotel to dress for the evening's outing. When they joined the men in the hotel foyer, several pairs of male eyes gave witness to the fact that their efforts had not been wasted. Lydia's fair complexion and blonde hair were admirably set off by her trained gown of pink spotted muslin, made in the prevailing classical style with a high waist and short puff sleeves; while the soft yellow of Corinna's similarly styled gown accentuated the deep golden lights in her hair and eyes.

"To present such a picture, ladies," remarked Landier, with a gallant bow, "is to capture our poor hearts completely! Permit me to escort you to the carriage."

Laurence made a grimace as he caught Sir Richard's eye, but that gentleman preserved an inscrutable countenance.

Arrived at the Cheveley's house, they were conducted by a liveried footman to an ornate drawing room with a painted ceiling. Here they were received by their host and hostess and introduced to the other guests. Corinna soon fell into conversation with Miss Frances Cheveley, a young lady of much the same age as Corinna with dark, glossy ringlets, a creamy complexion and hazel eyes.

"Do you find it strange in Paris?" asked Miss Cheveley. "I did, at first. But there are so many English families here, and like all compatriots in a foreign country, they tend to group together. It's like a season in London or Brighton — one meets the same people everywhere, all the time."

"But you must have met many French families, too," replied Corinna. "Do you find them hospitable?"

"Oh, yes. We've been invited to balls and evening parties and even to receptions at the Palais des Tuileries. There is to be another reception in a few days' time, and I expect your party will be included, since Sir Richard Beresford is acquainted with Mr Langham, who is at the embassy." She lowered her voice. "There are a few English people who won't go there, you know, as they refuse to meet Napoleon. It is a great embarrassment to Lord Whitworth, the ambassador, but there's nothing he can do."

Corinna nodded, not greatly interested in this, and went on to press for a description of the Tuileries palace.

"Oh, I'm not the least little bit clever at describing places, Miss Haydon! But you'll see it for yourself before long." She hesitated. "You have a French gentleman in your own party. Is he perhaps one of the emigres whom you met in England?"

"No, he lives in Rouen."

She proceeded to relate the circumstances of Landier's friendship with John, while Miss Cheveley listened with sparkling eyes.

"How vastly romantic!" she exclaimed at the end of the account.

"Well," replied Corinna doubtfully, "I'm not at all certain that it can be considered romantic, precisely, to be in danger of drowning."

"No, not that, but the rescue and then the friendship which followed, you know. It is just like something from the pages of a romance, don't you agree? Are you fond of reading romances, Miss Haydon, or do you consider them a waste of one's time?"

"I hope I am not so prosy! No, I read a great deal, but little that would be considered improving, I fear. Who are your favourite authors, Miss Cheveley? Do you enjoy the novels of Mrs Radcliffe?"

This was the prelude to a long, animated discussion which was only terminated by a general move to the dining room. Corinna was seated at one side of the table between Patrice Landier and an English gentleman whom she had met for the first time that evening. Miss Cheveley sat opposite her, with Sir Richard as one of her neighbours. Although Corinna herself soon became involved in a lively interchange with Landier, she could not help noticing how well her new female friend was going on with Sir Richard. They never seemed to lack for conversation, while Miss Cheveley's sparkling eyes and his smiles gave evidence that both were enjoying themselves.

As they drove back to the hotel, the evening was voted a great success by everyone except Laurence, who declared that affairs of the kind were too slow by half for his taste.

"But Cheveley and I have arranged an expedition of our own for tomorrow," he added, in a brighter tone. "Something much more in my line — there's to be chariot racing in the Champs de Mars."

"Even that may seem a trifle flat after lobster racing," remarked Sir Richard with a grin.

"What joy, to be spared your company for a whole day!" said Lydia, in a burst of sisterly candour. "I can only hope you'll contrive to keep out of mischief, Laurie, but it's more than I bargain for, I can tell you!"

The following day being fine, Sir Richard suggested that the rest of the party should go riding in the Bois de Boulogne. Landier was obliged to excuse himself as he had some business to transact in Paris, but the other three agreed readily to the scheme. A consultation with the landlord resulted in suitable mounts being supplied and they set off through the busy streets until they reached the quiet villages of Chaillot and Passy, surrounded by open fields and woods.

There were many other smartly dressed riders cantering along the bridle paths of the Bois de Boulogne, and frequently the party found themselves obliged to proceed in single file. Becoming impatient on one such occasion, Corinna headed her horse off the track into the trees, threading her way precariously among protruding roots and overhanging branches.

She soon heard a shout behind her. She reined in and looked back to see Sir Richard following. He drew level, and shook his head with an admonitory smile.

"I think not, don't you agree? These poor hacks do best on a path, though God knows their best is pathetic enough. I never crossed a greater slug in my life than this beast of mine — how do you find yours?"

"Never mind that!" she answered tartly. "Why must you come after me as if I were the merest child? I am quite capable of looking after myself, I thank you!"

This boast was unfortunately disproved at that precise moment. In her irritation, she had tugged hard at the rein and the horse reared, almost unseating her.

Sir Richard quickly leaned sideways in the saddle to steady her with one arm. She was an excellent horsewoman and soon had her mount under control again, then she turned its head to lead it back to the path. In silence he accompanied her until they were once more riding side by side along the bridle path a short distance behind John and Lydia, who had turned briefly to make sure that the others were following.

Corinna, too, was silent for a time, then she looked at him challengingly.

"I suppose you will say I have to eat my words?"

"I hope I have more discretion," he replied with a twinkle in his eye. "I've no wish to be left a mangled corpse in these woods."

"Do you know, you have the most abominable way of being always right?" she said, struggling not to laugh.

"You mistake," he answered ruefully. "I am seldom right where you're concerned, Corinna. Indeed, I seem fated always to set you at odds with me."

She flashed him one of her charming smiles, her golden eyes alight with mischief.

"Well, you know I have a quick temper. Besides, I must confess that I quite enjoy a little sparring match with you, now and then, just for the fun of seeing if I can get under your guard! But I never succeed," she added, thoughtfully. "You are so very—"

She paused.

"So very what?" he prompted, after waiting for a minute.

She shrugged helplessly. "Oh, I don't know! So very calm and unruffled — and when I'm in my high ropes, you counter it with cynicism, as if — as if — you didn't think it worth the trouble of becoming vexed with me, treating me almost as a fractious child! It's quite odious, I assure you!"

"I'm very sorry. Pray instruct me as to how you'd like me to go on, and I'll endeavour to mend my ways."

"Oh, if you don't know!" she exclaimed, bursting into exasperated laughter.

He raised a mocking eyebrow. "Would you like me to get into a passion with you? Shall I seize one of these branches and beat you with it, for instance? Such antics are not at all in my style, but I'm willing to oblige."

She laughed freely at that, diverted by the absurd images his words conjured up in her mind.

"Oh, Richard, you're so very droll!"

He gave an ironical bow. "Take care, madam. There are several branches conveniently near."

He joined in her laughter as they quickened the pace of their horses to come up with Lydia and John.

As Miss Cheveley had anticipated, Sir Richard's friendship with one of the British ambassador's entourage was sufficient to ensure an invitation for his party to a reception held a few days later at the Tuileries palace. As they made their way slowly up the grand staircase waiting to be received by the first consul and his lady, Corinna suffered a few tremors of awe. All about her were ladies resplendent in costly silks and muslins, many wearing brilliant jewels, and gentlemen either in correct evening attire or gold-braided military uniforms, with plumed helmets under their arms. It was a very mixed gathering, however, in spite of the seeming splendour; important embassy officials and *ci-devant* noblemen who had been given permission to return to France being ranged alongside Napoleon's officers and humbler individuals such as lawyers, financiers, and merchants.

"I feel quite overcome," whispered Corinna to her brother, who was standing beside her waiting for their turn to be announced.

"Pooh, at being presented to Boney?" scoffed Laurence.

"Hush! Pray lower your voice," entreated his sister. "Only think if you should be overheard and someone took offense! There's no saying what might occur!"

"D' you think I care a rush for that?" he replied scornfully, though in a much lower tone.

"No, but I should, and so would the others, you — you addle-pate! Now don't say another word, for it's our turn next, after Lydia and John."

As she made her curtsey, she raised her eyes in a swift appraisal of this man who held sway over a great nation without any benefit of royal blood. He was not as tall as she had supposed, and of stocky build; his complexion was sallow and his dark, piercing eyes gave him a sombre, brooding look.

There was an impression of power, she thought, and perhaps of ruthlessness. Madame Bonaparte, in contrast, was all soft seductiveness. She was undoubtedly a handsome woman, but Corinna was surprised to observe that she wore quite noticeable make-up.

She mentioned this to Lydia as they passed down the room among the other visitors.

"Oh, yes, I've heard that she purchases three thousand francs' worth of rouge every year from Martin, the fashionable perfumier," said Lydia. "Lady Cheveley told the story the other evening — did you not hear her? — of Napoleon's asking a lady of his court why she was so pale, and was she recovering from a confinement? When she denied this, he recommended her to go and paint her face, like Madame Bonaparte."

"Well!" exclaimed Corinna. "I trust he won't address a similar remark to us!"

There seemed little likelihood of this, since the first consul was very sparing of his conversation, passing down the room among his guests with few pauses and those of only short duration.

"Is it not a regimented affair?" whispered Patrice Landier with a grimace to Corinna. "For myself, I prefer private parties or the balls at Frascati's where one may relax a little. Do you like to dance, mademoiselle?"

"Indeed I do. At home, I attend all the assemblies."

"Ah, fortunate gentlemen who have the pleasure of partnering you! But I shall not despair — we are all bidden to a ball at Milady Northcote's, are we not? May I beg the honour, Mademoiselle Corinna, of a dance — perhaps, even, two? Now pray don't refuse me, or I shall be obliged to put a period to my existence!"

She laughed, enjoying the gallant nonsense.

"Oh, you're too absurd, monsieur!"

He assumed an expression of comical dismay.

"Alas, you mock at me! But I know that the English delight in absurdities, so I must take what comfort I can from that. And you will dance with me at the ball, will you not, mademoiselle? You cannot be so cruel as to refuse."

She glanced away momentarily to where Sir Richard was standing close by in conversation with Mr and Mrs Langham; she saw that his eye was upon her and thought it registered disapproval.

She tilted her chin defiantly, placing her hand upon Landier's arm and bestowing a brilliant smile upon him.

"Of course I will dance with you, nonsensical creature, but at present I would like some lemonade. Do you think we might move to the refreshment table?"

He responded with alacrity, steering her in that direction.

Sir Richard's friends moved away from him presently and he was joined by his brother and Lydia.

"There, what did I tell you?" demanded Lydia, her glance following Landier and Corinna. "Those two are dealing splendidly together, just as I hoped."

"Which two? Oh, you mean Corinna and Landier, I collect," replied John. Then, turning to his brother with a chuckle: "Did you ever know females when they weren't matchmaking? A man has only to do the civil, and they're looking for the banns to be called."

"Well, you may laugh, but I do think she's showing more interest in your French friend than in any of her beaux in Tunbridge Wells," said Lydia defensively.

"I dare say. They don't possess his Gallic charm, my love, and she's here to enjoy herself, ain't she? But I'll wager she doesn't mean anything by it, no more than he does. Why, for all we know, he may already have fixed his interest with some little French miss."

"Do you think so?" demanded Lydia, putting on a scandalised air. "Then he has no right to flirt with my sister in that abandoned way!"

"Well, I don't wish to cavil, m'dear, but what would you say *she's* doing?"

"She is not flirting!" Lydia was indignant. "Is she, Richard?"

Sir Richard raised his quizzing glass and inspected the couple under discussion with a solemn air. Corinna was laughing up into Landier's face at that moment with an undoubtedly provocative gleam in her golden eyes.

He lowered the glass quickly.

"You must hold me excused," he said languidly. "I fear I'm no judge. Would you care for some refreshment, too, Lydia? And after that, perhaps we should pay our respects to Lord Whitworth. I see he is over there with my friend Langham. It will not do to ignore our nation's ambassador — one never knows when one may require his services."

Lydia laughed. "You are always so provident, Richard! And guarded, too," she added, giving him a curious look. "I wonder if anyone, even your own brother, ever knows what you really think?"

"Or cares?" he parried. "But naturally, I study to be interesting, my dear sister. When a man cannot lay claim to Gallic charm, he must manage to rub along with English phlegm — what d'you say, John?"

CHAPTER FIVE

Lord and Lady Northcote came from London and had hired a house in Paris similar to that of the Cheveleys. She was a dashing young matron who was very popular with the gentlemen; he was an amiable fop whose slow wits were an excellent foil for her tireless vivacity. They had been present at Lady Cheveley's dinner party and, having been introduced to Sir Richard and his companions, had at once invited them all to attend their next ball.

Lady Northcote received them in a pale green muslin gown that was almost transparent, her auburn hair dressed in a tapering cone bound about with ribbons of an identical shade. She fluted a welcome, while her husband added an incoherent word or two in the same vein. As they passed on into the ballroom, which was already crowded, Sir Richard raised his quizzing glass, pausing to survey the scene.

"Dear me, quite an extravaganza," he murmured to Corinna, who was standing beside him.

The walls were festooned with swathes of pink silk wherever there did not happen to be full-length mirrors ornamented with ormolu, and flowers were banked in profusion before the dais on which the musicians were stationed.

She chuckled. "Yes, isn't it? Vastly different from the assemblies in Tunbridge Wells!"

"Well, after all, you came to Paris in order to enlarge your horizons," he reminded her. "Perhaps we have admired for long enough, and should now move about the room a little."

When they began to do so, they soon identified acquaintances among the crowd and were caught up in conversation. Although they had been scarcely a fortnight in Paris, already they knew several people; as Miss Cheveley had said, the Englishman abroad tended to gravitate towards his own countrymen.

Miss Cheveley herself had approached Corinna almost at once, isolating her from the rest of her party, who drifted onwards to converse with others.

"Now that we are in a fair way to becoming friends, Miss Haydon, I feel that I may perhaps indulge a little curiosity concerning one member of your party," she said, after a few social trivialities had passed between them.

"By all means. Do you mean Monsieur Landier? But I've already explained his connection with us, have I not?"

"Yes, indeed you have, but I didn't mean that gentleman," answered Miss Cheveley, a slight flush colouring her creamy complexion. "Perhaps, however, I shouldn't quiz you — you will think me a prying female, and in general I assure you I am not."

"No, I don't believe you are," returned Corinna, "and you've no occasion to feel guilty, for I'm the most quizzing female in the world, always curious about my neighbours," confessed Corinna, somewhat overstating the case in a friendly urge to reassure her companion. "I should suppose that the person you have in mind is Sir Richard Beresford."

Miss Cheveley shyly admitted the impeachment, still looking rather ashamed.

"You will already know that he is my sister's husband's elder brother — dear me, how clumsy and intricate that sounds!" Corinna laughed, easing the slight tension. "He has an estate in Sussex, Chyngton Manor, which he inherited a few years ago on his father's death. His parents and mine were old friends, so we have known the two brothers all our lives."

Miss Cheveley hesitated. "There is no Lady Beresford — the gentleman is not married?"

"Married? Richard? Oh, no!" declared Corinna emphatically, as if such an idea were unthinkable. "He's not at all in the petticoat line — or perhaps I should say that so far he has never shown a particular interest in any one female, and we would certainly know of it, if he did, being so closely associated."

"Yes, of course."

"I must admit that it had never occurred to me before," went on Corinna, wrinkling her brow, "but I should suppose that he must soon be turning his thoughts towards matrimony, for he is eight and twenty, you know. I only hope that when he does come round to it, he'll choose a female whom my family can like, for my mother has always considered the Beresfords almost as blood relations."

The conversation was interrupted at this point as the floor was being cleared for the dancing to begin. Corinna moved with her friend to join Lydia and Lady Cheveley in the seats provided at the sides of the room; as she did so, she thought over what had been said. It was clear that Frances Cheveley's query had not been prompted by idle curiosity alone. She must, reflected Corinna, possess at least the first stirrings of an interest in Richard. Was there anything on his side? She had not noticed, but then she had not been watching for the symptoms. Nothing had been further from her mind, and now she wondered why. Richard was a personable gentleman of title and estate, and as such a highly eligible parti. There must have been plenty of females who had set their caps at him, and before long someone would succeed in fixing his interest. Perhaps it would indeed be Frances Cheveley.

Corinna was quite at a loss to understand why she should find such a prospect slightly depressing. As both she and Lydia liked Frances Cheveley, surely there was nothing against a closer connection with her? Nothing against Miss Cheveley, no, she decided in a flash of self-perception; what she objected to was the notion of Richard's being married. But that was absurd! Of course he would wish to marry at some time, and probably soon, as she had just pointed out to her friend. She must accustom herself — they all must — to the likelihood of this.

She sighed. It seemed a pity; matters were very comfortable as they stood at present, but that was a selfish attitude.

Her reverie was interrupted by the prompt appearance of both Sir Richard and Patrice Landier to claim the two young ladies as partners in the dance. There was a moment when it looked as if Sir Richard would ask her; but Landier spoke first, reminding her of her previous promise. All four took their places in the set. At first, Corinna tried to watch the other pair to see if there could be anything to suggest a growing attachment between them; but she soon abandoned this when her partner complained of her inattention.

"I am not, I realise, the most brilliant talker in the room, mademoiselle, but for form's sake you must throw a word at me now and then, like a bone to a dog," he reproached her, his eyes twinkling.

"I beg your pardon — did you say something to me which I didn't answer?"

"Several things, but no matter! You are quite right to ignore them, for they were of a dullness *incroyable*," he replied, laughing.

"Then let us both mend our ways," she said, joining in his laughter. "You shall be your usual entertaining self and I promise to hang on your every word."

This seemed to answer, for from that moment they became one of the most animated couples in the room.

When Sir Richard claimed Corinna for the succeeding dance, she was still in high spirits and soon coaxed him out of an initial tendency to gravity into his more usual raillery.

They had just joined hands in the final movement when he suddenly felt her grip tighten convulsively. He looked up into her face and saw that her head was turned away towards the door, her neck muscles taut. He followed her gaze.

A gentleman had just arrived belatedly and was being greeted by Lady Northcote. He was strikingly handsome, with thick chestnut hair, classical features and a slim, upright figure. His evening attire was faultless, the dark blue coat smooth across his broad shoulders, the cravat of snowy linen intricately tied. Sir Richard recognised him instantly.

It was Fabian Grenville.

Corinna uttered an exclamation of annoyance as there was a faint tearing sound, and she looked down to see that she had stepped on the hem of her gown and ripped it slightly.

"How odiously clumsy of me!" she said as she gathered up the folds in one hand to make her concluding curtsey. "Pray forgive me, Richard, if I rush away from you, but I must pin this up at once."

"Of course — an unfortunate accident," he replied.

She darted off, still clutching her skirts with one hand, in the direction of her hostess.

Corinna ruefully explained her predicament.

"How tiresome," said Lady Northcote with spurious sympathy. "But my maid will soon repair the damage for you

— she's an excellent needlewoman. If you will go into the ladies' retiring room, I'll have her sent to you."

She ushered Corinna into a small room across the hall and left her there. Corinna was not sorry to have a few moments alone in which to recover from the shock of seeing Mr Grenville. She had scarcely expected ever to meet him again, in spite of her romantic daydreams; but to see him here in Paris had not entered even those rosy imaginings.

The uncomfortable flutterings of her pulses had subsided by the time she heard a deferential knock upon the door. She called out permission to enter.

A young girl of about her sister Irene's age came into the room. She was small and slender, with black hair demurely drawn back under a white lace edged cap, and large dark eyes. Her face took Corinna by surprise, for it was unlike that of the usual English abigail; it was fine featured, almost aristocratic, and wore a remote, withdrawn expression which suggested a nun-like serenity.

She dropped a curtsey. "I believe you need my help, milady."

Corinna realised then that the girl was French. Her English, though good, was faintly accented.

"Oh, yes, if you please. But I'm not milady, only plain Miss Haydon. What is your name?"

"Madeleine, ma'am. It is your dress, yes?"

Corinna ruefully displayed the rent in her gown.

"The most tiresome thing, and quite my own fault. I can't even blame a clumsy partner, I must confess! Can you do anything to make it last through the evening? I'll be so much obliged to you."

The girl knelt down to inspect the damage.

"Why, yes, I think I can manage to set a few stitches which will hold the material and not be noticed. Pray be seated, Miss Haydon."

Corinna obeyed, arranging the torn hem to one side of her so that the maid could work on it. Having provided herself with the necessary materials from a workbox which stood in the room, Madeleine knelt down on the floor beside her and set about the task.

"You are French, are you not?" Corinna asked, curious about this girl who seemed somehow above her station in life.

"Yes, ma'am."

"Did you come from England with my lady Northcote?"

"No, ma'am. Milady did not bring her own maid, so she engaged me here."

"I see. Is your home in Paris?"

Madeleine shook her head. "No, ma'am."

"Oh, then in the country somewhere?" persisted Corinna. "And you came to seek employment in the town?"

"That is so, ma'am."

"Do you miss the country? A large town such as Paris must be quite a change, I surmise."

A tremor passed momentarily across that serene countenance, like a ripple on a quiet lake.

"Yes, ma'am. I do miss my home. But one must accustom oneself, and this is a good post. I am fortunate to have obtained it."

Corinna was silent, reflecting that it must be a melancholy business for a female to be obliged to earn her own living. This girl seemed grateful for the employment she had found, but there was that about her which suggested that in reality she was above it, and had once known better days.

"There, I think that will do for the present," said Madeleine, rising to her feet. "Will you be pleased to inspect it in the mirror, ma'am?"

Corinna moved to a long mirror against one wall, and twirled about, studying her hem with a critical eye.

"Why, that is splendid!" she said, smiling at the girl. "Thank you so much — you've worked wonders!"

Madeleine inclined her head in dignified acknowledgement of this tribute; but when Corinna produced some money from her reticule and would have pressed it into the maid's hand, she drew back.

"Thank you, Miss Haydon, it is not necessary. I am happy to be of service," she said quietly.

Almost Corinna stared. It was something new in her experience for servants to refuse vails, and it gave her a momentary pang of shame for having made the offer.

"Then thank you again," she said, as she moved towards the door. "Good-bye, Madeleine."

The maid curtseyed. "*Au revoir*, mademoiselle," she replied.

The moment Corinna stepped once more into the ballroom all thought of the preceding interview vanished. She could think of nothing but Mr Grenville, and looked eagerly about her to locate him. This was difficult, as another dance was in progress; so after a few moments, she gave up the quest and made her way to some chairs at the side of the room where she saw Lady Cheveley and one or two other matrons seated.

"Oh, there you are, Miss Haydon," Lady Cheveley greeted her. "Sir Richard Beresford said you had suffered some mishap to your gown and had retired to adjust matters. I trust all is satisfactory now?"

Corinna replied suitably, and a desultory conversation followed while she continued to glance about the room. At last she espied Mr Grenville among the dancers. His partner was a brassy blonde female of some years older than himself, dressed in a very low-cut gown of pink silk which displayed fully her ample proportions. She smiled a great deal too much and from time to time made girlish, fluttering motions with her hands.

"Do you know, ma'am, who is that lady dancing with Mr Grenville — that's to say, the gentleman with chestnut hair in the blue coat," she added, realising that Grenville might well be a stranger to Lady Cheveley.

"Mr Grenville? Oh, so *you* are acquainted with him, are you?" replied her companion, giving her a quizzical look which Corinna did not altogether relish. "He's complete to a shade, is he not, and quite turns all the females' heads! But perhaps I should give you just the tiniest hint, since your Mama is not here with you, that he is not to be relied upon, my dear. In fact, not to mince matters, a gazetted fortune hunter. Sad, for he is quite an Adonis and has such charm! But so it often is, alas — the most attractive men are seldom the most eligible, as I've often warned Frances. It is rarely a girl has the good fortune to meet one such as Sir Richard Beresford, who is possessed of good looks and gentlemanly address in addition to his undoubted eligibility. Your family has been acquainted with him for many years, I collect?"

"We've known the Beresfords forever," replied Corinna dismissively, for she did not wish to be drawn into the same conversation with the mother that she had recently had with the daughter. "And Sir Richard is everything you say. But tell me, ma'am, who is that lady? Do you know her?"

"Not to say *know* her, for she is not quite in my style," said Lady Cheveley drily. "She has been in Paris for about a month and is, so I'm told, the widow of a wealthy London merchant. She is here with a married sister and the sister's husband. Their name is Collard and the widow is a Mrs Peters. Mr Grenville has been much in their company." She lowered her voice. "Lady Northcote is prodigiously free with her hospitality, and one never quite knows whom one will meet at her parties."

Corinna continued to observe Mr Grenville and his vulgar — yes, there was no other word for the female — partner. What Lady Cheveley had said suggested that Mrs Peters was the present object of his attentions. As she was wealthy, that must be the attraction, for she was scarcely in his style. Corinna could not repress a feeling of disgust that he should sink so low in his search for an heiress. Miss Pemberton, the lady whom he had courted so assiduously in Tunbridge Wells, had at least been his social equal and he need not have been ashamed to introduce her to his friends. For the first time, she admitted a doubt as to his conduct; hitherto she had always tried to justify this to herself as unavoidable when a gentleman lacked means.

She saw he was not dancing at present, but standing at the side of the room with Mrs Peters and several other people who were obviously their friends. He was conversing most particularly to the widow, whose behaviour towards him continued to be as boldly flirtatious as when they had been dancing together.

She watched them covertly for some time, but at last resolutely withdrew her eyes, feeling dejected and yet close to anger; she was almost inclined to plead a headache and return to their hotel. But to do so would mean curtailing Lydia's enjoyment, for she knew that her sister would never let her leave the ball unaccompanied; so she concealed her feelings as best she might, trying to show some interest in Lady Cheveley's conversation.

Lydia was dancing with her husband when she first noticed Fabian Grenville in the room. She gave a start of dismay.

"Of all the unlucky things, John! That man is here — the very person whom I brought Corinna to France to forget! Was ever anything so wretched! And just when I thought she was in a fair way to turning her interest elsewhere!"

"So you've spotted him," said John in a casual tone. "Knew he was here — Richard told me. No need to put yourself in a taking over that. Dare say his present company will open your sister's eyes to the kind of fellow he is."

It was only towards the end, when supper was over and some of Lady Northcote's guests were departing, that Corinna and Grenville came face to face. He was moving towards the exit, Mrs Peters on his arm and the rest of their group following; and he passed close by Corinna, Lydia, and Sir Richard, who were standing together in that part of the room.

For a second he halted as if about to speak; then, obedient to the pressure on his arm exerted by his impatient companion, he smiled, bowed, and departed.

CHAPTER SIX

A few days later, Patrice Landier was strolling in leisurely fashion through the gardens of the Palais Royal, enjoying the sunshine of an unusually mild April day. As usual on a fine day, the gardens were thronged with people, most of whom were as leisurely as himself; which was why his attention was first caught by one amongst them who seemed to be in a hurry.

She was a young female whose attire suggested that she was employed as a maid, and she was carrying a bandbox. As she walked briskly past him, he caught a glimpse of her face and at once gave a start of recognition. He quickened his steps to catch up with her and touched her lightly on the arm.

She halted, turning a startled look upon him which immediately changed as she in her turn recognised him.

"Mademoiselle Fougeray!" he exclaimed in astonished tones. "Why, what brings you here?"

She coloured as she sketched a curtsey in response to his bow.

"Good day, Monsieur Landier," she replied.

She was obviously somewhat shaken, though her voice was calm enough.

"But what are you doing in Paris, mademoiselle? I thought I had lost you, that we should never meet again! I went a month since to your uncle's house in La Bouille and was told that the good curé, alas! was dead, God rest him. I am so very sorry, mademoiselle — you must mourn for him — believe me, if there is anything I can do—"

"You are very good, monsieur, but there is nothing."

"You are here in Paris with some relatives, perhaps? When I inquired after you, no one knew where you had gone."

"No, monsieur, I have no relatives in France. One of the nuns brought me here on my uncle's instructions, to find suitable employment so that I can carry out his plan for my future."

"What employment? What plan?"

"I am personal maid to an English milady. Her name is Lady Northcote," she explained. "And as I am on an errand for her now, you will readily understand, monsieur, that I must not delay. Your pardon, but I should be on my way at once."

She sketched another little curtsey and turned away as if to leave him. He placed a detaining hand on her arm.

"But no! Now that I have found you again I cannot let you go so easily! I will walk along with you to Lady Northcote's house," he said with a determined air.

"Monsieur, it is not *convenable* that you should walk with me," she protested, her colour coming and going. "I am only an abigail, you realise, and such things are not done. If anyone should notice and tell milady—"

"Is not France a Republic?" he asked scornfully. "Are we not all equal citizens of our country? Moreover, mademoiselle, you and I are old acquaintances — for six months or more I have been visiting the curé and yourself whenever I could escape from my business duties. Can not one friend walk with another? But only tell me truly that you don't desire it — for *yourself*, mind, not for milady Northcote — and I will go away at once!"

This she could not bring herself to do; so she allowed him to walk along beside her and even to carry the bandbox, though she protested a little at this.

"And now tell me what was your uncle's plan for your future," he said as they went on their way.

"He wished me to go to an aunt of mine who lives in Brighton," she replied, stumbling a little over the foreign word. "That is a town on the coast in England, you know."

He smiled at her anxiety to ensure his understanding of this point.

"Yes, I do know, for at one time I was a prisoner of war in England not so very many miles distant from Brighton. And so you are hoping to save enough money from your employment to pay for the journey to England?"

"I shall save what I can, naturally. But milady has promised to take me back with her when she leaves France, and it is on that I depend chiefly, for I think I can scarcely save enough, even with what was left me by my dear, dear uncle."

Her voice shook on the last words.

"And so you will go," he said in a despondent tone. "Most likely then I shall never see you again. Can I not persuade you to change your mind, to remain here in France, to permit me to see you frequently and perhaps—" He broke off, then resumed in a low, passionate voice: "Mademoiselle Madeleine, this is scarcely the time or the place for me to tell you all that is in my heart — you have suffered a great loss, moreover you are very young still, and unprotected — I would be a brute to force my attentions upon you at present—"

She put up her hands to cover her burning face.

"Monsieur — I implore you!" she stammered.

He controlled himself with an effort, for indeed he had said more than he intended, though certainly not as much as he wished.

"I have done — I will embarrass you no further," he promised. "But I may see you again, mademoiselle, may I not, to talk over old times, to stand as your friend in case of need?"

"You are very good — and yes, it is comfortable to have someone whom I know from my past life, close at hand," she admitted. "But, monsieur, I don't see how I can arrange matters for us to meet. Whatever you say about being a family friend I cannot think it proper to be making assignations with you. Besides" — she put up her hand with a touchingly imperative little gesture when he would have interrupted her — "there is a practical difficulty. Situated as I am, you cannot call on me at milady's house, and I never know when I shall be at liberty to walk abroad."

"There are no errands that occur at regular intervals?" he queried. "No free time allotted to you?"

She hesitated. "Not so that I may depend upon it. But sometimes I walk a little by the banks of the Seine, in the early morning."

"Then I will meet you there," he said quickly. "Whereabouts do you go?"

"Close to the Pont Neuf. But, monsieur, you will not wish to rise so early. And truly, I do not think we should."

"At home, I am astir by seven o'clock. Do you rate me as one of these fashionable people with endless leisure? I am a businessman, mademoiselle, and have work to do in the world."

By now they had reached the road in which Lady Northcote's house was situated, and she halted.

"Do not, I beg you, accompany me to the door, monsieur. I may be observed."

"*D'accord*. It is arranged, then, and I will look for you by the Seine tomorrow."

"I cannot promise," she said hesitantly.

"But you will try — please? If you don't appear, I shall understand that you could not come."

She nodded and gave a brief curtsey.

"Thank you for carrying my bandbox," she said, relieving him of this encumbrance. "*Au revoir*, monsieur."

He bowed. "*A bientôt*, mademoiselle," he corrected her, smiling.

He stood there watching until she had disappeared.

During the ensuing week they met almost every day to stroll beside the sunlight-dappled waters of the Seine. They talked of the past — though not so very far back, a bare seven months ago — when Landier had first come quite by chance to Madeleine's village. He had fallen into conversation there with the Curé Vernet, who had civilly invited the young man into his house for refreshment. Madeleine had brought them coffee and stayed to listen to their conversation. There were few people of education in that neighbourhood, and her uncle had welcomed the opportunity to talk with Landier. As for the young man himself, he had been captivated by the gentle, quiet-spoken girl who employed none of the usual feminine arts to make herself attractive to him, but had sat silently by, listening, an intent expression on her serene countenance.

In response to the curé's invitation to call again any time he was passing that way, he had returned only a few days later; and soon he was a frequent visitor.

He spoke now of those comfortable hours which the three of them had passed together, recalling the lively discussions between the curé and himself.

"We could not agree on everything, you may remember," he said. "He held one view of what France ought to be, and I another. But he was always a generous opponent in our little arguments, bearing me no grudge for venturing to challenge his opinion."

It was evident that these reminiscences of her uncle brought Madeleine much solace in the sorrow which, until now, she had been forced to keep hidden. She encouraged Landier in them, and he was only too glad to indulge her so that he might the more easily avoid another, more compelling subject which he had resolved to postpone for a while. During those months when he had been visiting at the curé's house, he had been in a fair way to falling in love with her. He was making up his mind to speak of his feelings to the curé when pressure of business unfortunately curtailed his visits for several weeks. During that time, the curé developed his terminal illness; and when Landier was at last free to return, it was to find that the curé was dead and buried and that Madeleine had left the village for good. No one would admit to knowing where she had gone, neither had she left any message for him.

It seemed to him then that there was nothing else he could do but to try and forget her; but now that he had met her once again, he realised that his heart was irretrievably lost. There could be no forgetting.

All this was in his mind as they strolled together in the spring sunshine beside the river, but he knew he must not risk speaking of it yet. She was as easily startled as some shy woodland creature, he told himself fondly, and he must approach her as softly. Moreover, as she was now without the protection of a guardian, he must behave towards her as circumspectly as the honour of a chivalrous man required. The time might come when he could speak of marriage, but that time was not yet. Even to have persuaded her to meet him in this way was perhaps not what he should have done, he acknowledged to himself ruefully; but how else, in their peculiar circumstances, could he possibly pursue the acquaintance?

So far, their meetings had been safe from prying eyes, for none but humble folk intent on their own concerns were found beside the Seine at such an early hour of day. When Sunday came round, however, and Madeleine said she must forego their usual meeting in order to attend Mass, Landier's impatience to see her overcame her more prudent objections, and she was persuaded to accept his escort back from church to her place of employment.

This proved to be a mistake. They met no one who gave them a second glance until they reached the corner of the street in which Lady Northcote's house stood, and where Madeleine had decreed they must part. As they lingered for a few moments to take leave of each other, a young lady and gentleman turned into the street, almost bumping into them.

It was Corinna and Laurence Haydon.

All four looked surprised, though in different degrees. Corinna at once recognised the French girl.

"Why, it's Madeleine, is it not?" she exclaimed impulsively. "I suppose you've been to church — and you, too, Monsieur Landier?"

"Good morning, Miss Haydon," replied Madeleine with a curtsey.

Landier thereupon bowed and performed the necessary introduction between Laurence and Mademoiselle Fougeray with something less than his usual air of assurance. A few civilities as to the clement weather passed before Madeleine said quietly that she must be going, and took her leave.

"And so must we," said Corinna, while Landier stared after the slight grey figure. "We're on our way to make a call on Lady Cheveley and her daughter. Do you care to join us, sir?"

Landier declined somewhat hastily and they parted to go their separate ways.

"Who was that female?" asked Laurence curiously. "Pretty little filly — don't recall seeing her before. Landier seems to know her well, though — bit of a dark horse, our friend, what?"

"Yes, he does," agreed Corinna in a wondering tone. "It's odd, because she's Lady Northcote's abigail. She mended my gown for me when we attended the ball there last week."

Laurence whistled. "An abigail, what! I tell you something, sister, I reckon he's not just a dark horse, but a rank outsider! And to think he has the nerve to make up to you! Mind you, she don't look like any abigail I ever saw. Would have said she was Quality."

"She certainly is a most superior young woman, and I tell you, Laurie, you've no right to be jumping to conclusions," reprimanded Corinna. "I know their being together looks odd, but for all we know there may be some perfectly normal explanation."

"Ay, I dare say," chuckled the irrepressible Laurence. "The usual explanation, I don't doubt."

Corinna changed the subject quickly, for her own mind was not as easy as she would have liked her brother to believe. She had come to think almost as highly of Landier as the two Beresfords did, and it was something of a shock to discover him in what appeared to be an improper connection.

As for Landier himself, the incident haunted him. He realised only too well what conclusions could be drawn from his association with Lady Northcote's maid, and he longed to set matters right. More than that, he was now determined to make an attempt to do so. He would put his fate to the touch without further delay, win or lose all.

On the following morning, therefore, he arrived at their rendezvous a full hour before he could expect Madeleine to be there, and spent the interval pacing up and down in perturbation of spirit.

She came at last, her eyes troubled. "Mademoiselle," he began impetuously, "our position is intolerable! I cannot any longer permit you to expose yourself to such misapprehensions as must have been in the minds of those friends of mine whom we most unfortunately encountered yesterday! That they should think—" he broke off, flushing like a boy. "You must believe me when I say that it will not do. Mademoiselle Madeleine," he continued forcefully, "you must know how much I respect and admire you — I have loved you these many months past, and want you for my wife. I know that you think of me only as a friend, but could you not find a greater warmth for me in your heart? I would have waited to give you more time, but our present situation is intolerable, and I must speak now!"

She had lowered her eyes, her cheeks suffused with blushes. She attempted to speak, but could not.

He seized her hand and carried it to his lips. "Dearest Madeleine, you must answer me!" She withdrew the hand gently, raising her head again to look at him with eyes full of trouble.

"Monsieur, I cannot," she said after an effort. "I made a promise to my uncle before he died — a solemn promise which I cannot break — to go to my aunt in England and allow her to make a suitable marriage for me—"

"But why is not my offer suitable? Why cannot we go together and seek this lady's approval? I can't see the difficulty, provided only that you can care enough for me to become my wife."

"That is because you don't know my history. I see I must say what may cause you pain, but there is nothing else to be done. During those last hours, my uncle spoke of you. He said that though he considered you to be upright and honourable, I must not think of you as — as a husband. He guessed, you see, that such was in your thoughts."

"Well he might! But why, since you say he approved of my character? He knew, too, that I was a man of some substance and could offer you a comfortable establishment. What other objection could there be?"

"He said I must marry one of my own rank. You see, I am the daughter of an aristocrat — my father was the Vicomte de Fougeray. He and my mother—"

Her voice faltered.

"The guillotine?" he asked gently.

She nodded. "Ten years since, when I was only seven. My father's brother, too — it is his wife who is now in Brighton. There is also a son, three years older than I. My aunt and cousin managed to escape to England in time. As for me, I was smuggled out of our château by a faithful servant, who took me to the curé of his native village. It was thought wise that I should pass as the Curé Vernet's niece, so from that time he became my uncle — and thus I have thought of him from childhood, thus I shall always think of him! He has been all the family I had—"

She broke off, sobbing quietly. He moved towards her as if to take her in his arms, but checked himself, his face set.

"And you? You consider that this difference in rank matters? You consider me beneath you?"

She stretched out a hand towards him, looking up into his stern face with tear-dimmed eyes.

"Ah, no! I don't know what to think, except that I must keep a promise made to a dying man whose every thought was for my welfare! Please understand — you must try to understand!"

He made no reply for a moment, watching her grief with an unaccustomed hard look in his eyes.

"Then there is nothing left but for us to part," he said, at last, in clipped, unnatural tones. "I wish you well. *Adieu*, Mademoiselle de Fougeray. I am your very humble servant."

He bowed in exaggerated courtesy, then turned on his heel and left her standing there.

CHAPTER SEVEN

No one was particularly surprised when Patrice Landier announced on the following day that he must end his vacation and return to Rouen. It had always been understood that he could remain only a short time in Paris.

Before he took leave of his friends, Landier found an opportunity for a few private words with Corinna.

"I think you and I, mademoiselle, have been good friends during my stay in Paris, *n'est-ce pas?*"

"Indeed we have," agreed Corinna warmly. "You will be a sad loss to our whole party, monsieur."

"Thank you. But because of our friendship, I would not like to leave you under the shadow of a misunderstanding. Pardon me" — as she looked puzzled, not immediately seeing what his meaning was — "I refer to Sunday, when you met Mademoiselle Fougeray in my company. You may have supposed, could scarcely have been blamed for supposing—"

A slight blush coloured her cheeks. "Indeed, sir, you have no need of explaining anything to me. It is not my affair."

"Ah, but I must, with your permission, for the sake of Mademoiselle Fougeray's reputation. You see, I was a friend of the curé, her uncle, and in the past often visited at their home in a village close to Rouen. Until recently I was not aware that her uncle had died and she had been forced, through lack of means, to seek employment in Paris. The situation was difficult — I could not call on her in the ordinary way, so I was foolish enough to persuade her to meet me clandestinely. My conduct was misguided, my only excuse that I wished to make her my wife."

Corinna opened her eyes wide at this, but could find nothing to say.

"I fear I've shocked you, but what was to be done? I believe I need not tell you that our meetings were always as circumspect as that of Sunday — we met and walked together in public places."

"I assure you, monsieur, I was not shocked — only surprised," said Corinna, finding her voice. "That poor girl! She has been most unfortunate. But now I suppose all is well, and I can wish you happy?"

He shook his head dolefully. "No, I was not successful in my application, for reasons with which I need not trouble you. I leave Paris a disappointed man, mademoiselle, but I trust at least I haven't forfeited the good opinion of my friends."

"You haven't forfeited mine, I assure you, monsieur," she replied warmly. "As for the others, except only Laurence, they knew nothing of the incident, for Laurence and I haven't spoken of it. But I am so sorry for your disappointment — it is a melancholy thing indeed to be crossed in love! I can only hope that time will ameliorate your distress, as everyone says it must."

She said this with a softened expression, impulsively putting out her hand to him. He took it and carried it to his lips.

At this inopportune moment, Sir Richard walked in upon them.

He started to retreat at once; but Landier leapt up, protesting that he must go, as the carriage would be at the door. After he had left, Corinna sat pensively turning over in her mind what he had told her. Inevitably, it led to a consideration of her own disappointment in love. She had not seen Fabian Grenville at all since the evening of Lady Northcote's ball, and time had a little softened her feelings of outrage on that occasion. She wondered if she would see him again and whether on the next occasion she would learn that he was actually betrothed to that vulgar female, Mrs Peters.

"You appear in some danger of falling into melancholy," remarked Sir Richard in a rallying tone.

She started from her reverie. "Do I? Well, it is a little sad to part from such a lively member of our party, after all, don't you agree?"

"Of course, but I trust we can still contrive to amuse you. What do you say if we stroll over to Frascati's and try one of their famed ices?"

She jumped up at once. "Oh, yes, by all means let us be doing something."

During their walk he exerted himself to entertain her and succeeded so well that by the time they reached Frascati's restaurant she was in her usual sunny mood. They seated themselves at one of the tables in a room decorated in the classical manner with pillars and friezes of plasterwork. Corinna looked curiously about her at the assembled company, very mixed as in most public places in Paris. They nodded to some English acquaintances nearby, but otherwise saw no one whom they knew until a loud laugh drew their attention to a group at one table against the wall.

Corinna glanced in that direction, then stiffened. The laugh had come from a female in a showy purple silk bonnet adorned with three large curled feathers; one look was enough to identify her as Mrs Peters. She was accompanied by a middle-aged couple whom Corinna thought she recognised as having been with Mrs Peters at Lady Northcote's ball, and also by Mr Grenville. He looked as elegantly turned out as usual, and so much above his company that the effect might have been ludicrous, had Corinna felt in the least like laughing.

She turned her head away quickly, but not before Grenville had intercepted her glance, and given a brief bow. Sir Richard, who was still watching, saw him hesitate, rise, and say something to his companions, then start to move towards the table at which Sir Richard and Corinna were sitting.

"Deuced warm in here," said Sir Richard, getting up from his chair. "I see you've finished your ice. Shall we go?"

Nothing loath, she, too, rose. He tossed some money onto the table and, taking her shawl from the back of the chair, draped it about her shoulders. As he was performing this office, Grenville arrived before them. He bowed again, more deeply this time, a delighted smile on his handsome face.

"Why, Miss Haydon, what an unexpected pleasure to see you in Paris. It's an age since we last met. 'Servant, Beresford."

"Surely not, sir?" retorted Corinna, making a gallant effort to remain mistress of the situation, in spite of a fluttering pulse. "You saw me, I think, about a fortnight since, at Lady Northcote's ball. But I dare say you've forgotten — one meets so many people here — I had almost forgotten it, myself."

Sir Richard contented himself with returning Grenville's bow and murmuring "How d' you do?"

"Forgotten? Oh, no, indeed not — how could you suppose so? But at that time you were on the point of leaving with your party, so it seemed scarce opportune to hinder you."

"Of course," said Corinna sweetly. "And you, too, were very occupied with your party, Mr Grenville."

A slight diminution of the smile indicated that he had registered a hit, but he continued with unabated affability.

"I was referring to our meetings in Tunbridge Wells last summer, Miss Haydon — so many pleasant memories of that time crowd in on me! I declare I have never enjoyed myself half as well elsewhere, before or since! It is too much to hope that you, too, may retain some agreeable recollections of my visit?"

This was said with a tender, intimate look that made Corinna's heart turn over, and inspired Sir Richard with an itch in his fists.

"Our assemblies at home are *always* prodigiously agreeable," returned Corinna, trying for a careless tone. "Everyone must be pleased that you, a visitor to the town, found them so. But we must not detain you, sir," she added, ostentatiously glancing across the room to the table he had just left. "I fancy your party are waiting to leave."

His own eyes flickered in that direction and observed that Mrs Peters was not best pleased.

"Just so. Well, I must hope that we shall soon meet again, ma'am, in circumstances which will allow of a longer chat."

He bowed low to Corinna, more briefly to Sir Richard, and took himself back to his table companions, who were now standing awaiting him with ill-concealed impatience.

Sir Richard shepherded Corinna from the restaurant without saying a word; but his shrewd glance noted the signs of disturbance in her countenance and the slight trembling of her hands, and his jaw tightened.

She recovered a little as they walked along, although it was some time before she could subdue her confused thoughts sufficiently to converse with him. When she did, it was on indifferent subjects, and he saw that there were to be no confidences. He was by far too considerate to make any comments himself, so the encounter was dismissed. But like many emotive subjects barred from conversation, it occupied a disproportionate space in the thoughts of both.

When they reached the hotel they found Laurence there, with a glum expression on his face.

"Here's a deuced wretched business," he greeted them. "Cheveley's off back to London tomorrow — says there's no more sport to be had in Paris. What with both Landier and him gone, we'll soon find ourselves at a stand for company."

"Fustian!" exclaimed Lydia, laughing. "Why, we have so many acquaintances here now, that we're hard pressed to fit in all our engagements."

"Do they all go?" asked Corinna. "Miss Cheveley said nothing of it to me when we met yesterday."

"No, the rest of the family are to remain for the present, but nothing would do for Cheveley but to clear off for London. He has rooms in Albermarle Street, he tells me, lucky devil!"

He looked so like a sulky schoolboy that John and his brother were hard put to it not to laugh; but they restrained themselves nobly, suggesting that possibly he might care to accompany them to the Champs de Mars, where Napoleon was to review some troops that afternoon.

"It isn't an outing to appeal to the ladies, I fear," said Sir Richard, "but I don't doubt they'll contrive to exist without our company for a few hours."

This was agreed to, with what Sir Richard apostrophised as more fervour than civility, and the sisters settled down to a comfortable cose.

For some time they talked of Lydia's latest ball gown and dress in general, subjects which were barred when in the gentlemen's company. After they had exhausted this topic for the moment, Lydia switched to a more personal one.

"I hope you won't miss Monsieur Landier too much," she said with a sly look. "It seemed to me that the two of you were dealing famously together."

"Don't be such a goose, Lyddy! That is, if you mean what I think you mean, and I'm sure you do," said Corinna, with more emphasis than lucidity. "I shall miss his nonsense, of course, for he had an amusing way with him, but as for anything else — it's too absurd! And if only you knew—"

She stopped, uncertain how far she ought to reveal Landier's confidences to her. She had said too much for Lydia's natural curiosity, however; upon being pressed further and deciding that there could be no harm in it, she repeated what she knew of his association with Madeleine Fougeray.

"Well, it would certainly seem odd that he should seek out an abigail for a wife, but as you say, since she is of a clergyman's family, I suppose she is something above her present station."

Corinna agreed absently to this, then was silent for a few minutes.

"Richard and I met Mr Grenville at Frascati's," she said presently, in a careless tone. "He was with some of the friends who accompanied him to Lady Northcote's ball."

"Do you mean that vulgar widow, Mrs Peters, and her relations?" asked Lydia. "Lady Cheveley was telling me how he has been dangling after that woman ever since she arrived in Paris. It seems he made a try for one or two more acceptable young ladies at first, but his reputation has followed him here, as one might expect, so his efforts were to no avail. I wonder if he could indeed bring himself to marry such a female? If he did, he'd be obliged to bury her in that house of his in Eastdean, for she would be nowhere received in polite society."

A sigh escaped Corinna. Lydia looked at her, half in pity, half in exasperation.

"Dearest, you surely cannot still hanker after such a man? You must see that there are no lengths to which he will not go to marry money."

"And is he so much to be blamed for that?" Corinna demanded indignantly. "It is no new thing for gentlemen to be obliged to look for an heiress! He has been so unlucky as to have his inheritance wasted by his father—"

"That isn't all the story. You cannot but know that he has mounted up debts on his own account, what with gambling and extravagant living."

"Well, what could one expect, with such an example as that of his father? I dare say our own brother might have gone on in the same style, had Papa been the kind of gentleman to play ducks and drakes with his fortune! Indeed, Laurie has the same sanguine temperament as Mr Grenville, and could easily have developed into a gamester!"

Lydia saw that nothing was to be gained by pursuing this topic and wisely allowed it to lapse.

Gossip circulated as freely among the English visitors in Paris as in the drawing rooms of any fashionable resort at home. In a few days, the sisters learned by this means that all was over between Mr Grenville and Mrs Peters. It seemed that the gentleman had been indiscreet enough to pay too much attention to other ladies. High words had ensued, resulting in the abrupt departure of the widow and her relatives for England.

"Of course, she was insanely jealous," said Lady Northcote, one of their principal informants. "I did hear that the trouble was precipitated by an incident at Frascati's, but no one seems to know the exact details. However, it seems he's consoling himself at present in the gaming rooms, presumably until he chances upon another candidate for his affections."

Corinna studiously avoided meeting her sister's eye.

When she had spoken of Laurence's ability to become a gamester, Corinna had never for one moment imagined that her words might be prophetic. A week later, she received a shock, therefore, when he complained to her of losses at the roulette table.

"Gaming, Laurie?" she said, in a disturbed tone. "That's a new thing for you, isn't it? I've never heard you mention it before."

"No, well, a fellow must do something, and it's been devilish dull here since Cheveley left. I've taken to looking in at Perrin's gaming house in the Palais Royal — matter of fact, it was that fellow Grenville who suggested it to me."

"Mr Grenville — oh, no!"

"No need to set up a screech, Corinna," he said, eyeing her with disfavour. "Thought you rather liked the chap yourself. He's a rare good sport, I must say, even though he does have the devil's own good fortune! I've dropped a fair bit of blunt to him already. Not that it signifies — I'm not a pauper."

"Oh, no, but—"

She broke off, trying to choose her words. She wanted to say that as Laurence was a minor, it was highly improper of Mr Grenville to encourage him to frequent gaming houses, let alone to bet with him personally; but she knew that any comment of the kind would be ill-judged. Opposition only made her brother the more determined to pursue his course.

"But what?" he demanded impatiently. "Never say that you're turning into a spoil sport, like all the rest!"

"I hope not, though I can't but think there are better ways in which you could employ your time," she answered cautiously.

"I wish you may tell me of any, then. I've no taste for these balls and parties that the rest of you are forever attending," he said disgustedly.

Then, seeing she still looked troubled, he flicked her cheek with his fingers affectionately.

"Don't worry, sis, I'm not on the road to becoming a hardened gamester. Not really in my line. Just something to do."

CHAPTER EIGHT

Corinna continued to feel uneasy, nevertheless, and she soon mentioned her fears to Sir Richard, who at present had worries enough of his own. It was now the first week in May, and for days past rumours had been flying about that Lord Whitworth was on the point of leaving France, since diplomatic relations were breaking down over Malta. Some of the more prudent English visitors were already taking their departure for home, and Sir Richard urged his party to lose no time in following their example. He found to his chagrin that the others took a more optimistic view of the situation and were in no mind to quit France at present. There were balls, evening parties and excursions planned for the weeks ahead, invitations which they had already accepted.

"Besides," said Lydia, "even if the worst did happen, there can be no such desperate hurry to go. Why, only this morning John read in one of the journals that English visitors will find as much security in the justice of the French government as in the protection of our minister, so what can be fairer than that?"

Besides this graver matter, Corinna's uneasiness about Laurence seemed of very small account, and for once Sir Richard heard her with something less than ready sympathy.

"I'm not quite sure what you think I can do," he said, a little impatiently. "If you're suggesting I should act as a bear-leader to your brother, no, I thank you."

She flushed at his unaccustomed tone.

"No, of course not that, precisely. I thought perhaps you might just give him a hint, so that he doesn't become too much addicted to this new craze of his."

"You really believe that a word from me would influence him?" he demanded with an incredulous lift of his eyebrows. "Even though you, who are so much closer to the boy, have failed to produce any effect?"

"Well, at least you might try!" she retorted.

"I might, if I were fool enough not to know that it would only make him more stubborn."

This was so much what she herself thought that she found it distinctly unpalatable. "Oh, you are odious!" she snapped at him, stamping her foot.

"So you often tell me. I am beginning to believe that it's your settled opinion," he replied coolly.

"Well, can you blame me? If only you were not always so — so detached and uninvolved—"

"No doubt you would prefer me to lower my guard and become vulnerable?"

The tone was mocking; but as her eyes met his, for a moment she saw there a depth of feeling which made her catch her breath. A tremor ran through her. It was for a moment only, and then the look had vanished to be replaced by his usual nonchalant expression.

"Oh, what's the use?"

She shrugged helplessly and turned away.

In spite of what he had said to Corinna, Sir Richard decided to look in at Perrin's gaming house that evening. So far, he had never visited any of the licensed gambling establishments of Paris. He knew that some of them added females of dubious character to their other more obvious attractions, but did not seriously suppose that Laurence would frequent these places.

He had also learned from Edmund Langham that royalist intriguers could sometimes be found mingling with the genuine punters; this in its turn brought a number of Napoleon's undercover agents there. Altogether, more games than roulette or cards were played in the gaming dens of Paris.

Perrin's appeared, on the surface at any rate, to be conducted in an orderly manner; so, having settled himself at a roulette table alongside one or two other men with whom he had a nodding acquaintance, Sir Richard whiled away a few hours at play. There was no sign of Laurence; but quite early on he had noticed Grenville, evidently deeply engrossed in the play and frowning a little, as though his bets were failing to prosper. He did not notice Sir Richard.

After several hours during which Laurence had not put in an appearance, Sir Richard rose, gathered up his counters, nodded pleasantly to his acquaintances and passed into the cloakroom. The attendant was missing, so he was obliged to move amongst the stands which held the customers' outdoor garments in search of his own. He had just succeeded in finding them, when a voice which he recognised made him pause before emerging from what amounted to concealment.

"And how the devil d'you think *you've* anything to tell me to my advantage?" It was Grenville's voice, sounding unusually petulant. "Damn it, I don't even know you, and not sure I want to!"

"My name, monsieur, is Fouché, but that is of no importance. What I have to say will be of more interest to you."

"It had better be. Out with it, then! D' you suppose I've nothing more to do than stand here all night talking to you?"

"Things have not been going well for you, Monsieur Grenville, I believe, of late?" The tones were silky, the English heavily accented. "The wealthy lady eluded you, the play seldom goes your way—"

"Damned impertinence! Take yourself off, before I give you a leveller, you — you—!"

"Calm yourself, monsieur. There are more ways of making money than by marrying wealthy ladies or by games of chance. I will instruct you in this matter, if you will be patient with me."

"The devil you will! And how in thunder d' you come to know so much of my affairs?"

"It is my business to know such things. It is for that I am paid, and Napoleon pays well — to the favoured few, that's to say. Which you may come to know for yourself, monsieur, if you will but hear me."

"I'm listening, but so far I've heard precious little to the purpose! Come to the point, damn you, or take yourself off!"

"We approach the point rapidly, I promise you. You have a house in England near to the coast, I am informed?"

"Yes, a devilish dull hole — but what's that to say to anything?"

"I will explain, monsieur, but first let us adjourn to a place where there's no danger of interruption and where we may discuss this over a bottle of wine."

"A capital notion, though to my way of thinking you're castaway already! I'll go with you, though, if only out of curiosity."

Sir Richard heard their footsteps retreating. After a few moments, he ventured forth from his hiding place and stood deep in thought for some time before making his way out of the building. On his way back to the hotel, he pondered again over what he had heard. Some business proposition was evidently about to be put to Grenville by the mysterious

Fouché. Sir Richard recalled what Edmund Langham had told him of the intriguers who frequented certain of the gaming rooms, and speculated as to where such a one as Grenville might fit into their schemes. He could find no satisfactory answer.

He was able to assure Corinna that there had been no sign of her brother in Perrin's gaming rooms that evening, and that therefore this new interest of his could not be quite as compelling as she had feared.

"Oh, did you go there on his account?" she said gratefully. "That was extremely good in you, especially as I quite thought you considered I was making a fuss over nothing!"

"Well, now perhaps you'll see that it's no great matter," he replied, smiling. "I am, of course, unable to assure you that he passed the evening in a manner calculated to ensure his moral uplift."

She laughed. "That wouldn't be Laurie, would it? But you can have no notion how much I disliked the thought that he was becoming a hardened gamester!" Her expression sobered again. "So much damage can be done by embarking on such a course — I have seen the effects of it on others."

He nodded, but made no comment, understanding that she was referring to Grenville's situation. A wave of bitterness swept over him for a moment. Why must she persist in considering the fellow a victim of circumstances, when it was only too plain to the impartial observer that he was an indolent wastrel who lacked the strength of character to take any positive action on his own account to set his affairs in order?

During the week that followed, he had other considerations to assist him in banishing these sombre reflections from his mind. Uneasy rumours concerning the international situation continued to circulate, and several more English families took their departure.

"We've decided to leave," said Lady Cheveley, when they all met at an evening party. "My husband considers it wiser to go, in view of all this uncertainty. It's a pity, for Frances in particular is enjoying herself here and we have formed a delightful circle of friends. However, I trust we shall see you with your husband, Mrs Beresford, at our home in Rottingdean — and you, too, Sir Richard, for it is not much above an hour's journey for you. We shall lose no time in sending you an invitation, I promise you. And of course, Miss Haydon, if ever *you* should wish to make the journey from Tunbridge Wells, you can be assured of a welcome. Frances and you have become quite bosom bows, have you not?"

This was true. Corinna's friendship with Frances had grown with the passing weeks. Sir Richard had been much in Miss Cheveley's company, too; and Lydia thought Lady Cheveley's invitation to him to visit them in Brighton had been particularly significant.

"Depend upon it," she confided to Corinna later, "Lady Cheveley has quite settled it that there is to be a match between Richard and Frances. I think *she* is quite taken with him, but I'm not so certain of his feelings. What do you think?"

She found her sister disappointingly unwilling to speculate on this subject, however, so she tried it out on John.

He only laughed. "What, matchmaking again, puss? Give poor Richard leave to choose his own lady love! Not but what I've a notion—" He broke off, looking sober for a moment.

"Yes?" demanded Lydia eagerly. "You've a notion — what, dearest? Do, do, tell me!"

He folded her in his arms.

"Never you mind. There are more interesting things I'd like to tell you that concern only the two of us. Will you grant me an audience, ma'am?"

She gurgled with delight and nestled against him, everything else forgotten.

Laurence had been seldom with the others of late, having found one or two companions of about his own age with whom he went riding or on excursions into the surrounding countryside. He informed Corinna that Fabian Grenville had left Paris a week since.

"I don't go to Perrin's rooms since he left," Laurence said carelessly. "Not much sport without him, as I'm not acquainted with anyone else who frequents the place. Thought you'd like to know, as you set up such a screech about my gaming and going to the bad."

She protested indignantly against this remark, but was relieved to know that his activities were at an end in that direction. She was not at all sure whether she was sorry or glad to learn that Mr Grenville was no longer in Paris. No doubt the reason for his sudden departure was the rupture of his relationship with the wealthy widow. She did not judge him to be the kind of gentleman to be scared away by rumours of renewed war.

These gained substance alarmingly after a few days, when the French newspapers announced that Lord Whitworth had been recalled to London, and that consequently communication between the foreign offices of the two countries had ceased.

Panic ensued among the English. All the visitors wanted to quit France immediately, being unwilling to trust to previous French assurances of unimpaired hospitality even in the event of war. Who could wish to remain in enemy territory? Unfortunately, the return to their native country was not so simple. The seaports were two days' journey distant by carriage, and few English visitors had brought their own equipages with them. This meant a sudden demand for hired vehicles which far exceeded the supply.

Only after two days' energetic search did Sir Richard and the others finally manage to secure a carriage; and even then they had strong doubts that it would prove roadworthy.

The carriage was to be brought round to their hotel at seven o'clock on the following morning; so, after spending what remained of the evening in doing the last of their packing, they retired early to bed.

The next day, they assembled in good time in the hotel foyer.

"Now where the deuce is Laurie?" demanded John testily, running his glance over the luggage to make sure that nothing was forgotten. "The carriage will be here before long and we want no delay in setting out."

Sir Richard nodded and went over to make inquiries of the landlord, while John looked into the rooms on the ground floor.

"The *patron* says he saw Laurie go off about half an hour since on one of the hacks we hired for our use here," Sir Richard informed the others. "What a wretched fellow he is — I imagine he was up earlier than the rest of us and couldn't bear to wait about doing nothing. Oh, well, he knows the time planned for our departure, so no doubt he'll turn up presently."

But Laurence had not appeared by the time the carriage arrived at the door, nor even after the interval taken for loading the luggage.

Sir Richard looked anxiously at his watch, and John smothered an oath.

"Best tell the man to walk his horses a bit," John said, suiting the action to the word.

After twenty minutes of this, the coachman became understandably impatient. Did the English milords want the use of his coach or not? There were others, *voyez-vous*, who would be only too eager to claim his services — yes, and at a higher fee. He delivered his ultimatum; either they boarded the coach at once or not at all.

Sir Richard came to a decision. "You go ahead with the ladies, John. I'll wait for Laurence, and we'll follow as soon as possible."

John nodded. "Only sensible course. We'll await you at Dieppe, then."

"Best not. Take the first chance of a passage, for odds on it will be Bedlam in the ports. We'll look out for ourselves."

"If you think I shall stir a single step without my brother," put in Corinna emphatically, "you're faint and far off! Why, he may be lying somewhere injured at this very moment — a fine thing it would be for me to run off and desert him!"

"Don't be a goose, dearest," said Lydia, putting an arm lovingly about her. "What can you possibly do that Richard can't do equally well? Now do come along, like a good girl, before that odious driver decides not to take us at all!"

Corinna shook herself free, her face set in determination.

At this point the odious driver sought to force the issue by starting to loosen one of the straps which secured the luggage to the roof.

"Hold hard!" commanded Sir Richard. "You may hand down those two small cloakbags, though."

He indicated the overnight bags belonging to Corinna and himself, before stepping forward to help Lydia into the carriage.

"You two had best set off," he said in a calm, unruffled tone. "No time for further argument — in you get, John."

The cloakbags were deposited on the cobbled forecourt of the inn, and the driver mounted to his seat. There was just time for Corinna to run forward and plant a hasty kiss on her sister's cheek before the door of the coach was shut and the vehicle moved forward.

"Nothing much wrong with the horses, at any rate," remarked Sir Richard coolly, taking up the cloakbags. "They'll set a fair pace."

Corinna made no reply. She had won her point, but all the same she did feel a little foolish. She remained silent while they made their way indoors to the lounge, where Sir Richard ordered some coffee.

It was now almost half past eight, and Corinna's fears for her brother were mounting. He *must* have had an accident. There could be no other explanation.

She turned to Sir Richard, her lovely eyes dimmed with trouble. He understood at once, and placed a firm, reassuring hand over her trembling one.

"He'll walk in presently, as large as life, you'll see," he said calmly. "You know your brother — he gets caught up in something or other, and loses all sense of time, wretched fellow!"

"Why, yes, so he does," she acknowledged, clutching eagerly at this straw of comfort. "I dare say you are right."

The anxiety was returning, however, when a further quarter of an hour brought no sign of the absentee. Then, just as Sir Richard was contemplating taking other measures than merely sitting and waiting, the door of the room opened and Laurence strode in hastily. Beside him, to Corinna's amazement, was Madeleine Fougeray.

CHAPTER NINE

Corinna leapt to her feet, her eyes blazing with indignation. As most women do who have been anxious about a missing loved one, she relieved her feelings by heaping bitter recriminations on the culprit's head.

"I couldn't help it, I assure you," he explained apologetically. "The most devilish thing! The hack went lame while I was riding in the Bois de Boulogne, so I had to find a farrier and leave the cursed animal with him. It all took time, then I'd to walk back — no transport to be had, as you know. On the way I met mademoiselle here, and she was in the deuce of a coil, poor girl! Well, couldn't leave her crying her eyes out, now, could I? Deuced shabby thing to do! So she told me what the trouble was, and I brought her back with me, thinking we might be able to assist her."

Sir Richard turned to the girl, who had been standing uncertainly beside them.

"Pray be seated, mademoiselle," he said gently. Then, turning to Laurence with a weary air, "I suppose it never crossed your mind that on this morning of all times it would have been wiser to forego your usual ride?"

"I was so curst anxious to be ready betimes that I woke up at the crack of dawn," replied Laurence apologetically. "There was no going off to sleep again, so what was I to do? I finished packing, breakfasted, and there was still time to kill until seven, so I went out. And but for my deuced bad luck, I'd have been back here in plenty of time!"

Sir Richard shrugged fatalistically. "No profit in holding an inquest now."

He turned to Madeleine, whose flushed cheeks and troubled dark eyes showed her embarrassment.

"How may we serve you, mademoiselle?" he asked quietly. "What is the trouble?"

"You are very good, monsieur, but it is unthinkable that you should be burdened with my affairs," she replied, with an attempt at dignity belied by her trembling lips.

Corinna, recovered now from her outburst of temper, saw that the girl was in real distress, and gently persuaded her to explain. Thus encouraged, Madeleine repeated what she had already confided to Laurence; that Lady Northcote had always promised to take her back with the family to England, but at the last moment there had not been sufficient room in the conveyances, so she had been left behind.

At first, none of her listeners could understand why she should be so desperate to leave her native country; so Madeleine was obliged to reveal all the details of her story as she had told them to Patrice Landier.

They regarded her for a moment in silence.

"So you are a French aristocrat," Corinna said thoughtfully.

"Yes, by birth I am so, but for many years now I have been accustomed to think of myself as a curé's niece. It was safer thus, during the Revolution. And I would have been content to remain so, but my good uncle wished otherwise. I am bound, Miss Haydon, by my promise to him on his deathbed. I must — I *must*" — she clasped her hands together in a gesture of strong emotion — "by some means reach England in order to fulfil that promise."

"Oh, we must help her, Richard!" exclaimed Corinna, much moved. "Can we not take her with us?"

"Must say, that's what I had in mind myself," put in Laurence, "when I brought her back with me."

"At the present moment, there seems small likelihood that we ourselves will succeed in reaching England," Sir Richard said drily. "You may recall our extreme difficulty in obtaining transport before, and now it's all to do again. However, you and I will set about that without delay, Laurie. Meanwhile, I'll have a word with the landlord about retaining our rooms for a further period, if that should prove necessary."

When he had moved away to do this, accompanied by Laurence, Madeleine looked doubtfully at Corinna.

"I do not think that Sir Richard Beresford wishes me to go with you, Miss Haydon, and for that I do not blame him. If only I were not in a situation of the most difficult, I wouldn't for a moment consent to accept your so very kind offer of assistance! But what am I to do? You see, mademoiselle" — she paused, her cheeks flushing again — "I have not quite money enough to pay for the whole journey myself, though I can manage something. And then, of course, when I reach my Aunt in Brighton, I am sure she will at once reimburse you."

Corinna gave the girl a warm smile and patted her hand reassuringly.

"Why, of course she will — I never doubted it. As to your acting as my abigail, there's no need of that. I'll have a word with Sir Richard, if you'll excuse me for a moment."

She rose and went over to Sir Richard, who had just concluded his business with the landlord.

"That's all arranged," he said to her. "We may keep our rooms for as long as we wish. But as to this French demoiselle—"

"Yes, I want to speak to you about her. Laurie, go and talk to her for a minute, will you? I wish to have a private word with Richard."

Laurence, anxious to make what amends he could for his misdeeds, obediently went to join Madeleine.

"The poor child feels that you don't really wish to have her with us, Richard, but—"

"No more do I," he cut in brusquely. "For one thing, it will mean an extra person for whom to find transport, and numbers may be vital. For another" — he paused and shot a searching look at her — "Corinna, does it not occur to you that she may be using us in more than the obvious way? Her story is odd, don't you think?"

"Perhaps, but *I* find it convincing. What do you mean when you say she may have some ulterior motive in asking us for help?"

He sighed. "I fear you're altogether too trusting, Corinna. Recollect that we are now at war with France and it's not unknown for spies to seek entry into enemy territory."

She stared at him with angry incredulity. "*Spies!*" she repeated scornfully. "You truly think that gentle creature could be possessed of so much cunning?"

He glanced warily about them, but there was no one close at hand.

"Hush, keep your voice down. One cannot afford to overlook such a possibility, that is all."

"You may think as you choose, but I have the utmost faith in her integrity!" she exclaimed fiercely.

"Forgive me, but have you never had cause to question your own judgment in such matters?"

She was speechless with anger for a moment, her blazing eyes glaring into his cool blue ones.

"You — you!" she burst out at last. "Oh, of all the odious, despicable creatures! I detest you!"

He bowed mockingly. "That is understood, but at present we must preserve an armed neutrality, since we are all in the same boat — and a devilish leaky vessel, at that! Come, let us put our differences aside and concentrate instead on the tricky business of getting back to England."

His last words were spoken in a placatory tone. In spite of her spurt of anger, she was too sensible not to realise that he was right, and that this was not the time to quarrel.

"I think you should know," she said, forcing herself to speak more quietly, "that Madeleine Fougeray was known to Monsieur Landier — in fact, he wished to wed her. It was because she refused him that he returned so abruptly to Rouen. Surely this must put an end to your suspicions of her?"

He raised his eyebrows, evidently surprised.

"So that was it," he said after a pause. "I did wonder… however, as you say, this does put a slightly different complexion on the matter. Let us join the others and discuss our plan of campaign."

The discussion was brief, for they had only one course to take, and that was to find a conveyance speedily. This could be done only by a great deal of tramping about from place to place making interminable inquiries.

For three days Sir Richard and Laurence had no success. By now, war had been officially declared and Sir Richard was growing uneasy lest the ports should be closed. He kept these fears to himself, however, merely saying to the others that when they did succeed in hiring a carriage, he intended to make for Rouen.

"Landier will know more than we do of how matters stand at Dieppe, I dare say, and he'll give us the benefit of his advice."

"Oh, yes, I'm sure he will," said Corinna. "But do you truly think there's any hope at all of our finding a conveyance?" she went on doubtfully. "I must say, it doesn't appear likely, judging by the results so far."

"Nonsense, it's only a matter of time," Sir Richard said bracingly. "Some of those carriages which went off to the coast a week or so ago must arrive back in Paris before much longer."

This proved correct, for on the following day the landlord offered one of his own coaches which had just returned. The fee he asked was exorbitant, and he also warned them that there might be some difficulty in obtaining changes of horses on the road; but by this time, the visitors were in no mood to meet trouble halfway, and hastily made ready to set out on their journey.

They had to cover a distance of seventy-six miles to Rouen; what with the indifferent horses offered for hire and the poor state of the roads, they were unable to average more than six or seven miles an hour. Their coachman therefore suggested an overnight stop halfway, saying that he could recommend the inn at Magny-en-Vexin. It turned out to be tolerable, though not at all what the English party had been accustomed to patronize.

The next morning they took to the road again, partially refreshed by an indifferent night's sleep on lumpy beds, but heartened by the thought that they were now on the last day of their journey. By the time they reached the outskirts of Rouen in the early evening, however, the two girls were decidedly jaded and looking forward with relief to reaching shelter. There was no hope of finding a hotel since most had been commandeered by the military and other officials.

"I'll go straight to Landier," Richard said. "I'll be back shortly. Meanwhile, make yourselves as comfortable as possible here."

Less than an hour later they were sent for, and Corinna was feeling more at ease than she had for the past four days. Madame Landier conducted her to a pleasant bedchamber with white dimity hangings and a luxuriously soft bed, instructing an abigail to bring her plenty of hot water and whatever else might be required in the way of aids to her toilette. She had removed the dust and some of the aches of travel, and now stood in her petticoat awaiting the return from pressing of the only muslin gown contained in her overnight cloakbag.

A gentle tap came at the door and she called out permission to enter. Instead of the expected maid with her gown, however, it was Madeleine who answered the summons. One look at the girl showed Corinna that she was deeply troubled.

"What is it?" she asked gently, for there was something about Madeleine that called forth her protective instincts.

"Oh, mademoiselle!" burst out Madeleine. "I should not be here, indeed I should not! I don't know how to look at him, let alone speak to him! And his mother everything of the kindest and gentlest — imagine to yourself my embarrassment!"

"Truly it *is* an awkward situation," agreed Corinna. "But there was nothing else to be done, and recollect that it's only for one evening. Tomorrow we'll be on our way to the coast. Come, Madeleine! You've but to eat your dinner at the same table — and I'll sit beside you and shield you from his conversation."

"You are so good to me, mademoiselle, more than I deserve. For your sake, I'll do my best."

At that moment, the maid entered with Corinna's gown and would have helped her visitor into it, but Madeleine took that office upon herself. Corinna dismissed the abigail.

"There, that looks charming," Madeleine pronounced, turning Corinna about to inspect herself in the long glass. "Stand still, mademoiselle, while I tie the sash."

She fastened a pink ribbon sash about the waist of the white muslin gown sprigged with small pink flowers, then stood back to study the effect.

"And now I shall arrange your hair," she announced.

Corinna laughed. "There's no gainsaying you, as I know from experience, but truly I'm quite capable of doing it myself."

"But you shall not, while I am with you. It is one little thing I can do to prove my gratitude."

When Corinna entered the dining room, she certainly looked fresh and dainty, and not in the least like a travel-weary female with a limited wardrobe. Three masculine pairs of eyes expressed approval, even if one pair quickly switched to her companion. Madeleine was wearing her dove-grey gown with a simple gold cross and chain about her neck, and her black hair drawn back into a thick coil. A faint flush tinged her cheek as Landier drew forward a chair for her, while his father performed a similar office for Corinna.

Talk during the meal was chiefly among the men of the party concerning details of the journey to Dieppe and the subsequent passage to England.

Corinna noticed that, although Landier seldom took his eyes off Madeleine, he never addressed her throughout the meal; but she fancied that his mother's shrewd glance at each of the two in turn was not deceived by this lack of communication. Corinna herself kept her promise to Madeleine by constantly involving the girl in the conversation with madame. She was pleased to see that the two seemed to have a mutual liking. Madeleine listened to and answered the older Frenchwoman with respect, and in return her few remarks were treated with indulgence.

"Do you intend to enlist again in the navy?" Laurence asked Landier, at one stage in the meal.

Patrice shook his head decisively. "Not unless I were to be conscripted, and I don't think that likely, for Napoleon also has great need of his financiers and men of commerce. No, a serving life was well enough when I was young and adventurous, like yourself; but I grow old, now, *voyez-vous*, and think of a hearth and someone to sit beside it with me."

His glance flickered slightly towards Madeleine, but quickly returned to Laurence.

"Dear me, and I can give you two or three years," drawled Sir Richard, with a wry smile. "Dashed if you don't make me feel quite in the sere and yellow, Landier."

Patrice burst out laughing and raised his glass. "Perhaps I was doing it too brown — isn't that your expression? Nevertheless, I think perhaps you may agree with me that we have both reached an age when we think of marriage."

"Ah, but who would have us?" asked Sir Richard in the same tone, raising his glass in response.

"Well, I'll tell you who would have *you*," Laurence said to him, grinning. "You've but to go as far as Brighton, I'll wager!"

Corinna was suddenly conscious of a curious sinking feeling inside which made her lose track of the conversation for a few moments. When she recovered, it was to find that Sir Richard had smoothly switched it into other, less personal channels.

It had been arranged that they were to proceed to Dieppe on the following day in the Landiers' travelling carriage, escorted by Patrice himself. When Corinna came downstairs to breakfast, therefore, she was surprised to find that, instead of preparations for departure, some kind of serious consultation was in progress among the gentlemen. They looked up with grave faces as she entered.

"Is anything wrong?" she asked quickly.

Sir Richard rose to pull out a chair for her at the table beside Madame Landier and Madeleine.

"Perhaps you should have your breakfast first," he suggested.

"There *is* something amiss!" she exclaimed, refusing to sit. "Pray tell me at once — I will *not* be treated like a child!"

"I will tell you, mademoiselle," said the elder Landier, and now she noticed that he was in his outdoor clothes. "I have but just returned from our banking house, where I learned tidings of the most distressing for your friends. Napoleon has issued a decree that all English males between the ages of eighteen and sixty at present in France are to be detained as prisoners of war."

CHAPTER TEN

Corinna sat down abruptly, staring at their host in painful concentration.

"Oh, dear God," she said at last, in a whisper.

"The decree doesn't apply to females, of course," said Sir Richard, seemingly unperturbed. "Monsieur Landier has most generously offered to escort you to one of the neutral ports and put you aboard a ship bound for home."

"But what will you and Laurie do?" asked Corinna, finding her voice.

"We're going to make a run for it!" said Laurence energetically. "Landier has a scheme for smuggling us out of the country with the aid of a man who was his boatswain in the navy. He was explaining it all to us before you came downstairs."

Corinna made no reply, but listened with strained attention as Patrice Landier outlined his plan.

"This man Bonnet has a farm at a little place near the coast not far from Dieppe. He also owns a small fishing boat, and I've good reason to believe that he knows more than he should of the activities of certain smugglers operating between France and England. I've kept in touch with him, and I know he would do me a favour for old times' sake, especially if the price was right. I foresee no difficulty if I can but get you to the coast — how to accomplish that?" He spread his hands in a Gallic gesture. "All exits from the town are bound to be watched by officials scrutinizing papers. Once outside the town walls, I could take my coach along country lanes where there would be little risk of that, but how to quit the town itself in safety?"

"On foot!" exclaimed Laurence, who seemed to be actually enjoying himself. "There must be plenty of pedestrians passing out of the town, and if we mingle among them — with the fog to help screen us from close scrutiny—"

"It's possible," said Landier. "But they are all humble persons, *voyez-vous*, and even in the fog, your attire would set you apart."

"Then we must change it." Sir Richard spoke decisively. "How can we obtain a couple of suits of fustian, farm workers' smocks, or something of that kind? Have you any suggestions, Landier?"

"*You* are the difficulty," replied Landier, eyeing him. "One of our grooms is much of a size with Haydon, but you're too tall to fit into any of the servants' clothes. If we could procure a smock for you, though, you might make do with breeches and woollen hose. I'll go down to the market for one, then we can roll it in the dirt to give it a more realistic look."

Sir Richard wrinkled his nose fastidiously.

"My thanks to you, Landier, but I beg you won't choose the stableyard for the operation."

"How can you possibly jest?" asked Corinna with a tremor in her voice. "It is all too monstrously serious!"

He moved towards her and placed a firm hand on her shoulder for a moment.

"We shall come off safe, never fear, my dear," he said lightly. "My only misgivings are for you."

She seized his hand as he withdrew it, looking up into his face with a pleading expression in her brown eyes.

"Richard, let me come with you! I don't want to go back home on my own — oh, not that I am too cowardly to face the journey alone, do not think me such a poor creature! But I cannot *bear* not to know what is happening to Laurie and — and to you — to be wondering all the while if you've managed to escape, or if you are mouldering in a French prison! I won't be any trouble, I promise you" — as she saw him shake his head — "I could go with Monsieur Landier in the coach, for they won't question me, will they, since you say females are exempt from their monstrous decree? And no matter what difficulties and hardships are to come afterwards I can face them all if only we remain together! Oh, please, Richard — dear Richard — please don't send me away!"

At the endearment, an exultant light flickered momentarily in his eyes. Then he turned to Patrice Landier, who had been about to hurry off on his errand.

"What's your opinion, Landier? Is it at all possible? Could we bring it off?"

The other shrugged. "Possible, yes, though it would obviously be simpler for two men alone." He paused as Corinna let out a dismayed exclamation. "But since Miss Haydon feels so strongly," he went on, "perhaps we can manage."

"And I?" put in Madeleine, who had so far said nothing. "I, too, wish to go to England. May I not accompany my friends?"

Patrice looked into her dark eyes for the first time since she had entered his house.

"If you must, mademoiselle," he replied quietly. "But I beg the favour of a private word with you when I've returned from the market."

Her face lost some of its serenity. "*D'accord*, monsieur. But I think it is better that *I* go to the market, not you. You are known in the town, and the purchase of a peasant's smock may be remarked and remembered hereafter. But no one will wonder at it if I, a country girl, should make such a purchase. Besides," she added naively, with a fleeting smile, "I will get the better bargain."

Madame Landier chuckled. "She is right, Patrice, trust a woman for marketing. You have a shrewd head on your shoulders, *petite.*"

Madeleine looked pleased at the compliment, and rose at once to set out on her errand. She was no stranger to the streets of Rouen; she soon returned with a coarse smock of the kind worn by peasants in the fields and of sufficient length to accommodate Sir Richard. She had also procured a shapeless, much stained hat for him to wear.

"Faugh!" he exclaimed, lifting this with the tips of his fingers and inspecting it dubiously. "Where did you obtain this revolting object, child? Must I wear it, Landier?"

"I had it from one of the countrymen in the market," she explained. "But, indeed, monsieur, I think you must cover your hair, for its altogether too fashionably cut, *n'est-ce pas?*"

Landier nodded. "Mademoiselle is quite right, *mon vieux.* I had not thought of it myself."

"Needs must when the devil drives," sighed Sir Richard. "Come, Laurie, let's don our disguises, while your sister has some breakfast."

While everyone else was thus occupied, Patrice Landier led Madeleine out of the parlour into a small room adjoining it, where they could be alone.

"There is not much time, mademoiselle," he began, looking into her troubled dark eyes with an intensity which made her lower her glance. "I am about to ask you again to reconsider your decision, to remain here in France and become my wife. Mama guesses how it is between us, and you must have seen that already she approves you. As for me, there are no words to express my unchanging devotion. I would not persist did I think you totally indifferent to me; but although I am no coxcomb, I believe I've seen signs that you could in time come to love me. Say that it is so, my dearest! And even if you must bid me wait until that comes to pass, I will be patient. Only say that you will remain here in France, and give me a little hope that you will one day be mine!"

She was trembling with the intensity of an emotion which matched his, but to which she would not give way. She gripped her hands together, forcing herself to look directly at him, yet almost losing her senses before the passionate depths she found in his eyes.

"I — I — could love you, monsieur," she stammered. "Oh, so easily! But—"

He waited for nothing more, but swept her into his arms, holding her close to his heart. His lips sought hers, and for a moment she yielded them to him.

Then she resisted, pushing him away with trembling hands. He tried to put his arms about her once more, but she stepped back, shaking her head.

"No! No, it cannot be! I must go — I must keep my promise!"

"But everything has changed, Madeleine! We are now at war, and the journey you might before have made in safety will be fraught with danger. As an enemy alien, you will not be welcome in England. France is your country, my dearest — stay here and make your life with me!"

"What has France done for me but rob me of my parents and my birthright?" she asked bitterly.

"It is for us, the youth of France, to make of our country what we wish it to be," he said vigorously. "The past is gone, Madeleine, and we must let it die! No sensible man desires war, but peace will come again and with it opportunities to make ours a great nation. There's so much to be done — will you not stay and be a part of that glorious future, Madeleine? I think if the Curé Vernet could have known all, that is what he would have now wished you to do!"

"There is much in what you say, but I cannot," she said brokenly. "Don't you see that I must keep that most solemn deathbed promise? I think you are a good man, monsieur, and perhaps there is hope for France with men such as you to work for her. But it is useless to tell me what my uncle *might* have wished me to do. I only know what he *did* ask, and that I will perform."

His hands dropped to his sides and the light died out of his eyes.

"So be it," he said wearily, turning away. "I must go now and set about repaying a long-overdue debt to my English friends. But would to God John Beresford had left me to drown all those years ago."

The fog had thickened by the time Landier handed first Corinna and then Madeleine into the carriage. Corinna felt its clammy touch on her face, and shivered as she settled herself against the comfortable upholstery before staring apprehensively out of the window into the shrouded street. Vague wraiths passed slowly to and fro, feeling their way along suddenly unfamiliar pavements, their footsteps muffled by this atmospheric blanket that deadened all sound.

"We'll need to go slowly," said Landier as he took his seat beside Corinna. "No difficulty about those two on foot catching us up, but I hope this clears quickly once we're outside the town. It does as a rule."

She made no reply; her every nerve was stretched taut with anxiety over her brother and Sir Richard. They had slipped out of the house by the back entrance to make their way along a deserted alley which would bring them into the street. As the carriage moved slowly forward, she strained her eyes to try and identify them among the shadowy forms on the pavement, but without success.

The short distance to the town wall seemed interminable, but at last they reached it to join a short line of other vehicles waiting to go through. As Patrice Landier had supposed, officials were stationed at the gate, shadowy figures holding aloft flares and challenging all who sought to leave the town. To Corinna they appeared full of menace. A sudden shout from one of them made her start almost from her seat, but Landier placed a restraining hand on her arm. She heard the word "English" amid the outcry, and a moment later two figures were being hustled past their carriage under arrest.

She looked at Landier, her eyes big with terror, her heart beating so fast that it seemed as if it must choke her. In that agonising moment, she did not know whose fate mattered most to her — the brother she had loved from childhood, or the man whom until now she had always taken for granted.

"I do not think it is our friends," whispered Landier encouragingly. "One can't see clearly in this fog, but one of them looked too short to be Richard. Courage, mademoiselle!"

He signalled to Madeleine to change places with him, which she did, placing a protective arm about Corinna.

In a few moments, it was their turn to go through the gate. One of the officials held up his flaming torch, exchanged a few words with the coachman, then abruptly pulled open the door.

Patrice quietly gave his identity and the man seemed satisfied, but his glance lingered curiously on Corinna.

Before Landier could reply, Madeleine leaned quickly forward to shield Corinna partly from view.

"Madame is unwell, *citoyen*," she said sharply. "She should not be troubled."

The official mumbled an apology, evidently daunted by this display of feminine claws; and, slamming the door, signalled to the coachman to proceed.

None of them spoke until they were well clear of the gate and turning towards open country. Already the fog was changing to drifting mist; after they had gone a short distance, Landier ordered the coachman to draw in to the verge.

"We'll wait here for them," he said. Silence fell over the waiting coach. Corinna was tense with anxiety. After what seemed an interminable time, footsteps were heard approaching, at first faint but gradually becoming louder. Corinna's heart began to pound again as she peered through the window into the misty scene.

At last two figures appeared, halting beside the coach to scrutinise the passengers. The next moment Landier flung back the door and they stepped hastily inside. A sob caught in Corinna's throat as she threw herself into her brother's arms.

For two days the fugitives stayed concealed at Bonnet's farm while they awaited the arrival of the smugglers who were to take them across the Channel. Bonnet's wife did her best, but the accommodation was primitive. Corinna forced herself to utter no word of complaint, mindful of her promise. She and Madeleine gave what comfort they could to each other and in so doing, their affection grew. The French girl was indeed sorely in need of her English friend's support, for by now she realised that she truly loved Patrice Landier. Not even at the last moment, when he held her clasped to his heart in farewell, would she change her determination to keep her vow; but it was a bitter decision, and the parting was almost unbearable for both.

"Promise me, my dearest, that if everything does not turn out as you hope in England, you will get word to me," he pleaded in anguished tones. "Depend on it, Sir Richard will find a way to discover these smugglers and they can bring a message to Bonnet for me. And then, my only love, I'll come to fetch you, though all the armed might of England should stand in my way!"

With such words to remember, it was no wonder that Madeleine's spirits were at a low ebb when at last the fugitives boarded the smuggling vessel bound for the coast of Sussex. But she rallied courageously, never allowing her grief to prevent her from helping Corinna to endure the hardships which still confronted them. They were obliged to pass the long hours at sea confined in a small space among kegs of brandy and other contraband, in constant fear of discovery. Moreover, the vessel reeked of fish, for fishing was the ostensible business of these men. Increasingly, Corinna and the others came to rely upon Sir Richard's calm judgment and unfailing optimism.

Once, and once only, when Corinna's nerves were strained to breaking point, did she lash out at him in the old way.

"I won't stay down here another moment in this airless, stinking hole!" she stormed. "I don't care what you say, Richard, I am going up on deck!"

She started to scramble out from the corner where she and Madeleine were crouched together, but he seized her in a firm grasp.

"You will stay where you are, if I have to hold you down by force," he said roughly. "No, don't argue" — as she began a heated protest — "this is no time for the vapours. Disobey me and you put us all in peril."

"For God's sake, Corinna, do as he says!" ordered her brother impatiently. "Else we shall wish we'd never brought you along!"

This was enough to recall her to her promise. With a muttered apology, she subsided; and Sir Richard released her, patting her tangled curls in a consoling gesture.

"Courage, my dear. You've done splendidly so far, and we're on the last lap."

Almost in tears, she crept into the comfort of Madeleine's arms.

Several more uncomfortable hours were to elapse before they were transferred with their few belongings to a small rowing boat with two sturdy men at the oars. Presently the bottom of the boat grated on pebbles and one of the men shipped his oars to step overboard into shallow water, bearing the baggage ashore.

"This be Cuckmere Haven," the other man informed them.

The two girls were lying slumped in the boat, weary and dishevelled. Corinna found herself lifted like a child into Sir Richard's arms as he stepped out of the boat. She let her head droop onto his shoulder and clasped her nerveless arms about him. She felt his embrace tighten as he bore her to the beach, where he set her gently down, steadying her for a few moments before reluctantly releasing her to return and parley with the men.

Laurence had likewise assisted Madeleine ashore, and the group stood waiting until Sir Richard came over to them as the men put out to sea.

"Well, here we are, on English soil at last," he said cheerfully.

"Call these dashed pebbles soil?" scoffed Laurence. "Still, I'll grant it's better than being cooped up in a stuffy vessel. What's to do now, Richard? You say your house is only a couple of miles off, but how are we to reach it? The females are deadbeat, in no case for walking."

It was not yet dawn, but a lightening of the sky heralded its approach and enabled them dimly to distinguish surrounding objects. To their right loomed the shadow of a huge cliff, while at a little distance across the beach on their other side they caught the pale gleam of the Cuckmere river.

"There's a boat," said Sir Richard suddenly. "See it, up-ended by the river? The smugglers told me there's a farm about half a mile up river where we may be able to hire some kind of conveyance. Come, ladies, we'll assist you."

The river wound in large S bends through marshy meadows; when they had laboured on for half a mile, it bent towards a rough track which ran at right angles down to a lonely farmhouse. The first rosy fingers of dawn were creeping across the grey sky as they reached this point, where a mooring post was driven into the bank.

Sir Richard stepped out of the boat and made it fast to the post.

"This is it," he said. "You stay here while I go and try my luck."

He vanished along the track.

He was gone for some time, but at last they heard the welcome sound of wheels and heavy hoofs approaching, and Sir Richard came into view, driving a wagon pulled by a powerful farm horse.

"Had to knock 'em up," he explained, as he halted the beast and jumped down. "Took some time to get it into their heads what I needed, but this was the best they could manage. I fear it's not over clean for the ladies, but we haven't far to go now."

Weary though she was, Corinna managed a wry smile. She dreaded to think what kind of picture she must present, dirty, dishevelled and with her hair tumbling about her shoulders. A dirty wagon could not worry her now.

She glanced at her companions, who were in a similar state; then thought in surprise that she had never seen Richard appear to greater advantage, even when attired in the full glory of ball dress. His head was bare, his fair hair wind-tossed and damp with sea spray; his face, though a trifle unshaven, was tanned and glowing with exercise. He had long ago discarded the soiled smock, and now wore a shirt, admittedly also soiled, open at the neck and with sleeves rolled up to reveal brown, muscular arms. He had always looked the elegant gentleman; but now he was primeval male, the strong, resourceful protector.

She suddenly felt as though she had never really noticed him before.

CHAPTER ELEVEN

In her younger days, when Sir Richard's father had owned Chyngton Manor, Corinna had frequently stayed there with her family. She loved every inch of it. This was the first time, however, that she had been a guest there since Sir Richard had inherited the property.

She awoke to the scent of flowers coming in at her casement window. Stretching herself luxuriously, she realised after a few minutes of wonder that she was actually lying on a soft down mattress in a carved oak four-poster bed. She sighed with relief. This was one of the bedrooms in the Tudor wing of Chyngton Manor, where Richard had brought her safely after so many hazards.

They had arrived at dawn; what time was it now? She slipped out of bed to consult her watch, and saw that it was close on noon. Vaguely she recalled their arrival; the shocked surprise of the staff on seeing their master and his companions in such a state. She had been escorted upstairs, assisted to undress and bathe by a maid with deft, gentle hands, then tucked into bed. Thereafter, all was oblivion.

She crossed to the window and leaned from the casement. The warmth of the sun touched her face; below her was a green expanse of lawn and flower borders bright with blue and pink lupins, sweet williams with velvety petals, and roses of every hue. She revelled in the calm beauty of it, the peace.

Sir Richard came into view, strolling across the lawn. He halted opposite her window and, looking up, caught sight of her. He raised a hand in greeting, but she drew back quickly, conscious of the impropriety of being seen in her nightgown.

Even as she did so, she thought that there was surely no need for her to be so missish after all the enforced intimacies of their flight from Paris. She shook her head; the fact remained that a return to normal circumstances at once restored the normal patterns of conduct.

Yet in some indefinable way she felt that her relationship with Richard had changed. They all met shortly afterwards around the dining table in the lovely oak-panelled parlour which had low chintz-covered window seats looking out on the garden, and a stone fireplace emblazoned with a Tudor rose and the Chyngton arms. He now looked very much the English country gentleman in fawn riding breeches, tasselled Hessians, an olive green coat of impeccable cut and snowy white linen; but there flashed into Corinna's mind that picture of him as he had appeared by the first light of dawn, unkempt and dishevelled, yet challengingly masculine. She felt unaccountably shy of him, the old, easy relationship for the moment banished.

They all looked more civilized now, and they were young enough for rest to have restored them to their normal healthy state. The ample meal provided by Sir Richard's excellent housekeeper was being consumed with dispatch.

"I fear it was nothing short of a nightmare for you ladies," remarked Sir Richard when their appetites had been somewhat sated. "You were splendid, too — pluck to the backbone!"

"I'm not so sure that I altogether deserve your praise," replied Corinna with unusual diffidence. "But just to be safe home again has been enough to banish the horrors of that journey! That's to say" — glancing at Madeleine — "it is for us, but possibly you may feel differently, Madeleine, since you're in a foreign country, where everything is strange."

"It will not seem strange once I have found my kin and accustomed myself," said Madeleine staunchly. "And I would like to express my deep gratitude to both you gentlemen for permitting me to accompany you and for taking such good care of me throughout all our trials."

In one breath, they both assured her that it had been a privilege to serve her.

"You are very good. There is yet one more service which I am obliged to ask of you," she continued, "since I do not know this neighbourhood and cannot manage without assistance. I must find a lodging for a day or so, until I can seek out my aunt. Perhaps, Sir Richard, you may know of one of the villagers who would have a small room at a modest rent? I shall be infinitely grateful if you can recommend me to such a one."

"Oh, there's no need for that!" exclaimed Corinna. "My sister Lydia will be happy to accommodate you, I assure you, Madeleine."

"Of course she will," put in Laurence. "And I intend to escort you myself to Brighton to seek out your relatives, so that's all settled."

"You are very good, monsieur, but perhaps Mrs Beresford may not find it convenient to receive someone who is a stranger to her."

"Lord, what a pother over nothing!" exclaimed Laurence with scant ceremony, for he had come to treat Madeleine almost as a sister. "Lydia will like nothing better than to take an interest in your concerns, I'll wager, for she's the nosiest female ever!"

"For shame, Laurie," reproved Sir Richard, marring the effect with a broad grin.

"Well, ain't she, now? She's forever matchmaking, as you must have seen for yourself when we were in France. If she didn't do her utmost to push Corinna off on L—"

He broke off abruptly as Sir Richard's boot made contact with his shins.

"You'll be able to find out from Lydia herself in a little while," Sir Richard said, adroitly reverting to the original topic of conversation. "I sent a message over telling of our safe arrival and saying that we would present ourselves at Friston House later today."

The Beresfords' house was a pleasant, creeper-covered house of only moderate size that had been built about forty years since and had chanced to come on the market just before Lydia and John were married. Its grounds were small, but this was not seen as a disadvantage by John, whose profession made a large estate unsuitable at present. He was pleased to be near his brother, while Lydia found it agreeable to live among neighbours who were already acquainted with her husband's family, instead of being obliged to settle down among total strangers.

When the carriage party arrived at the house, they found Laurence, who had ridden ahead. He was sitting out of doors with Lydia and John, on a terrace overlooking the flower garden. It was evident that he was well launched into an account of their adventures, for his sister and her husband were hanging on his every word.

Both jumped up at once when the others appeared, however, and Lydia ran to clasp Corinna in her arms.

"Oh, my poor, poor love, what you must have suffered! And we've been nigh frantic with anxiety over you! Laurie seems to think it all a great game, you must know, but I am certain you could not have done so!"

Madeleine had been hanging back diffidently during these greetings, but now Corinna drew her forward.

"You may recall my mentioning Mademoiselle Fougeray to you, Lyddy? Madeleine, this is my sister, and her husband, Lieutenant John Beresford."

Madeleine made a curtsey. Lydia looked blank for a moment before recollecting who the girl was, then smiled warmly and held out her hand.

"How do you do? Are you also a fugitive from France, mademoiselle?"

"Pray call me Madeleine, madame. Yes, in one sense, I am" — she smiled wanly — "because I've forsaken my own country to seek relatives living in Brighton. I hope soon to be with them."

"In the meantime," put in Corinna, "I'm sure you would not object to Madeleine staying here for a few days? After all the travelling of the past week — and in such conditions! — it's more than she could support to dash off at once for Brighton. Besides, I've no wish to lose her so soon. I don't know how I should have gone on without her!"

"Nor I without you," said Madeleine warmly. Then, turning with a slight blush to Lydia, of whom she felt a little shy: "But indeed I wouldn't wish to put you to any inconvenience, madame. I dare say I may easily find a lodging nearby."

"I shan't hear of such a thing," exclaimed Lydia hospitably. "And now that I think of it, you will be doing me a good turn by keeping Corinna company while I am absent for a few days. Of course, you don't know about this, my love" — turning to her sister — "but John has been recalled and must set off for Portsmouth tomorrow."

117

Corinna exclaimed in dismay and looked commiseratingly towards her brother-in-law. By now, they were all seated, and he was holding an animated conversation with the other two men.

"Oh, you need not think *he* minds," said Lydia, "and why should he, indeed? He is bred to the sea and loves it. As for me" — she tilted her chin courageously — "I am a sailor's wife, so must expect partings. I had intended to remain here until I had news of you, but now I shall accompany John to Portsmouth. I can stay with our friends the Dawsons until John and Lieutenant Dawson sail. And if Madeleine is here with you, you won't mind my absence, I'm sure."

"Of course you must go, Lyddy. And perhaps Mama may not object if I stay on with you a little while after you return. She has Irene and Anthea to keep her company, so will not miss me."

Lydia's face lit up. "Oh, I'm so glad you've suggested that yourself, for it's the very thing I was about to ask of you! I shall become accustomed in time to John's absence because I must, but just at first—"

She broke off, biting her lip. Corinna patted her hand comfortingly.

"Talking of Mama," Corinna said, in sudden contrition, "how much does she know of the delay in our arriving home? Poor love, she must be almost out of her senses with worry."

"That's what we wished to avoid, John and I, so we were guilty of a small deception. As soon as we arrived home, I wrote at once to say that we were *all* safely back, but that you and Laurie were quite worn down with travelling, so wouldn't be returning home just yet."

"Mama is as full of misgivings as an egg is of meat," declared Laurence with an unfilial chuckle. "She always fancies the worst — no doing anything with her! John and Lyddy were wise to keep her in the dark. Only think what a Cheltenham tragedy she'd have made of it had she known we'd been left stranded in France!"

"The less you say on that head, the better," Corinna reminded him tartly.

"D' you expect I shall go about in sackcloth and ashes for the rest of my days, sis?" he retorted indignantly. "For Lud's sake, pick a quarrel with Richard instead, can't you? Come to think of it, it's some time since you've come to cuffs with him — won't do to neglect him, y' know!"

To her annoyance, Corinna felt a blush rising. She dared not look at Sir Richard to see how he was taking this remark, even though at that moment he was engaged in conversation with Madeleine. Lydia stared at her sister for a moment, sensing that something was wrong, but puzzled as to what it could possibly be. Perhaps, she reflected, the answer lay in some part of their adventures which had not been heard, but which Corinna found particularly embarrassing. With an instinct to protect her sister, she abruptly changed the subject.

"What do you suppose? The most extraordinary event! Mr Grenville has arrived at his house in Eastdean, and shows every sign of actually settling there, after all his neglect of the place! Workmen are busy restoring it to rights, and moreover, he has established some distant relative as his housekeeper. I hear that the lady is an elderly widow and eminently respectable, not at all like that creature with whom he took up when he was in Paris. She has been engaging staff from among the village people — it seems no servants are being brought down from London, except his personal valet."

She realised belatedly that her choice of fresh subject could not be considered entirely happy, and threw a look of appeal towards her husband.

"It's given the neighbourhood something to gossip over, at all events," he said, smiling at her. "So in that way, the fellow's performed a service. Speculation is rife as to where the blunt's coming from, the favourite theory being that he's come into an inheritance."

Sir Richard looked thoughtful, but made no comment. He was recalling the conversation he had overheard in Perrin's gaming rooms between Grenville and the unseen Frenchman. Had Grenville indeed inherited a fortune since returning to England? Or had he heard of something to his advantage in Paris, as the Frenchman had promised? It might be important to know.

CHAPTER TWELVE

Lydia and John set off for Portsmouth on the following morning by post chaise. Sir Richard rode over from the Manor to say good-bye.

"You'll look after Lydia while I'm gone?" asked John as the brothers exchanged a warm handclasp. "Corinna will stay with her for a while, but it will relieve my mind to know that you're keeping an eye on things."

"You may safely rely on that, old fellow. I'll be looking in frequently." Then, on an unaccustomed serious note: "God keep you, John, till we meet again."

Meanwhile Lydia was giving some parting instructions to Corinna, mainly concerned with domestic affairs.

"Mrs Bolton is an excellent housekeeper, and you may depend upon her to keep matters running smoothly in my absence. She'll spare no effort to make you feel at home." She hugged Corinna to her. "Oh, my dear, I can't tell you what a prodigious comfort it will be to me to find you here on my return, instead of being obliged to come back to an empty house!"

She smiled tremulously; then allowed John, who looked very distinguished in his naval uniform, to assist her into the waiting post chaise. The postilion cracked his whip, and, with a crunching of gravel, the vehicle disappeared down the drive.

Soon afterwards, Sir Richard took his leave. Corinna saw him go with mixed feelings. One moment she wanted him there; the next an unaccountable shyness took hold of her that made his presence almost a strain. Sensitive to her every mood, he observed her attitude without being able to account for it to

121

his satisfaction. He pondered over this on the short ride home, where such thoughts were immediately banished for the time by a lengthy consultation with his land agent.

As soon as the others had gone, Laurence, already impatient to be doing something, asked Madeleine when she would like to go to Brighton.

"Not that you're to be thinking we wish to be rid of you," he concluded, with a disarming grin. "Stay as long as you like, and welcome."

"I would like to go as soon as possible," replied Madeleine.

"Why, it's not much above an hour's journey away," Laurence advised. "We could jaunt over there this very afternoon — it's famous weather for a spin along the coast! Since there are three of us we will have to take the carriage, I suppose, but I shan't take John's coachman. I'll tool it myself."

"A rare treat for us," Corinna remarked drily to Madeleine. "Don't be surprised if the wretch puts us in a ditch."

"Oh, I am sure he is much too skilled a driver for that. But yes, I think perhaps I will go there this afternoon, for it is much simpler to explain oneself face to face than in a letter."

After partaking of a light nuncheon, they set off along the road leading to the coast, a pleasant stretch which lay between gentle downland slopes and woodland. It was a fine summer afternoon, and when they reached the Cuckmere Valley, the winding river glinted attractively in the sunlight.

"Who could believe now," said Corinna, "that our circumstances should have been so different when last we were here? Only recollect how wretched we were — exhausted, cold, hungry — yet now it all seems like a bad dream!"

Madeleine assented, but her dark eyes were troubled.

"What is it, my dear?" Corinna asked gently. "Are you perhaps anxious as to your welcome when you reach your aunt's house? Pray tell me."

"Yes, it is partly that," the other said slowly. "My dear uncle seemed so certain that she would be overjoyed to see me, and I never doubted it until now. Yet how can one be sure? I don't at all remember her, and she will find me greatly changed from the child she once knew. It is possible that she may not desire to provide a home for me."

Corinna placed a reassuring hand over Madeleine's own.

"Come!" she said in a rallying tone. "You mustn't lose heart now, when you have ventured so much to come here. All will be well — and even should the worst occur, you have other friends who will not desert you, I promise."

At this, Madeleine's long-pent-up feelings overcame her, and she buried her face on Corinna's shoulder, shaken by sobs.

"I think — I think — my heart is broken!" she stammered incoherently. "I left him — I wanted oh, so desperately to stay! He will never know — that I love him truly — deeply — forever—"

The words dissolved in her grief.

For a time, she gave way to it, while Corinna soothed and comforted. Then she sat upright again, resolutely wiping away the tears from her ravaged face.

"You will think me but a poor weak creature — and, indeed, I am ashamed," she said contritely. "It was your kindness. I don't know how it is, but" — her voice shook — "kindness is in some way more liable to overcome my feelings than if one is harsh to me."

"My dear child! If you must know, I think you one of the most courageous females I've ever met. But you'd be less than human, you know, if your admirable self-control did not occasionally break down. I do realise how difficult was the choice which you felt it your duty to make — I wish I could find anything to say to console you," she concluded in a helpless tone, "but a wiser head than mine would be at a loss."

They fell silent for several minutes, while both stared abstractedly from the windows of the coach. Presently Madeleine roused herself, however, declaring resolutely that she was quite recovered.

"And we will speak no more of sad things, *chère* Corinna, but you will tell me what manner of town is this Brighton where we are going?"

"Brighton? Oh, it's a prodigiously fashionable place, for the Prince of Wales comes down from London every summer, and most of the London *ton* follow him. There are balls held at the Castle Inn, which has a magnificent assembly room. It is too early yet in the season, Madeleine," she continued, "but later on, you may like to indulge in sea bathing."

"You mean one immerses oneself in the sea?" asked Madeleine, evidently shocked. "Is not that most unwise? Besides, for a female, it would be immodest!"

Corinna chuckled. "Oh, it's all most proper, I assure you! Boxes are provided on the beach for disrobing — the gentlemen's on the west side and the ladies' on the east, well separated. Then the boxes are drawn into the sea by horses, and some prodigiously muscular persons known as dippers open the doors and assist the occupants into the water."

Madeleine shuddered. "Bah! I think it would be very cold, and not at all pleasant!"

"Then perhaps you'd prefer a donkey ride?" asked Corinna mischievously. "It's a favourite sport for some of the females, and famous fun to watch, for they frequently tumble off — oh, not to hurt themselves, you know, for it's only on the sand, and not far to fall from a donkey's back."

Madeleine laughed. "You wouldn't have much sport with me, for I can ride — a horse or a donkey, it makes no difference."

They chattered away in this lighter vein until their carriage swung under the archway of the Old Ship, one of Brighton's leading hostelries situated on the seafront. Ostlers came hurrying to the horses' heads, and Laurence jumped down from the box to give his orders.

"Well, here we are," he announced, pulling open the carriage door. "Right as a trivet, and no complaints, I trust?"

Having been reassured on this point, he suggested that his passengers might like to take a glass of lemonade in the coffee room while he refreshed himself with a tankard of ale. While they were being served, he made inquiries of the waiters as to the whereabouts of the house they were seeking, and discovered that it was situated in one of the lanes not more than five minutes' walk away.

Presently they took their way there, and soon located the house, a small half-timbered building with latticed windows. In answer to Laurence's knock, the door was opened by a sharp-featured female of middle years with an unwelcoming aspect. She did not invite her visitors to enter, but quickly gave them to understand that not only did Madame de Fougeray *not* reside there, but that she knew nothing of the whereabouts of such a person. Pressed to say how long she had been living there, she gave the period as five years or so; stating at the same time that it was none of her visitors' business, and she had something better to do with her time than stand at the door answering impertinent questions.

"Well, I'm dashed!" exclaimed Laurence indignantly, as the door closed in his face. "What a virago! You're sure we have the number of the house right, Madeleine?"

She produced the letter again, and they all studied it; the heading was quite clear.

"It's dated nine years ago," remarked Corinna dubiously. "It's quite likely that in so long a time your aunt may have removed elsewhere. But how are we to discover where? If only Richard were with us, I feel he might know what to do."

"We don't need Richard," declared Laurence roundly. "Tell you what, some of the neighbours must know something. I'll inquire this side, and do you two try your luck on the other."

He knocked vigorously on the door of the adjoining house. Meanwhile, the two girls approached their objective rather more timidly, having been put off by the previous reception. Their cautious knock this time brought a more rewarding response, however; for they were greeted by a comfortable-looking matron with white hair under a lace cap, who smilingly bade them enter.

"You'll mean the French lady who used to live next door before the Prestons came," she asked with a slight grimace as she named her neighbours. "Ay, I mind her well, pour soul, turned out of her own country by them murdering heathens, and neither kith nor kin in England! And the lad, too — a little gentleman if ever I met one! Though later on, when he took to working for the fisher folk, he became more like the other lads, which was only natural, you'll allow, ma'am."

Madeleine, who had been looking downcast, here shared a triumphant glance with Corinna.

"Do you by any chance know where they went when they removed from here?" asked Corinna.

"Now there I can't help you, ma'am. But maybe some of the fishermen might know something, seeing as the lad earned a trifle working for them."

"Can you tell me the names of these men, or where they may be found?"

The woman shook her head. "Nay, I know nothing of the fisher folk, save that at this time o'day you'll likely find some of them down on the beach at their nets."

There seemed nothing further to be learned; so, having thanked their informant graciously, they took their leave.

Laurence had received no answer to his knock on the other door, and now awaited them hopefully.

"I see you gained admittance — any luck?"

"I'm afraid we didn't discover much to the purpose."

Corinna then repeated the gist of her conversation with the kindly occupant of the house.

He pursed his lips. "Mm. Not much to go on, is it? Still, we'll leave no possibility unexplored. Tell you what, I'll escort you two back to the inn and you can await me there while I pursue inquiries on the beach."

Presently he left them in the Old Ship while he crossed the road to go down to the beach. He soon espied a little farther along a number of boats drawn up on the shingle and some men nearby busy with nets. He approached quickly, his boots crunching on the pebbles, but no one favoured him with so much as a glance when he halted.

He accosted the nearest, a surly-looking individual dressed like the others in a dark jersey, stained breeches, and high sea boots.

"A word with you, if you please, my good fellow."

The man looked up, eyed him contemptuously, spat, then continued with mending one of the nets.

Suppressing an instinctive urge to teach the fellow better manners, Laurence moved away to another of the men. Here he encountered the same lack of interest, though shown with less incivility. He jingled some coins together in his pocket, and was given a hard stare from very blue eyes set in a weather-beaten face.

He stated his business as briefly as possible. The man heard him out, as did another who was working close by, and had paused to listen. Both shook their heads.

At first, he believed that the ignorance expressed by them was genuine enough; but as he went from one to another of the group, always receiving the same kind of evasive replies to his questions, he began to gain the impression that they were deliberately withholding information. He turned his back on them in disgust.

He was about to give up and stalk back to the inn, when he noticed a solitary fisherman standing at some distance from the others who had obviously been watching. He strode purposefully towards him.

The man began to retreat, but Laurence caught up with him, laying a detaining hand on his shoulder. The fellow turned with a snarl.

"Take yer 'ands off me, young buck!"

He raised a threatening arm.

"Shouldn't if I were you," warned Laurence, opening his fist to disclose a guinea. "No need, anyway. All I want of you is to know the whereabouts of some friends of mine, and I'm willing to pay for the information."

The man dropped his arm, his eyes glinting at sight of the gold.

"What friends?" he demanded.

"They're French, name of Fougeray, and there was a boy who used to work with you fishermen. They left the town about five years since, but no one seems to know where they went. This is yours" — he thrust forward the guinea — "if you can help me to find them."

The man's eyes shifted momentarily to Laurence's face, before returning to the guinea.

"There was a lad," he admitted grudgingly. "Worked for some o' us until he took up wi' more risky business."

"What d'you mean by risky business?"

"Smugglin' an' the like. Not 'ere — nobody 'ere don't meddle in suchlike," he added hastily. "Law-abidin' folk, we be."

He held out his hand expectantly, but Laurence shook his head.

"You'll need to tell me more than that," he said firmly. "Where do these smugglers operate?"

A scared look came over the weather-beaten face.

"Don't do to meddle wi' they," he said almost in a whisper. "Cut out yer liver an' lights, that lot would, as soon as look at yer. I'm tellin' naught else — keep the blunt, so long's ye let me be."

He began to turn away, but Laurence detained him with a hand on his arm.

"Answer one question only — just nod your head, if you're scared to say more. Do these gentry operate down the coast towards Eastbourne?"

The man hesitated, then gave a quick nod. Laurence passed over the guinea, which was quickly palmed.

On his way back to the Old Ship, he meditated over what he had learned. It seemed likely that Madeleine's cousin had been working for the very same smugglers who had recently brought himself and the others across the Channel. There would scarcely be two gangs operating in the same area.

If that were so, then it was possible that the de Fougerays had moved somewhere nearer to the centre of operations, and might even be in the neighbourhood of Eastbourne. The devil of it was that he could scarcely tell Madeleine what he suspected. It would not be pleasant news for the poor girl that her cousin was — or had been — in league with a gang of smugglers!

CHAPTER THIRTEEN

When Laurence told Madeleine that he could obtain no more certain information than that her aunt and cousin had most likely removed to the vicinity of Eastbourne, she was deeply disappointed.

"No matter for that," he said encouragingly, seeing her crestfallen look. "It's only five miles from here, y' know, and I expect a few inquiries there will soon find them."

She thanked him for his trouble, but remained acutely conscious of being obliged to rely on his elder sister's hospitality for a longer period than she had envisaged. Her independent nature chafed at this, and she determined to set about obtaining a lodging elsewhere. She lost no time, therefore, in questioning one of the housemaids about the possibility of finding accommodation in the nearby village.

"There is a large house in the village, I think," she said to the girl, recollecting something which had been said by Lydia Beresford on the day of their arrival. "It belongs to a gentleman who has recently been engaging servants. I wonder, do you know the name of the lady who manages the household?"

"Oh, yes, miss," answered the girl, pleased at being able to oblige. "'Tis Mr Grenville's house, called Eastdean Place, an' the gennelman's never been nigh it for I dunnamany years, but now 'e's doin' it up good an' proper, spendin' a mort o' money on it. The lady in charge there is called Mrs Benton — a regular Tartar, so our Sukey says."

Madeleine asked how far it was to the village and where Eastdean Place was situated. She was given directions, and told she could easily walk there. She said nothing of her intentions to Corinna and the others. She arose early the next morning before they were astir, partook of a light breakfast, then set out on her solitary walk.

She went through and beyond the village of Eastdean until she reached the track which she had been told led eventually to Birling Gap. After a short distance, she turned into a narrow lane and soon came upon the house she sought, approached by a neglected drive full of weeds.

Eastdean Place was a large, flint-built house with a pillared portico surrounding the front entrance and bay windows on either side. It was being redecorated, she saw, for some scaffolding had been erected and workmen were busy.

She hesitated for a few moments, doubtful if she should approach the front door on her particular errand. Presently she walked round the house until she came to a side entrance, and here she knocked.

The door was opened by a footman in shirt sleeves and a green cloth waistcoat. He had evidently been polishing silver, for he held a vase and a rag in one hand. He stared at her, dumbfounded.

"I wish to see Mrs Benton, please," she said firmly.

Evidently he was uncertain of the status of this visitor, for he hesitated.

"Madam b'aint receivin', miss," he said, in broad Sussex tones.

"I am come on business," said Madeleine, with more assurance than she felt. "If your mistress is at home, pray have the goodness to conduct me to her at once."

The tone was enough. With no more hesitation than was necessary to rid himself of the articles he was carrying and to don his coat, he conducted her along a passage, through a green baize door and across a checkerboard hall to a small parlour.

He knocked timidly on the door, and a sharp voice bade him enter.

An angular female of middle years was sitting before an oak bureau writing a letter as Madeleine was shown into the room. She was wearing a modish grey morning gown and an attractive lace cap which did not succeed in softening her thin, shrewish face. She put down her pen and turned towards them, raising her eyebrows.

"A lady to see you, if you please, ma'am."

Madeleine came forward and curtseyed.

"My name is Madeleine Fougeray, ma'am."

Mrs Benton favoured her with a cold nod as the servant withdrew.

"May I ask to what I owe the favour of this visit?"

"I apologise for intruding upon you, ma'am, but I understand that you are in need of maidservants, and am come to offer myself. I have a testimonial here from a lady with whom I have been previously employed, milady Northcote."

She handed over the fulsome letter which she had begged from Lady Northcote before they parted in France. Mrs Benton took it reluctantly, looked Madeleine up and down for a few moments, then condescended to read it.

"Very pretty," she acknowledged grudgingly. "I see this lady says you're an accomplished needlewoman. Well, I can certainly do with one such here, for the household linen is deplorably neglected. But why is it that you are no longer in Lady Northcote's employ, my good girl? I see she gives her London direction, so I can easily verify anything you may tell me."

"You are welcome to do so, madame," replied Madeleine with dignity. "I was employed by milady as her personal maid while she was on a visit to Paris. She has her own abigail in London, so when she returned to England she no longer required my services."

Mrs Benton looked at her curiously. "Yes, I had guessed you were French, although your English is sufficiently good. But since there was no post for you in Lady Northcote's London household, why have you come to England?"

Madeleine had given serious consideration as to what she would say at this interview, and had come to the conclusion that it would be wiser to keep as far as possible to the truth.

"I have now no surviving relatives in France, madame, so came here thinking to find a home with an aunt who lived in Brighton, as I understood. But when I went to the house, I learned that she had moved away, no one knew where. I am left, therefore, with no home and very little money. I must find a post."

Mrs Benton studied Madeleine acutely for several moments. The girl had a certain air of breeding and shapely hands, very different from those of the country housemaid whose clumsy ministrations she was at present obliged to support. Cousin Fabian — she called him cousin, but the actual relationship was more remote — had expressly forbidden her to advertise for an experienced lady's maid. He would have none but local staff with the sole exception of his valet, a smooth-tongued, deceitful creature whom Mrs Benton privately detested and almost feared, and who had been with him for many years.

"Very well," she said at last. "I will engage you as my personal maid on a fortnight's trial. Be here at seven o'clock in the morning to commence your duties. I'll summon the creature who is at present maiding me, and she will instruct you as to the times at which I expect various services, besides making you acquainted with my wardrobe. You will thereafter present yourself here at seven each morning and leave the house each evening after you have dressed me for dinner."

"But — but shall I not live in, madame?" stammered Madeleine, dismayed.

"Certainly not — none of the other servants do so, with the exception of Mr Grenville's personal man and certain of the stable hands," snapped Mrs Benton.

"But I have no lodging," protested Madeleine. "Please, madame, the smallest room — almost a cupboard — would suffice! And then I would be at hand," she added with a hint of guile, "to assist you to retire for the night, madame, which now I must suppose you are obliged to do unaided."

Mrs Benton's first impulse had been to send the girl at once about her business; but this final remark gave her pause. Why should Cousin Fabian have the benefit of a valet constantly in attendance, while she was obliged to make do with a daily maid? It was a ridiculous foible of his that all the household staff should leave the premises after dinner had been cleared away. It relegated the house to the level of a country inn rather than a gentleman's residence. She made up her mind.

"Very well, for the present you may sleep in one of the smaller attics, but understand that this is a temporary arrangement only. The maid will show you where it is. Ring the bell for her."

When Madeleine returned to Friston House, she found Corinna and Laurence had long since breakfasted and were wondering at her absence. She quickly explained where she had been and the outcome of her visit. At first they protested that it was absurd for her to take such a step; but her quiet resolution at length prevailed.

"I regard it as of the utmost importance that no one in my place of employment shall know on what friendly terms I stand with you and your sister," she said, smiling to soften her firm tone. "It will make for questions, *n'est-ce pas*? And I don't wish to be thought other than I seem. Once I find my aunt — if, indeed, I ever do! — all these matters will arrange themselves, and we can meet as equals."

"Never say you don't intend us to meet at all in the meantime!" protested Corinna. "How else will we keep you informed about the search for your aunt?"

"I shall hope to walk over here most afternoons, for I was informed this morning that I can usually expect to be free between the hours of three and five," said Madeleine. "But one must be discreet, I think, so I will enter by the garden gate and wait for you in the shrubbery, so that your servants do not see me."

"Yes, by Jove, and I tell you what!" put in Laurence, fired by this hint of mystery. "When you get the chance, Madeleine, examine the grounds at Eastdean Place for some suitable spot there where we could creep in to meet you or leave messages, y' know! 'Pon honour, it should be capital fun! And I was thinking how slow things would be after our escape from France!"

Madeleine could not but smile at his eagerness.

His final words to her were that he intended to waste no time in pursuing the search.

"Corinna and I will set out this very afternoon," he promised. "Pluck up, there's a good girl."

She pressed his hand earnestly. "You are very good, Laurence, far more than I deserve. I have been thinking that perhaps the simplest way to find them would be to engage a lawyer — but that is a costly business, and—"

"No, no, we might have recourse to that in the end, but I have other plans first," he assured her heartily. "Leave all to me."

She exchanged a warm embrace with Corinna and went on her way.

"Of course, I couldn't tell her a lawyer was out of the question, seeing that her cousin is most likely breaking the law," Laurence said to his sister when Madeleine had gone. "In the circumstances, he'd be scarce likely to come forward in answer to a lawyer's advertisement, now, would he? But I think our best bet is to find those smugglers who brought us across the Channel. They operate somewhere in this area, or they wouldn't have chosen to land us at Cuckmere Haven, so they're bound to be this chap Fougeray's lot.

"Tell you what," said Laurence. "Let's try our luck in the villages — I remember Richard saying that he and other local landowners suspected that their villagers might be involved with the smuggling fraternity, but since there'd been no outrages, they didn't concern themselves to probe into the matter. West Dean's on our way. Let's try there first."

"But it's on Richard's estate," objected Corinna. "Would it not be more proper to call and explain to him what we're attempting to do, and allow him to put the questions?"

"Pooh! I tell you, sis, you seem to have developed a devilish silly notion all at once that Richard is the best person to handle everything! I suppose you think just because he brought us safe out of France — and I'd remind you he wasn't the only one concerned — he's some kind of hero!"

Corinna blushed painfully, relaxing her grip on the rein momentarily so that her horse faltered. She soon set it right, grateful for the incident because it enabled her to keep her face hidden from her brother.

"Stuff!" she said roundly. "Very well, do it in your own way."

They turned off the high road by an ancient farm along a path which climbed for a while before descending steeply to the small, sequestered village surrounded by trees. Having dismounted and tethered their horses to a convenient post, they strolled towards a group of lichen-covered cottages. In one of these an elderly woman in a coarse fawn gown and white apron was standing in the open doorway. As they halted before her, she curtseyed, surveying them with a fixed, slightly hostile stare.

They attempted to engage her in friendly casual conversation, Laurence doing most of the talking; but she seemed disinclined to cooperate, answering in monosyllables and staring beyond them at the path by which they had come, as though expecting someone.

"It must be lonely here of nights," Laurence said after a time, in desperation. "And the sea's close at hand. D' you ever get any unwelcome visitors — smugglers, say? I've heard rumours that this is smuggling country."

Halfway through his speech, he was conscious of footsteps approaching behind him. He swung round quickly as a harsh voice spoke in his ear.

"Ye've 'eard a deal too much, mister. Who be ye, and what d'ye want wi' honest folk?"

He faced a burly, menacing farm labourer. Corinna retreated a step and tugged at her brother's arm, but he stood his ground.

"Nothing in the world," he said airily. "Only passing the time of day, y'know."

"Well, pass it otherwheres," growled the labourer.

As if others had been watching behind curtains, a small group now converged on the scene. They surrounded the pair, so that Laurence began to wonder if he would need to fight his way out, and how Corinna would fare in such an undignified affray. On her account, he was hesitating what he should do next, when the clopping of hooves made the villagers look round.

To Laurence's relief, the approaching horseman was Sir Richard. He reined in, surveying the group with raised eyebrows.

"Well, well, what have we here?" he demanded.

There was much bobbing and pulling of forelocks among the villagers, who at once began to disperse as silently as they had arrived. The woman in the cottage door and the burly labourer took the hint and retreated into their cottage.

"And what exactly was all that about?" asked Sir Richard, having swung out of the saddle to walk beside them towards their horses.

Laurence explained.

"Good God, you must be all about in your head to think you can ask questions of that kind without setting up their hackles! And when your sister is with you, too!"

"And why should I not be with him?" demanded Corinna hotly. "Disabuse yourself of the notion that I am a helpless, half-witted female!"

"You well know that I hold no such notion. Though I might be forgiven for supposing," he added, not altogether wisely, "that your wits would provide a safer solution to the problem than this."

She turned an indignant face towards him, her eyes sparkling with golden fire.

"You are altogether odious! Don't speak to me again!"

She gestured to Laurence to help her into the saddle, then urged her horse forward into a pace suited to her turbulent emotions. She was indeed angry, but mixed with the rage was a strange feeling of exhilaration and challenge. She realised suddenly that she was actually enjoying herself. She wanted to fight him, to goad him out of his habitual calm detachment into — what? She was in no mood to seek an answer.

"Ay, that's more like it," said Laurence encouragingly, as they both brought their horses up to join hers. "Quite like old times! But honestly, Richard, how the deuce else am I to set about the business? Seems to me if we can but track down some of these smugglers, we shall find Madeleine's cousin and, through him, her aunt."

Sir Richard agreed, and was about to say more when they saw a horseman coming towards them along the road into which they had just turned. He drew level, gave a start of surprise, then swept off his hat and bowed with a flourish. It was Fabian Grenville.

"Why, Miss Haydon!" he exclaimed in lively pleasure. "What brings you to these outlandish parts? But I forget — Beresford's estate is here, and your sister also lives close by."

He bowed again more briefly to the gentlemen.

"'Servant, Beresford — Haydon."

"My brother and I are staying with my sister Lydia for a while," replied Corinna, not too cordially, for she had not forgotten Mrs Peters.

"I am relieved to see that you came safe out of France," continued Grenville. "I took myself off as soon as matters looked chancy. You may not know that I've decided to settle in at Eastdean Place, my old family home? Old is the operative word, for the house and grounds need a deal doing before the place can be considered fit for a gentleman's residence. I've been there some weeks now and made good headway. Curst workmen all over, though, getting under one's feet. Still, I hope to see the back of 'em before long, and then I'll give a housewarming. Trust you'll all be able to come to it — how long do you intend to remain with Mrs Beresford, Miss Haydon?"

"My plans are uncertain, but I think at least a month."

"A month only! Then I must hasten to rid myself of those fellows. My party would be quite spoilt, ma'am, I assure you, if you could not be present."

She returned a thin smile to this compliment, and they parted with the usual civilities.

"Dare say it won't ruin his party if *we* aren't able to be present, though," remarked Laurence.

Corinna made no reply, and Sir Richard merely grunted, something approaching a scowl on his usually pleasant countenance.

CHAPTER FOURTEEN

Sir Richard's reproof to Laurence had not altogether fallen on deaf ears, so that young man decided that whenever possible in future he would try to exclude his sister from his investigations. He still considered that something might be learned in the nearby villages, and set off for Eastdean, but this time resolved to proceed more warily. He had not previously visited the village, the first sight of which affected him in much the same way as it had Madeleine. It was difficult to connect such a pretty, seemingly sleepy place with the dark doings of smugglers. He was reluctant to abandon his theories without putting them to the test, however; and, having pondered for a moment, he strolled casually into the Tiger Inn. He ordered a tankard of ale and seated himself on one of the settles beside an aged countryman with blackened teeth and a lined, weather-beaten face.

"Morning, gaffer," said Laurence affably.

The old man returned the greeting, then quickly drained his pot of ale, with an eye to the main chance.

"Allow me," said Laurence handsomely. "Landlord, fill up, will you?"

The innkeeper, a large, red-faced man in shirt sleeves, obliged, at the same time subjecting his stylish customer to a searching scrutiny. Strangers, especially those of the Quality, were rare in Eastdean.

Having pledged the old man's health, which privately he considered none too robust, Laurence proceeded to engage him in casual conversation.

His companion seemed ready enough to talk, but his endless stream of chatter conveyed no useful information. Either the man was obtuse, or else he was not to be drawn on the subject of his neighbours' activities.

After a while, Laurence gave up the attempt as hopeless. He rose to leave, setting down the price of another drink beside his unrewarding informant.

Reluctant to return home without having achieved anything, he decided to take a look at Grenville's house. Following Madeleine's description, he soon came to the drive, but did not turn along it, as this was decidedly no social call. What he had in mind was to try and discover some kind of rendezvous for the three of them on occasions when Madeleine might not be able to come to Friston House.

To either side of the drive a boundary wall enclosed the grounds of the house, with a narrow lane running alongside. The wall curved round to enclose the ground at the rear of the house, and he came to a back entrance in the shape of a battered wooden door which looked as though it had not been used for years.

He tried the door, delighted when he found it gave way to his touch. Trees were planted at intervals inside the wall; after carefully closing the door behind him, he took cover behind one of these and peered out across the grounds.

These were not extensive; no gardeners were at work in them, though it was evident that much needed doing. A wilderness of overgrown shrubs and unkempt grass stretched from the trees across to a small formal garden enclosed by low hedges. Confident that if he kept to this end of the grounds, he would be too far from the house to be overlooked, he began to explore the wilderness.

Thrusting his way through a jungle of overgrown rhododendron bushes, he found in its centre a small, ornamental wooden hut which must once have been intended as a summerhouse. Obviously no one had been near it for years, for it was in a dilapidated state, with peeling paint and windows encrusted with dirt. Pushing open the rickety door, he disclosed a similarly neglected interior. The once pretty white-painted bench with chintz cushions was filthy and festooned with spiders' webs; the ironwork of a marble-topped table was covered in rust.

"It's the very place," he said enthusiastically to Corinna and Madeleine later. "But perhaps you'd best clean the hut up a bit, Madeleine, or you'll both be setting up a squawk about soiling your clothes."

She nodded. "And you think we should meet there, instead of here?"

"Not altogether, for I dare say you'll be glad to walk over here now and then, for a change. But I thought we could use it in an emergency, especially for leaving messages. There's a small wall cupboard beside the bench where we could stow notes for each other, if anything turns up on days when we can't meet. I dare say even when you're confined to the house, you'd manage to slip out to the hut without being noticed."

Madeleine agreed that this seemed likely, and promised to visit the summerhouse daily in search of messages whenever she was unable to walk over to Friston House.

Lydia returned the following afternoon, tired from her journey but determined to put a brave face on her parting from John in all the uncertainties of war.

"And I'm so glad that you're here, my love," she said to Corinna, "for you and Laurie will make me laugh whenever I feel mopish! But where is the charming little French girl? Has she already gone to her relatives in Brighton?"

Corinna explained about this.

"Oh, dear, how distressing for her! She need not have taken a post until they are found, though — she would have been very welcome to stay here. And at Fabian Grenville's house, too! That may be a trifle awkward."

"No, for Madeleine insists on keeping her friendship with us a secret. She thinks it not at all proper for an abigail to be on visiting terms with Mr Grenville's neighbours. I do see her difficulty, so we've arranged clandestine meetings in the shrubbery. It's all capital fun!"

Lydia laughed. "Well, I'm sure Laurie would think so. You're such children, the pair of you — you make me feel a positive centenarian! Where is Laurie? I thought I would send him over to the manor to fetch Richard back to dine with us, then we shall be a cosy family party."

Sir Richard duly arrived, to be greeted warmly by Lydia but with restraint on Corinna's side. He raised his eyebrows questioningly at her as they stood together for a few moments before entering the dining room.

"I'm not yet forgiven, I see," he said, smiling wryly. "It's unlike you to bear a grudge, though. Usually you're ready to overlook our little tiffs."

"We shouldn't have any tiffs if it were not for your odious habit of interfering in my concerns!" she countered swiftly.

"True. Would you like me to promise not to do so again?"

There was a mocking expression on his face, but his blue eyes momentarily gave another message. She looked very lovely tonight, in a high-waisted gown of yellow muslin that brought out the gold lights in her hair.

"If I had the faintest expectation of your ever keeping to such a promise, I'd say yes, but I know you better, alas!"

"I was afraid you might. How shaming it is, to be read like an open book."

"You underrate yourself. Far from being easy to read, you're positively inscrutable at times."

"Ah, but you like mysteries, do you not? I know Mrs Radcliffe is one of your favourite authors."

"Mysteries are all very well between the covers of a novel," Corinna answered, laughing in spite of herself, "but I am by far too curious to tolerate them in real life!"

"One day perhaps I will elucidate the mystery for you."

She saw the intense look again in his eyes, and was forced to lower her own. When she looked up once more, it had vanished, to be replaced by his usual nonchalance. Then Lydia gave the signal for them to repair to the dining room, where conversation became general.

The talk ranged from Portsmouth and naval friends there to concerns in the immediate neighbourhood. Sir Richard told them that he had received certain instructions in his capacity as magistrate for procedure in the event of an invasion by the French.

"Invasion!" exclaimed the sisters, in horror.

Laurence's eyes kindled. "D' you think it may come to that, Richard?"

"Frankly, no. They must first run the gauntlet of our navy, and you may judge for yourselves how likely they are to succeed against Nelson," he replied, with quiet confidence. "But it's only prudent to make preparations, however unlikely the event."

"What kind of preparations?" asked Laurence.

"Warning beacons are to be erected at strategic points and the semaphore signal system extended. Volunteer forces are being raised to fight on the beaches and in the countryside, if need be. But all this makes dismal hearing for the ladies. Let us change the subject."

"Volunteer forces?" repeated Laurence. "Say you so? B' God, I've a good mind to join them — d' you know of one hereabouts, Richard?"

"Indeed I do. As a matter of fact, I'm off to Brighton tomorrow to see my old friend Colonel Wexham on that subject."

"Take me with you," Laurence urged. Then, his face clouding: "But where's the use? Mama would never agree, I suppose."

Sir Richard considered this. "I can't vouch for the success of it, but we might try to persuade her by laying stress on the fact that such forces are unlikely to see any action."

"Now you're roasting me," complained Laurence. "If it ain't like you to make the whole affair sound deuced tame!"

"No such thing. They *may* be called upon to play their part, though personally I doubt the French will ever reach these shores. Nevertheless, you'd be receiving useful training for a military career later, should you still wish to engage in one when you come of age. By all means, accompany me tomorrow, and then we'll discuss this further."

The conversation turned to other topics, and presently Madeleine's affairs were mentioned. Laurence related his unsuccessful attempts to glean some information in Eastdean concerning the whereabouts of the smugglers.

"Oh, pray don't meddle in such matters!" begged Lydia anxiously. "I never heard talk of any smugglers hereabouts myself, but I do know how dangerous such people can be if anyone starts prying into their affairs, so I beg of you, Laurie, leave well alone!"

"You may not have heard anything of local smugglers, but Richard has, for he told me so."

Lydia looked questioningly at Sir Richard, who nodded.

"Landowners hereabouts have always suspected that their own villages are involved in the trade, but as long as there was no violence, we chose not to inquire into it too closely. After all, smuggling has been a way of life along the Channel coast for hundreds of years, passing from father to son as if it were a legitimate trade. It's difficult to stamp out anything like that, and the preventive men have too much territory to cover to be effective. Lydia's in the right of it, though, Laurie — they can be ugly customers. Best not meddle."

"That's all very well, but how else can we hope to trace Madeleine's relatives? We daren't employ a lawyer—"

"True, but I see no reason against advertising privately in the local journals. An appeal to write to Mademoiselle de Fougeray care of a newspaper would surely cause no alarm."

"What a capital notion!" exclaimed Corinna. "I wonder we didn't think of it before."

"I'm not so sure," said Laurence, a trifle sulkily, for he had been enjoying his active part in the search. "Females don't read newspapers, and I'll wager smugglers don't either!"

"Who says females don't read newspapers?" demanded his sisters in chorus.

"Oh, well, I don't count bluestockings like you two!"

"Before you embark on a lengthy and doubtless stimulating family wrangle," put in Sir Richard, with a grin, "let me remind you that some friend of the family is sure to see this advertisement and bring it to their notice. But I suppose we ought to consult mademoiselle before taking any action. One wouldn't wish to be high-handed."

Corinna gave him a saucy look. "Would you not? How you are changed!"

"Thanks to your tireless efforts, my reformation has made rapid strides of late. A little more endeavour on your side will soon see the process completed."

"Small likelihood of that," she countered, laughing. "But I'll be seeing Madeleine tomorrow and I'll ask her permission."

But Madeleine failed to put in an appearance on the following afternoon. After awaiting her in the shrubbery until after four o'clock, Corinna decided that she must leave a message for her in the hut which Laurence had found at Eastdean Place. She had some qualms about attempting this, but she reminded herself that she had boasted to Sir Richard of her intention to take an active part in the search for Madeleine's relatives; this strengthened her resolution.

Having written a brief explanatory note to leave in their improvised post office, she set out for Eastdean Place by paths which avoided the main part of the village. Normally she would have enjoyed the walk; but as she drew nearer to her objective, she grew more and more tense.

She breathed a sigh of relief when she was safely past the entrance to the drive, and hurried on until she came to the door in the wall.

It took all her courage to enter and stand within the cover of the trees. Her heart was beating fast as she ventured out into what Laurence had aptly described as a wilderness. His directions had been plain, and she soon came upon the hut.

Bolder now, she pushed open the door. Then she started back in alarm. Someone was inside.

Evidently the occupant was equally startled, for she uttered a faint cry as she turned to face the intruder.

"*Mon Dieu!* Corinna, it is you — but how you scared me!"

"Not more than *you* scared me!" exclaimed Corinna, entering with lifted skirts, for the floor was none too clean. "I came to leave a note for you, but now I can tell you myself."

"And I to leave one for you! I could not get away until now, and it was too late to come to Friston House. You may sit on this bench, I think, for I have done my best to clean it."

They sat side by side while Corinna explained what was intended.

"Why, yes, I think that is an idea of the most clever! And it will not be near so costly as a lawyer, *n'est-ce pas?* As to that, you will allow me to defray the cost, of course."

"Of course," agreed Corinna glibly, knowing better than to argue over this. "But tell me how everything goes on with you, Madeleine."

"It is well enough. The workmen have almost finished inside the house, and I have been helping madame to refurbish the rooms. She says Monsieur Grenville will soon be receiving visitors, but he and the valet Thomson are absent today. A visitor arrived for him last night, and at such an odd time — it was past midnight! My attic room overlooks the stableyard, and the sound of a horse woke me. I looked out, and the moon was bright, so I could see a man dismounting, with Monsieur Grenville there beside him. I did not wish to pry, you understand, but always it is so quiet at night, and I wondered who it might be. The visitor did not stay overnight, for no guest room is occupied this morning. Perhaps Monsieur Grenville and his valet went away with him for no one seems to know when they left — but that seems odd, too. However" — with a Gallic shrug — "it is none of my business.

150

"And now, my dear Corinna, I must go, for soon I shall be wanted. Since I can expect no news from the advertisement for several days, there will be no need for me to come and visit you at your house every day as we arranged, I suppose."

Her tone was wistful, and it reminded Corinna once more how friendless Madeleine must feel herself to be at present.

"But indeed I hope you will," she said warmly. "Come every day, if you are at liberty to do so, and should I be obliged to be absent for any reason, I will leave a note for you in the little arbour where we sit in the shrubbery. And when news does arrive, either Laurie or I will bring a message here for you, if need be. Only think, Madeleine, it cannot be long now before your quest is ended, and then we'll have no further need of subterfuge!"

They parted in a cheerful mood; Corinna to remove herself speedily and thankfully off the premises, and Madeleine to return unobtrusively to the house.

The master of Eastdean Place had not returned home by dinnertime, so Mrs Benton took a solitary evening meal. As usual, the staff all departed for their own homes by nine o'clock, leaving their mistress and Madeleine alone in the house.

Mrs Benton went early to bed, instructing Madeleine to lock up the house securely before herself retiring for the night.

Unfamiliar with this duty, which was normally performed by Thomson, Madeleine spent some time in examining the several doors and windows to make sure that all was secure. She had reached her attic room and was about to undress, when she suddenly realised with dismay that she had overlooked the servants' entrance through the kitchen.

By now it was past eleven; Mrs Benton, a heavy sleeper, had been in bed for an hour, so there was small likelihood of disturbing her. Nevertheless, Madeleine, candle in hand, was careful to creep silently down the three flights of stairs which led to the kitchen. She gently eased open the door, then started in alarm as she saw a dark figure moving across the room.

"*Mon Dieu! Qui est là?*"

Almost she dropped the candlestick in her fright.

It was seized from her as a firm hand clamped itself over her mouth.

"Screech and I'll wring your neck," growled the intruder, also in French. "Keep quiet — not a sound — understand?"

She nodded, trembling. He put the candlestick down on a shelf nearby to take hold of her with both arms and draw her into the kitchen.

"I mean it," he whispered menacingly. "Do you speak English?"

She nodded again, too frightened for speech. She could not have cried out, even had she wished.

"But you're French?" Another nod. "Who are you? Why are you here?"

He was speaking in English now, with a strong Sussex accent.

She found her own voice, low and quavering.

"I am Madame Benton's abigail — she sent me to lock up."

"Ah, so." He nodded, seeming less ferocious now. "Now, see here, you — what's your name?"

"M-Madeleine," she stuttered.

"Well, Madeleine—"

He broke off, and raised the candle to scrutinise her for a moment in silence.

"I think I've seen you somewhere before," he said slowly and suspiciously.

She stared back at him, gradually recovering a little of her confidence.

"I, too, monsieur."

He put down the candle, grabbing her in so fierce a hold that she could barely suppress a cry of pain.

"You have *not* seen me," he hissed, "not tonight, not ever! If you dare to breathe one word to anyone of having seen me, I'll discover it, and make you pay! You're a pretty wench, Madeleine, *now*, but what man will look at you when I've been at work on you with this, eh?"

Suddenly there was a cruel-looking knife in his hand, its point just touching her cheek. She froze in horror, afraid to move, afraid even to breathe.

Seeing the effect he had produced, he chuckled in a way that sent cold shivers down her spine. He removed the knife, stowing it away.

"I trust you understand me, mademoiselle," he said in perfect French.

Madeleine nodded. She understood very well.

"Then go back to bed."

She did not hesitate to obey.

CHAPTER FIFTEEN

When Corinna reached home after parting from Madeleine at Eastdean Place, she found that Sir Richard and Laurence had just returned from Brighton. While they were there, they had chanced to meet the Cheveleys walking on the Steyne; and an invitation had at once been given to spend a day with the family at their home in Rottingdean, a village a few miles east of Brighton.

"They were very pressing that we should go tomorrow, if that chanced to be convenient," said Sir Richard. "Of course, I could not venture to promise definitely for you ladies, but Laurie and I accepted. Miss Cheveley was delighted to learn that you're staying here for a while, Corinna, and trusts that you'll both be able to meet frequently."

"Oh, yes, I should like it of all things," declared Lydia. "We've no previous engagements, as so far there's been no time to make any, but I hope to remedy that without delay! What do you say, Corinna? You'll be at liberty to go, will you not?"

Corinna agreed, reflecting that she could leave a note for Madeleine explaining her absence, as they had arranged.

It turned out another fine day, so they decided to make the journey by curricle, Sir Richard taking his own and Laurence borrowing John's. There was some discussion as to which of the sisters should be driven by her brother; but Lydia settled it by declaring that Laurence and Corinna were safer parted.

"You're such a wild pair, there's no knowing what starts you'll get up to! No, I'll go with Laurie to see he behaves himself."

"Serve you right if I put you in a ditch for that," grinned her brother. "Lord, though, I'm looking forward to handling those bays of John's! As neat a pair as ever I set eyes on, give you my word!"

During the early part of the journey, Corinna was unusually silent. She had not yet completely recovered from the unaccountable shyness with Sir Richard which had overcome her since their return from France. She managed to conceal it well enough when they were in company with the others; but to be sitting in close proximity to him in the curricle cast her into a state vexingly near to confusion. She stole a glance from time to time at the firm profile and strong, capable hands so admirably controlling his fresh horses; and there flashed into her mind the many instances during their escape from France when his cool head and swift decisions had brought them safely through danger. Laurence, the rebel and hothead, had unquestioningly accepted his leadership; a tribute, she felt, not so much to seniority as to strength.

He looked down at her, his blue eyes quizzical.

"I fear I'm in the suds again," he said, smiling wryly. "Wherein have I erred this time?"

She coloured a little. "No such thing — I was merely watching the way you handle your horses."

"Admiringly?" He shook his head. "No, that's too much to expect. Critically, then? Perhaps you will like to set me right — shall I change places and let you tool the curricle?"

She laughed. "Not on this road, I thank you, though I wouldn't object to trying my skill in a country lane!" Her tone changed. "But why should you suppose I was being critical?"

He shrugged. "Force of habit, my dear Corinna. I so frequently have the misfortune to incur your displeasure."

155

"I suppose I *am* a wretch at times," she acknowledged. "Why do you put up with me, I wonder?"

He made no reply, but concentrated earnestly on negotiating a bend which she suspected he could very well have managed without taking so much trouble.

"If I were to study for a flattering reply," he answered presently, with a sardonic smile, "I should say that blame from you is preferable to praise from any other female."

"Pray don't study for flattery!" she said tartly, half annoyed, half disappointed. "I prefer you to be yourself!"

"Which is to say—?"

She made a strong effort not to inform him. "I positively *refuse* to quarrel with you, Richard, on such a lovely day. I shan't say another word!"

"What, not even a monosyllable?" he pleaded, turning a mocking face towards her. "You must say something, you know, if only to keep me awake."

She dissolved into helpless laughter.

"You are truly the most absurd creature!" she said unsteadily, wiping the tears from her eyes.

"I know, but I throw myself on your charity. Even queens were indulgent to clowns."

"You choose to play the clown, and a vast number of other roles besides. But don't suppose you deceive me."

He cast a quick glance at her. "Do I not?"

"Not a whit."

"Yet you have been known to say I am inscrutable."

"So you are. But I do know when you're play acting, even if I can't always understand why, or what lies beneath the façade."

"Dear me, we become too analytical, I fear. Shall we try for a change of subject? You'll be pleased to know that I've arranged for your little French friend's advertisement to appear within the next few days in two of the local journals."

"Oh, that is capital! How long do you think it will be before she can hope to receive an answer?"

"That depends upon several unknown factors, but I should say we could reasonably expect to hear within a week or so."

"It will be quite long enough for her to stay in — in Mr Grenville's house" — she stumbled a little over the name, looking self-conscious — "for she's not too happy there, though she doesn't complain."

"The female in charge is somewhat of a dragon, I collect?"

Corinna nodded. "Yes, and Madeleine is lonely, for none of the domestics except the valet sleep in the house." She paused. "She told me of an odd incident that happened a few days ago, but I dare say there is some perfectly simple explanation."

He looked at her keenly. "What was that?"

She explained about the midnight visitor. Sir Richard listened attentively, but offered no comment.

"Mr Grenville is exactly the kind of gentleman who *would* entertain at all hours of the day and night," she said, with a laugh, "and go off without a word to anyone, too! It's vastly more interesting to live in that kind of style than to be a creature of fixed habits, don't you agree?"

"Indeed I do," he said stiffly.

At this point, they turned inland to Rottingdean, past some attractive flint and brick cottages and up a hill leading to the ancient church overlooking a pretty green and a duck pond. The Cheveleys' house lay a little farther on, a square, early Georgian building of moderate size.

The second curricle had been closely following, so that both arrived within a matter of minutes. The visitors were given a very warm welcome before being invited to partake of a nuncheon of cold meats, salad, and fruit.

Conversation during the meal was filled with reminiscences about their recent stay in Paris.

"By the way," Lady Cheveley remarked presently, "whom do you suppose I met in Brighton a few days since? You will never guess — Mr Grenville! And in quite a new and unexpected guise, that of a country landowner! He told me he has quite decided to settle at that place of his not very far from your estate, Sir Richard, and is putting it in order. What is more, he has invited us to his housewarming."

She was a little disappointed to discover that this was no news to her visitors. She dearly loved a gossip and would have reminisced over Fabian Grenville's affair with Mrs Peters in Paris, but found herself side-tracked by Sir Richard.

The afternoon passed pleasantly in wandering about the gardens. Corinna and Frances were able to enjoy a comfortable chat together while the gentlemen were inspecting some new horseflesh in Sir George's stables; but afterwards they became separated by a determined move on Lady Cheveley's part which brought her daughter walking beside Sir Richard. Corinna, while recognising the strategy, was bound to admit to herself that Sir Richard did not appear to resent it in the least. On the contrary, he seemed well pleased with his companion and made no effort to release himself from her company.

It scarcely came as a surprise, therefore, when at the conclusion of the visit he issued a cordial invitation to the family to dine at Chyngton Manor, and insisted upon fixing a date there and then. She was not best pleased, though she could scarcely have told why. She felt in no mood for driving back beside Sir Richard, so insisted on taking Lydia's place in their brother's curricle.

CHAPTER SIXTEEN

Corinna and Laurence were both at home to meet Madeleine in the shrubbery on the following afternoon, and at once imparted the good news that the advertisement would be appearing in the next day or two. She received it with rather less enthusiasm than they had expected, and Corinna then noticed that the other girl appeared pale and had dark rings under her eyes, as though she had not slept well.

"Is something distressing you?" asked Corinna. "You do not look at all the thing, my dear."

"No, no, it is nothing, only I have the headache a little," replied Madeleine hurriedly.

"Why do you not come indoors and lie down for a while? You don't need to return for another hour, and then Laurie can drive you back, to save you the fatigue of walking."

"Oh, no, I must not — I dare not!"

"Dare not!" repeated Laurence, his curiosity aroused by her evident distress. "That's coming it a bit strong, ain't? I know you don't wish to blazon it abroad that you're on visiting terms with us, but surely once in a way it wouldn't hurt to be seen together? Mrs Thingummy might have sent you here on some errand, for all the servants would know."

"No, no — it's not only that — but I can't be sure that it's safe for me to come here at all!" exclaimed Madeleine, wringing her hands. "I may have been followed!"

"Who the deuce would *follow* you?" demanded Laurence. "There's more in this than meets the eye, I'll be bound! What exactly has been happening over at Eastdean Place to put you in such a taking?"

"I dare not tell you!" replied Madeleine with a shiver. "Not for my life!"

"For your—!" Corinna broke off, staring. "Surely, Madeleine, you must be exaggerating? What *is* all this about? You must tell us, my dear!"

It required some strong urging from both before Madeleine could be brought to confide in them; but when at length she did, they listened to her story in stunned silence.

"Good God! No wonder you're scared out of your wits!" exclaimed Laurence at last. "But you say you recognised this ruffian?"

"Yes. I saw him once only, for he was not among those who brought us to England. But I could not mistake. It was when we were staying at the farm where" — her voice faltered for a moment — "where Monsieur Landier took us. This man was talking to the farmer one night when I entered the kitchen. I was sent out at once, but I gained the impression that they were discussing arrangements for our passage."

"So he *is* one of the smugglers, and most likely a prime figure in the business, by the sound of it. You say he speaks both languages well? One thing puzzles me, though — what in thunder would he be doing at Grenville's place, snooping about at dead of night?"

"That I cannot say," replied Madeleine, with something of her old spirit, "for I was too afraid to ask questions, *voyez-vous!* But he spoke as one who was acquainted with Monsieur Grenville, almost as if he had expected to meet him there."

Laurence considered this for a moment. "Well, if he saw *you* in France, he didn't set eyes on any of the rest of us, and I'll wager he wasn't told our names, either. As far as he was concerned, we were simply items of contraband to be smuggled across the Channel. That means he knows of nothing to connect you with us, so I don't think you need worry. He was probably warning you against blabbing to any of the other servants. Keep to your own quarters after dark, and you should be safe enough. In any event, I may be snooping around up there myself at nights, in future, so I'll keep an eye on you."

"Good heavens, Laurie, what on earth are you contemplating now?" protested Corinna.

He made no reply to this until later, when Madeleine, somewhat reassured, had returned to Eastdean Place.

"The thing is, Corinna, I've got a suspicion about all these havey-cavey doings at Grenville's place, so I thought I'd investigate up there after dark, see if I can confirm it."

"Suspicion?" she repeated sharply. "What on earth can you mean? What do you suspect?"

"I'd tell you, but I've a notion you won't like it above half," he said, eyeing her warily.

"Don't be so idiotish! You can't leave it at that — you've got to tell me now!"

Laurence lowered his voice, though there was no one remotely within earshot. "I reckon Grenville's hand in glove with the smugglers!" he said triumphantly.

She started violently. "*What?* You can't be serious!"

"Why not? The house is less than a mile from Birling Gap, which in case you don't know, is a natural cleft in the cliffs where one can get down to the beach. If Grenville had come to some arrangement with the gang for storing contraband on his property, say, until they could run it farther inland—"

"Laurie! This is the wildest notion — I won't listen to any more!"

"Please yourself, but you must see it would account for everything — these midnight visitors, his sudden affluence, even the fact that the servants don't sleep in the house—"

"You must be all about in your head!" declared Corinna scornfully. "As if a member of the *ton* would consort with smugglers!"

"Well, you may say what you choose, but I wouldn't be surprised at anything Grenville might do. He's a rum touch, take my word for it."

Corinna made no answer, but stalked off in high dudgeon. It was quite ten minutes before she recovered her temper, an unusually long time for her; but when she did, she began to review what her brother had said in a more objective frame of mind.

Was it so very unlikely that Fabian Grenville might be in league with the smugglers to the extent of leasing part of his premises to them for storing contraband? Doubtless such assistance would be well rewarded, and he certainly did not seem short of money at present. When one considered the depths to which he had been prepared to sink in his search for a wealthy wife, she reflected resentfully, it was not so difficult to suppose that he might turn to even more desperate measures. She had no illusions about his character; he was a hardened gamester used to playing for high stakes, and the risk attaching to such a venture as this could be part of its attraction.

She was forced in the end to admit that it was within the bounds of possibility; and the admission made her angry both with herself and with him.

She turned towards the house, seeking relief from her gloomy reflections in Lydia's company. She entered the family parlour on the ground floor, then stopped abruptly.

Of all people, Mr Grenville was sitting there with her sister.

He rose at once, bowing gracefully and offering her his hand. She took it in a daze, her cheeks colouring at the thought of her recent speculations about him.

"Delighted to see you again, Miss Haydon," he said, smiling and retaining her nerveless hand for a few seconds longer than mere civility required. "I should have called on you before, but this confounded business of setting my house in order seems to preclude every pleasurable activity! However, as I was just telling Mrs Beresford, the worst is now over, and I hope to be entertaining my neighbours to an evening party in a few days. I had Friday in mind — I do trust you have no prior engagement for that day, ma'am?"

"I — no, I don't think so," stammered Corinna.

Lydia allowed a moment's irritation to show in her expression. Even if the sight of Fabian Grenville was sufficient to throw her into confusion, there was no occasion to allow the gentleman to see it so plainly.

But then Corinna redeemed herself by making a rapid recovery. She seated herself gracefully beside Lydia and proceeded to join in the ensuing conversation with all her normal poise.

After a short while, Mr Grenville rose to take his leave. He was still in the middle of this when the door opened to admit Sir Richard.

"Beg pardon, Lydia, I came straight in, not knowing you were receiving," he said, halting on the threshold.

"That's quite all right, Richard, it's only Mr Grenville come to invite us to his housewarming party."

Both men eyed each other for a moment, then exchanged the usual civilities.

"You, too, of course, Beresford," said Grenville, "if you're at liberty. Dare say you'll be better acquainted with most of the guests than I am myself. Still, one must make a beginning, don't you think? I'll hope to see you all on Friday, then, at eight o'clock."

An elegant bow, and he was gone.

The housewarming party was a great success. Some thirty guests were present, all local people well known to Sir Richard and Lydia; no one from Grenville's somewhat rackety London set had been invited.

During the course of the evening Sir Richard heard many speculations on the reasons for Grenville's changed way of life. It was not long before Corinna quietly confided to him Laurence's views on this subject, beginning with an account of Madeleine's confrontation with the intruder at Eastdean Place.

He heard her out in silence.

"Well?" she demanded impatiently. "What is your opinion? Do you believe there can possibly be anything in what Laurie suspects?"

"Hard to say, on the evidence we have," he replied with a shrug. "The girl was quite sure that she recognised this intruder?"

"Yes, indeed she was, and you know for yourself how reliable Madeleine is, even though she was naturally upset."

"Of course she would be," he replied absently.

At that moment, Sir Richard observed their host approaching them, and touched Corinna gently on the arm.

"Perhaps this isn't the ideal place for such a discussion," he warned her in a low tone. "We'll continue it some other time."

He moved away to join the Cheveleys; and Corinna turned to confront Grenville, a willowy, elegant figure in a dark brown coat which set off his rich chestnut hair.

For once, her pulses remained steady.

"It won't do," Grenville reproached her gently. "You have been in my house for a full hour, and so far we've exchanged nothing but a few conventional words of greeting."

"You have your duties as a host, sir," she said demurely.

"True, and when I look at you, I could wish them at the devil," he answered with an intimate glance from his hazel eyes.

At this, Corinna's pulse gave the familiar quick leap.

"How are you amusing yourself in Sussex?" he continued, keeping his eyes on her face.

"Much as I do at home — riding, walking, paying calls." She tried to speak casually.

"Doubtless a trifle tame after life in Paris, where there was so much going on. But perhaps it is not places or entertainments which determine our pleasure, but people — the right kind of people, delightful companions who are able to make us think that an hour with them is better than months with anyone else. Do you not agree, ma'am?"

"It is possible," she replied, refusing to be drawn.

"Ah, now you are being cautious, and it's not as I remember you from the past. I always admired your decided opinions, your impulsive wholeheartedness! Do not say you are changed — that would be melancholy indeed."

"I am a little older since we first met, and perhaps also a little wiser," she replied primly.

"In seven months?" he asked incredulously. "You see, I know precisely how long ago it is — a desert of time, an empty age!"

"Is it?" Her tone was careless. "I forget — much has happened since you quitted Tunbridge Wells. Not least to yourself, I fancy," she added with slight emphasis.

"Ah, you are determined to punish me, I see. But believe me" — looking earnestly into her eyes — "you were always in my thoughts. The tenderest images—"

She returned his look coldly.

"What an accomplished flirt you are," she said admiringly. "I do believe I have never met your equal, not even in Paris, where all the gentlemen made a habit of gallantry."

A shadow of annoyance crossed his face, to be banished quickly by a rueful expression.

"I see how it is, you are determined on teasing me. Is there nothing I can do to prove my sincerity?"

She appeared to consider this. "I shouldn't think so," she answered at last in a negligent tone. "But, truly, it's of no account. Pray excuse me, sir — I see Mrs Malling desires a word with me."

She turned away to join this lady and her two daughters. While she was in conversation with them, an undercurrent of thought was running through her mind. Mr Grenville still had the power to stir her pulses. But she was not so ready now to be taken in by his smooth flattery.

Nevertheless, she was not averse to being made the object of his attentions once more, even though in a lesser degree she shared this honour with one or two other nubile young ladies present. She offered him no encouragement, however, maintaining her cool reception of his compliments in a way she certainly could not have achieved last summer. Far from discouraging him, this treatment seemed only to urge him to make greater efforts to please.

He invited her to ride with him on the following day, but she was ready with an excuse. It was difficult to manufacture excuses for every successive day, though; so she was finally brought to promise, albeit in the most off-handed way, that she would go out with him one morning next week, should the weather prove suitable.

During their various brief interchanges, she noticed Sir Richard's eye upon them in spite of his being frequently in Frances Cheveley's company; for some reason this seemed to give her a perverse pleasure. When next she spoke to that gentleman, she made a point of telling him that she was to ride with Mr Grenville.

"Delightful for you," was his terse comment.

But Lydia made no attempt to appear pleased at the news.

"I did think, Corinna," she said severely, on their way home, "that you would feel too disgusted at his past conduct to encourage him to dangle after you again. Mama would be most distressed to know that you have taken up with him once more."

"I tell you what, Lydia, it would be a splendid thing if my family would allow me to manage my own affairs!"

"But, dearest, you know we only desire your happiness," protested her sister.

"Very likely, and so everyone always says who tries to interfere with one!"

Lydia saw that she was angry, and thought it wiser to say no more. She subsided into her corner of the carriage, looking so hurt that presently Corinna relented.

"I'm sorry — I know you mean well," she acknowledged in a quieter tone. "But truly, Lyddy, I mean only to flirt a little. I am in no danger, I assure you."

Lydia was not so certain of this; but Corinna, having said it partly to reassure her sister, found herself wondering if in fact it might not be true.

CHAPTER SEVENTEEN

During the week that followed, Lydia resumed her usual social round and Corinna became caught up in morning calls, dinner engagements, and evening parties. They were all invited to Chyngton Manor when the Cheveleys dined there a few days after Grenville's housewarming party. Frances looked particularly charming, thought Corinna, in palest aquamarine sarsnet, with her dark hair piled up into a topknot from which curls dangled to the nape of her neck. She was sitting beside Sir Richard at table, and when she turned to speak to him the ringlets danced. Vastly fetching, thought Corinna, with a touch of acerbity of which she was instantly ashamed; for she was really quite fond of Frances, and knew her to be a girl who did not study for effect. Even so, she might shake her curls at any other man with Corinna's goodwill, wryly reflected that young lady; but Sir Richard Beresford was Haydon property, and it did not suit Corinna's notions for him to be thinking of matrimony.

She said as much to Lydia when she went into her sister's bedroom to say good night at the conclusion of that evening. Lydia had remarked that it really began to look as if there might be something serious between the two.

"Oh, what fustian!" exclaimed Corinna scornfully. "She's a prodigiously pretty, unaffected girl, of course, and any man would find her company pleasant — but Richard! You must know, Lyddy, he's the most complete cynic when it comes to female charms. I believe he's cut out to be a bachelor, and I must say that would be the ideal solution for our own family. Imagine how Mama would go on, if she could not always rely upon Richard's support and advice — she would be quite lost! Oh, no, he mustn't marry!"

"Well, I must say," protested Lydia, laughing, "it comes to a pretty pass if poor Richard must remain a bachelor simply for the convenience of our family! You can't be serious!"

"But I truly believe that is what he desires himself," insisted Corinna. "He's not at all in the petticoat line, as Laurie would say."

"Perhaps not, until now, but I do detect signs of an awakening interest in Frances Cheveley, and I think you must do, too, if only you'd admit it."

But this Corinna was not at all prepared to do. The mere notion was repugnant.

She had been meeting Madeleine frequently, although not every day, but so far there had been no news to give her of any reply to the advertisement.

"I begin to despair, Corinna," said the girl sadly.

"No such thing! It is being repeated regularly, and I feel sure will produce a response before long. Such matters often take a little time, you know."

"Yes, and if nothing comes of it soon," put in Laurence, who was present on this occasion, as on several previous ones, "I'll carry on with our former scheme. I'm getting a trifle bored with hanging about night after night up at Eastdean Place, and nothing to show for it."

"Well, at least Madeleine has seen no more of that dreadful man whom we think to be one of the smugglers," said Corinna. "That's something to be thankful for, at all events."

"No such thing — he's the very man I *do* want to see," insisted Laurence. "That fellow's the key to the whole, give you my word! Only thing that keeps me haunting the place is the hope that he'll turn up again."

Oddly enough, it was on the very next night that his hopes were realised.

He had been patrolling the house as usual and was hovering in the vicinity of the kitchen door when his quick ear caught the muted sound of footsteps approaching. He had just time to take cover behind a large stack of logs for firing when the dark figure of a man passed close to his hiding place, pausing before the kitchen door to rap gently three times upon it with his knuckles.

The sound was barely audible to Laurence, and could not possibly have aroused anyone who was not immediately behind the door waiting for it. Nevertheless, the door was opened at once, showing a light within. A second figure appeared on the threshold, whom Laurence identified as Grenville.

"Is that you, Jack?" he asked softly. "Come inside."

For a brief moment as he obeyed this order and moved into the light, the man addressed as Jack became visible to the watching Laurence. He was of medium height, slim and dark haired; with nothing to go on but the description given by Madeleine, Laurence decided with a tingle of excitement that this must be the intruder she had encountered.

The door closed firmly but quietly behind the pair. Allowing a few moments to elapse, Laurence ventured out from his place of concealment and crept towards it. Hopefully he applied first his eye and then his ear to the keyhole, but without result.

He swore under his breath. There seemed nothing to be done but wait for this fellow Jack to come out of the house and follow him. Accordingly, he concealed himself again behind the stack of logs, prepared for a lengthy vigil. To his surprise, the man emerged in less than ten minutes, the door closing firmly behind him.

It was not easy to follow his quarry in the gloom of the clouded sky, even though Laurence's eyes had by now become somewhat accustomed to the dark. Jack, on the other hand, walked forward confidently, as one who knew every inch of the way. He took a grassy path which led round the back of the stables to a gate which was evidently the stable exit. Laurence followed him through the gate, which fortunately did not creak, and continued down the narrow lane beside the boundary wall, keeping well into the wall in case his quarry looked back.

Presently they emerged from the lane into the wider track which led back to the village in one direction and down to Birling Gap in the other. Jack turned towards the sea and Laurence followed, nerves taut, for now there was no cover at all, but only the open cliff.

They had covered almost a mile, the track descending all the time, when Laurence saw the dark shapes of a few small buildings ahead. It seemed likely that his man would enter one of these cottages, if such they were, but it was too risky for him to approach any closer.

Cautiously, he lowered himself to the ground; and now he could hear the surge of the sea against the pebbles at the foot of the cliff. Presently the dark blur of Jack's figure merged into the surrounding gloom as it drew farther away from him.

He remained where he was, motionless, until he was rewarded by a gleam of light from one of the cottages, by which he could see the outline of a man's figure as he stepped inside the opened door. The light vanished, and all was dark again. After a short interval, he rose to his feet and made a stealthy advance towards the building where he had seen the light.

As he had thought, it was a small cottage, one of some three or four in a row. Now that he was close up to the door, he espied a chink of light coming through one of the windows. He moved cautiously across to it, but not cautiously enough. His foot encountered some object on the ground, he stumbled, put out a hand to save himself, and in so doing came into contact with the window.

The noise was slight, but it was sufficient to rouse the inhabitants. Before Laurence could take to his heels, two pairs of rough hands had seized him and hauled him into the cottage. Naturally, he put up a strong resistance, but was forced to yield when a knife was held at his throat.

Corinna went out riding with Grenville on the following morning, having evaded the issue as long as she could. She told herself that the outing had not the smallest significance for her, yet perversely took a great deal of trouble over her toilette. Her dark blue riding habit and matching hat set at a jaunty angle on her gold-brown curls brought praise from Lydia.

"Indeed, you look charmingly, my love! But I wish it were for some other gentleman."

"Do females dress for gentlemen or for themselves?" laughed Corinna. "In any event, this is new and it's high time I gave it an airing. I bought it in Paris, you'll remember."

"Yes, I do recollect. What a slug-a-bed our brother is! Here it is, going on for noon and he hasn't deigned to put in an appearance." Corinna knew very well how Laurence spent his nights, but had agreed to say nothing to Lydia unless it became essential. She returned some airy reply, therefore, and shortly afterwards Grenville was admitted.

Not long was spent in civilities before the pair departed on their ride. The day was ideal for riding, neither too hot nor too breezy; and the green downs, emblazoned with yellow gorse and scented by wild thyme, stretched invitingly before them. After a short, exhilarating gallop, they slowed their horses to a walking pace and he drew closer, putting out a hand to her rein.

"That was capital! Quite like old times!" he said, laughing down at her. "I can never forget the rides we had together in your home country."

She could not altogether remain impervious to the intimate look he gave her, but her voice was casual as she replied that Kent, too, was splendid riding country.

"Ah, but I refer to the company," he persisted, sliding his hand up the rein to cover hers. "Did I not tell you so but a few days since?"

She removed her hand gently. "I fear you are at your old game of flirting, sir."

"Are you still determined to punish me? All that is past — I swear it! And now I am free to please myself. You must know—"

He broke off, frowning, as a horse and rider rounded the bend in the track and came suddenly upon them.

It was Sir Richard, mounted upon a handsome bay which at once drew forth an admiring comment from Grenville after the first greetings. The two men exchanged a few words on that subject, then Sir Richard touched his hat and prepared to ride on; but Corinna stopped him, saying that as they were about to turn towards home, he might as well accompany them.

He hesitated, looked at Grenville but could read nothing in that urbane expression, then finally agreed. They rode together, idly chatting of this and that, until the gates of Friston House were reached. Here Grenville made his excuses, hoped to have the pleasure of calling upon the ladies another day, and with one parting, significant look at Corinna, rode away.

"You'll come in, won't you?" Corinna asked Sir Richard. "That is, unless you're upon an urgent errand elsewhere."

"Thank you, I'll look in for a moment."

His voice sounded constrained, and she herself was not quite at ease. She had acted on impulse in suggesting that he ride back with them, not wishing for the moment to be alone with Grenville after the turn their conversation had taken. She felt that Sir Richard had sensed this, and it created an atmosphere of embarrassment between them.

They rode side by side up the drive and turned towards the stables. Halfway there, they were suddenly confronted by Laurence, looking rather less than his usual jaunty self. A piece of court plaster covered one side of his mouth and his face was further disfigured by a black eye.

"Laurie!" exclaimed his sister in horror. "What in the world have you done to yourself?"

"No need to set up a screech," said Laurence repressively. "Got something to tell you — Richard, too, once you've got rid of the horses. Not indoors, though — in the shrubbery."

Having handed the animals over to a groom, they followed him to this retreat, agog with curiosity.

"Long and short of it is, I've found the smugglers!" he began. "The one who threatened Madeleine, too — name's Jack something or other."

"Yes, you bear the appearance of one who's flushed out some violent customers," said Sir Richard with a wry grin.

"Almost put a period to my existence. But I'd better tell you the whole."

He proceeded to do so, his sister listening with several involuntary exclamations of horror, and Sir Richard impassively but with close attention.

"They'd got the knife to my throat — and b' God they meant business! — when I managed to croak out the one word 'Fougeray'. I wanted to try and tell 'em that I'd come there only to look for that fellow, but I could see they didn't intend to waste any time in listening to explanations, so I shot out the name as a last desperate throw! Never expected it to work like it did, though! This fellow Jack was holding the knife, and at that he raised it an inch or two away from my throat, thank God. Asked what I meant. Well, I started to explain — said I'd no interest in the smugglers but as a means of finding this man Fougeray. Halfway through, he stopped me, turned the others out, then had the full story from me."

"Laurie, how dreadful!" shuddered Corinna. "You should never have attempted it! You might have been killed!"

"Did you learn anything to the purpose?" asked Sir Richard.

Laurence looked a trifle crestfallen. "Not precisely. He didn't divulge the whereabouts of Madeleine's cousin, but he did say that he knew where the fellow could be found, and would inform him. So I suppose that Madeleine will hear from her aunt eventually — that is, if this man's word can be relied upon."

"And then he allowed you to go? That seems odd."

Laurence nodded. "Sent me off with a warning — won't be so lucky next time, he promised, and I believe him, give you my word! Ugly customer, that one. Also said to keep mum, as they knew how to deal with informers. Well, I thought it best to say nothing to Lydia, so told her I'd walked into a door coming home after dark last night. She thought I was foxed, of course, and raked me down devilishly, but that don't signify."

"This is dreadful!" exclaimed Corinna. "Will you take any action against them, Richard? It is all so awkward with Madeleine involved!"

"I propose to take the course so expertly followed by our politicians, at least for the present," he replied. "I shall keep a watching brief. If I might venture a word of advice to you both, I'd recommend you to keep out of this altogether. You'd do well, Laurie, to abandon your nocturnal vigils at Eastdean Place."

"Ay, I dare say I must," conceded Laurence reluctantly. "All the same, I'd like to know where Grenville comes into all this — there's something devilish smoky going on up there. Told you before this what I think, Richard — what's your opinion?"

But although Sir Richard had his own views on this subject, he preferred for the moment to keep them to himself.

CHAPTER EIGHTEEN

Madeleine had been delayed by her duties that same afternoon, and when at last she was at liberty, it was too late to go over to see Corinna. Mindful of her promise to the Haydons to look in every day at the summerhouse in case there should be a message left there for her, she cautiously slipped out of the house.

As she pushed open the rickety door and rushed to the cupboard she could see at once that there was nothing, but that did not deter her from making a thorough search to ensure that the precious missive had not become lodged in some crevice.

Presently she was obliged to accept the fact that there was no letter. Shutting the cupboard, she sank down upon the bench to abandon herself momentarily to despondent thoughts.

She was roused abruptly from her reverie as the door opened and a man strode purposefully towards her. She started up in terror, and had opened her mouth to utter a scream when a hand was clamped firmly over it. A dark face hovered close to hers — a face she had good reason to remember.

"Quiet!" he hissed, holding her tightly. "I mean you no harm, but I must speak with you! Promise you won't shriek, and I'll let you go."

She nodded. Although his hold on her was firm, it was not as brutal as it had been on the occasion of their first encounter, nor was the expression in his eyes so terrifying. Nevertheless, when he released her, she sank trembling on to the bench, her knees giving under her.

"I am sorry," he said, speaking in excellent French. "I see I've frightened you, and such is not my intention on this occasion. I did not know who you were when last we met. You are Mademoiselle Madeleine de Fougeray, daughter of the deceased Vicomte de Fougeray?"

The formal title somewhat restored Madeleine's dignity. The fear died away from her face, showing its fine aristocratic lines as she lifted her chin proudly.

"I am."

He achieved a creditable bow which went oddly with his rough fisherman's attire.

"I made the acquaintance — or so one could call it," he said drily "— of a friend of yours last night, a young Englishman. I understand from him that you have come to England seeking some relatives."

"You mean Miss Haydon's brother, Laurence? How did it come about that you spoke with him?"

"He was so unwise as to follow me when I came visiting at this house. I soon detected him, and a confrontation followed."

"Oh, *mon Dieu!*" Some of the fear returned to her eyes. "You — you did not hurt him, I trust? He and his sister have been such good friends to me!"

He shrugged. "Be easy. There was a scuttle, and he most likely sustained a few bruises, but nothing worse. He is fortunate — those who attempt to spy upon us seldom live to tell the tale," he added grimly.

A shudder ran through her.

"Monsieur, I do not know who you are, or what you want with me," she said in a nervous tone.

"I am about to tell you that. I had your story from this youth, and it seems you and his family were transported from France by my agency. Now that I look at you closely, I recognise you. You came into the kitchen at Bonnet's farmhouse, did you not? I never set eyes on the others, but such arrangements are a commonplace with me. I merely give the orders."

He shrugged again, then looked at her keenly.

"This youth Haydon, mademoiselle — how close a friend of yours is he?"

She was puzzled by his tone, which was almost proprietorial.

"A very good friend, both he and his sister, but not, I think, the kind of friend you are supposing. He is just a boy, Laurie, *voyez-vous*! But, monsieur," — her voice was diffident, for she did not wish to antagonise him — "I still do not see what it is you want with me."

"Simply this — I have news of your relatives."

Her face lit up. "You have? Oh, monsieur, that is wonderful! I have been almost in despair — we inquired for them in Brighton without success, and then I advertised — but tell me at once! Where are they?"

He turned a look of compassion on her; and when he spoke, it was in a gentler tone than she would ever have believed possible from that source.

"My poor child, I fear I am about to inflict a sad shock upon you."

Her eyes widened as she waited for him to continue.

"Your aunt is no more," he said quietly. "She died three years since and is interred in Eastbourne, where she had lived after quitting Brighton."

She crossed herself. "God rest her. I cannot really remember her, for I was only seven when she left France, but somewhere in my mind an impression lingers of a lovely, gentle lady—"

"She was so," he said harshly. "Torn from her own country and people, to try and make a life among strangers. She lived in tolerable conditions at first, but once she had sold all her jewels, her life became insupportable for one of her upbringing. Nothing but poverty and hardship! I know she was relieved to quit that miserable existence, her only regret being that she must leave her son to find a living as best he might."

Madeleine's eyes had filled with tears.

"My poor, poor aunt! How much misery was caused by the Revolution! But what of my cousin, Jacques-Philippe? Have you news, too, of him?"

"I am your cousin, mademoiselle."

She started violently. "*You?* Is it possible? But you are—"

She broke off, afraid to finish.

"I am a smuggler, you would say? Yes, I admit it. What would you have? My mother and I needed money desperately, so when we were in Brighton I found casual employment among the fisherfolk. She did not like it, but there was nothing else open to me. In a few years, I chanced across a man who was involved in the smuggling trade in this area, and I managed to edge my way into the business. That was when I was obliged to remove my mother from Brighton to Eastbourne, to a poor hovel where she eked out her life. I began to do well in my chosen trade" — his voice was bitter — "but too late to benefit her. Now I am what you might call an organiser, quite an important man, I assure you, cousin!"

"But — but—" stammered Madeleine. "You are the Vicomte de Fougeray, since both our fathers are dead! It is not fitting that you should be involved with criminals!"

"The Vicomte de Fougeray," he repeated, in tones of deep scorn. "Not even in the country of my birth is such a title permitted to exist! It means nothing to me. Here I am known as Jack, with no one to trouble about a surname. I have no lands, no money but what I can earn for myself. I must make a living as best I can."

"But surely there must be other occupations open to you. More honourable than this!"

"Such as yours, for example? Do you consider it fitting that Mademoiselle de Fougeray should be an abigail?"

"I did what I must, for I could not accept the charity of my English friends," she said defensively.

"Precisely. You did what you must, and so do I. It is fruitless to argue on this head. Let us consider instead what you mean to do now that my mother is no more, and you are therefore without a home in this country."

She brooded in silence for a moment, then asked, "Are you married, Cousin Jacques?"

He gave a snort of laughter. "Not I! Oh, there have been females from time to time, you understand, but marriage, no."

"I was thinking that perhaps if you were, I might make a home with you," she said slowly.

"A home with a smuggler — *mon Dieu*, that would be something!" He laughed mirthlessly. "No, I have no settled home. I am a bird of passage, with a *pied-à-terre* here and also across the Channel, but I would not describe either place as a home."

"Then there is nothing for me but to remain where I am," she answered sadly.

"At Grenville's house? No, that you shan't do." His tone was firm. "Have you no friends in France to whom you could return? There must be someone. I can offer you no protection here."

She did not answer. He looked at her sharply, and saw a slow blush mounting to her cheeks.

"There is, I collect, a man in the case. You had better tell me."

Haltingly, she told him of Patrice Landier. He heard her out in silence, watching her keenly all the while.

"I see you love this banker," he said when she had finished. "Him I did meet at Bonnet's farm, and judge him to be a man of decision and fair-dealing. I am not inexperienced in making quick assessments of men, for often my safety depends on it. He is of suitable age for you, too, and should be able to offer you a creditable establishment. Do you wish to return to him?"

"With all my heart," she said simply.

"And he awaits only a word from you to bring him hotfoot to Bonnet's farm to receive you. You will write that word at once, and somehow I'll see it delivered. As for taking you to France, that is not so simple." His brow furrowed. "This is not the time of year for shipping contraband — the nights are too light. We have other business, however, which cannot wait on convenience, and should such business crop up, that would be your chance."

She wanted to ask what the other business might be, but held her tongue. She was content that he should tell her only what he wished her to know. The thought of being reunited with Landier filled her with a wild longing, and nothing else signified.

"It may take some time," he continued, "and when the opportunity occurs, you'll have little warning. But in the meantime, I'll find you a lodging away from this house, though you may continue to work here if you insist. While you remain under this roof, however, have a care. Do not make the smallest attempt to pry into anything that goes on here, and keep to your room at night. Do you understand?"

He turned a fierce look upon her, and she nodded obediently.

"Now go, and write your letter. I will collect it from you later — never mind how, but carry it around with you until I do."

She rose to leave him, but paused at the door.

"My friends — I may tell them of this?"

"Very well, you may tell your friends, if you're sure you may rely on their discretion."

"Oh, yes, indeed I am." She paused as another thought came into her head. "But I cannot be easy about you and this way of life, Cousin Jacques. Why do you not return with me to France? Monsieur Landier would find you some occupation more suitable."

"Return to Napoleon's France?" he asked scornfully. "Bah, what is there for such as I? It is but one degree better than the Revolution, and can never again be the France of our childhood."

"That is what I said to Monsieur Landier. And he replied that it is for the people of France to build for themselves the nation they desire. I did not agree with him then, but now I think differently."

He laughed tolerantly.

"But of course! Well, *petite*, we shall see, but I think your Landier is a very lucky fellow."

He took her hand; and with some memories of a more cultured upbringing under his dead mother's influence, carried it to his lips. In spite of his rough appearance, she did not find this incongruous, and responded with a low curtsey.

Meanwhile, Corinna had been impatiently awaiting Madeleine in the shrubbery at Friston House, eager to pass on the news she had received from Laurence. Since her friend had not put in an appearance on the preceding day, she was tolerably certain of seeing her; but as time wore on, her disappointment became intense.

Her impetuous disposition refused to entertain for a moment the thought of delaying her news until tomorrow. She would have dispatched Laurence with a note to leave in the summerhouse at Eastdean Place, had not the wretched boy ridden off with Sir Richard to Chyngton Manor. Since Laurence was not available, she must herself go to Eastdean Place. She had managed it once without the slightest difficulty, she told herself, so there was no occasion whatever for the qualms which beset her at the notion.

She hurried indoors to dash off a note for Madeleine, successfully evading her sister, who was chatting in the parlour with a visitor. As before, she managed to reach Eastdean Place without meeting anyone at all, and, conquering her misgivings, was soon inside the summerhouse.

This time, it was empty. She did not linger, but concealed her note in the cupboard and hastened out of the grounds. She had turned out of the lane into the road leading to the village when the sound of an approaching vehicle made her move over into the verge. She saw it was a curricle drawn by a pair of matched greys, and wondered that the driver should bring it along such a narrow, rough track. The next moment she recognised Grenville, evidently returning to the house.

He reined in his horses and saluted her.

"This is a pleasant surprise, Miss Haydon! I cannot hope that you've been calling on me, since you're unaccompanied, so can only suppose you've been taking a solitary stroll. What a pity I didn't know you were at liberty, or I would have begged the pleasure of taking you out for a drive. Are you returning home, ma'am? May I drive you there?"

She tried not to look self-conscious as she declined his offer, saying that she had come out for the exercise. He would not hear of her continuing on foot, however, so presently she allowed him to assist her into the vehicle.

"Do you often walk this way?" he asked as he took the vehicle back to the lane so that he could turn it.

"Oh, no, but" — an inspiration occurred to her — "I've heard some mention of Birling Gap, and thought I would walk down there to see it."

"You must be an intrepid walker," he said admiringly. "There and back from your sister's house would be about three miles, a distance to deter most ladies. But there is nothing whatever there to reward such effort, only a steep descent to a strip of pebbly beach. Moreover, the track deteriorates as one proceeds, and would be very rough for a lady's footwear."

"I am regardless of obstacles when I have an objective," she said, laughing.

"That is what I so much admire in you — yet it is only one of many attributes which make you quite the most fascinating lady of my acquaintance," he replied, giving her an ardent look from his fine hazel eyes.

"Fie, you say pretty things to all the females, I don't doubt. It's of no use to try and gammon me, sir, for I've seen you often enough paying attentions to others."

He said nothing for a moment, and she knew the shaft had gone home.

"I will not pretend to misunderstand you," he said, in a serious tone. "To my shame, I admit that in the past I have been *forced* — yes, it's not too strong a word — to pay court to females for whom I had no deep, sincere feelings. But if only you could understand my situation — if only you could know the agony of mind of a man who must attempt to please and flatter one female, while his *whole heart* is set upon another!"

Her pulses leapt and she found difficulty in breathing. He was confessing what she had so often urged to herself in extenuation of his conduct. Was it then true? Was she indeed the one he truly loved, as she had always tried to believe? She could not speak for emotion, but turned expressive eyes on his face.

He gathered the reins in one hand and leaned towards her to place his free hand over hers.

"Miss Haydon — Corinna!"

He broke off suddenly with an exclamation of annoyance. They had reached the gates of Friston House simultaneously with another vehicle which had swept into view from the opposite direction.

Sir Richard was driving this, with Laurence a passenger. Both noticed at once the intimate gesture which now Grenville quickly corrected.

The greetings which passed were cool on the part of the gentlemen, while Corinna managed only a confused mumble. The two carriages went in procession along the drive, with Grenville's leading. When they reached the entrance to the house, he leapt down and assisted Corinna to alight.

"Will you come in, sir?" she asked in a formal tone.

He shook his head. "Not now. Some other time I would like to continue our conversation, though, when there is some possibility of privacy. Dare I hope — perhaps tomorrow? May I take you for a drive in the afternoon?"

She found it difficult to resist the pleading in his eyes when her own emotions were in so much confusion. She hardened her heart, however, for two reasons. One was that she had already promised in her note to meet Madeleine tomorrow afternoon; the other, that she had too much pride to allow him to suppose her an easy conquest.

He showed some chagrin at her refusal, made on the score of a previous engagement, and pressed her to name another time. But at that moment her brother and Sir Richard returned from stabling the latter's curricle, and she would not remain with him any longer. He drove off and she entered the house with the others.

"Turning you up sweet, Grenville, ain't he?" remarked Laurence with a laugh. "What a complete hand that fellow is — remember how he was dangling after that vulgar widow in Paris? You must feel flattered, sis, to be following such a one!"

Corinna's face flamed; but before she could think of a sufficiently cutting reply, Sir Richard intervened, recommending his young friend to take a damper. By this time, they had been admitted to the house, and Corinna ran thankfully upstairs to her own room.

Tossing her bonnet heedlessly on the bed, she sank into an easy chair to give herself up to her thoughts. If she could credit what Fabian Grenville had implied that afternoon, she had been all along the real object of his affections. Circumstances had compelled him in the past to seek out a wealthy wife, but now in some way the situation was changed, and he was free at last to follow the dictates of his heart. It was what she had always tried to believe.

Tried? She caught at the word, frowning. Often enough she had insisted to Lydia that she *did* believe it; but now she realised that this had been self-deception. There had always been a doubt. Was that doubt now removed? She flinched away from the question.

It was replaced by another, even more disturbing. Mr Grenville still had some power to stir her emotions, but did she truly love him?

CHAPTER NINETEEN

Madeleine found both Corinna and Laurence awaiting her in the shrubbery on the following afternoon, and it was not long before she had given them her astounding news.

"Well, I for one am not so very surprised to learn that this smuggler is your cousin," said Laurence, after they had discussed the matter thoroughly. "Fact is, I had it from one of those fishermen in Brighton that he'd become involved in that business. I've been trying all along to get on the track of the smugglers, hoping it would lead me to him."

"You have been so good!" exclaimed Madeleine penitently. "And look how you've suffered as a result! I cannot tell you, Laurie, how sorry I am, and how prodigiously grateful!"

"Oh, fustian, my dear girl — I don't mind a bit of a mill now and then, especially in a good cause," he replied casually. "Come to think of it, I'm more than half sorry it's all over, for it was rare sport. Be a bit tame, now, unless—"

His voice tailed off, and he looked thoughtful.

"Unless what?" demanded Corinna sharply.

"Never you mind. So you're returning to France, Madeleine? Don't say it isn't your most sensible course, but we'll miss you."

"And indeed I shall miss *you*, my dear, faithful friends," she replied sadly. "But it may not be for some weeks yet, since my cousin says he must wait on circumstances." Her brow furrowed. "I don't know what he means, but it was plain that he didn't wish to tell me, so I refrained from questions."

Both Laurence and, to a lesser degree, Corinna would have liked to know more about the activities of Jacques Fougeray;

but both tactfully refrained from open speculation. Later, however, when Laurence was repeating the story to Sir Richard, he voiced his doubts.

"Know what I said to you about Grenville? Well, it looks as though I'd hit the nail on the head, eh? Why else should this smuggler fellow go there to see him secretly by night? And what of these others who've been there, too? All in the same game, if you ask me."

"Grenville doesn't necessarily need to be as deeply involved as you suppose, old chap," replied Sir Richard lightly. "He wouldn't be the first gentleman to arrange for a keg of brandy to be delivered secretly at his back door for his own use. Quite a common occurrence in these parts, I'd say."

"D' you really think that?" Laurence sounded crestfallen. "If it's no more than that, well, I suppose there's not much harm, after all."

"No, indeed. I tell you what, Laurie, how'd you like to accompany me to Brighton tomorrow to see how my friend Colonel Wexham's progressing with his volunteer force? There was some mention of the men he's already raised going off on exercises shortly. I can't promise anything, of course, but it may be possible for you to join them."

Laurence's eyes kindled with enthusiasm. "I say, do you really think there's a chance? That would be famous! It's the very thing I could wish for, now that Madeleine's little mystery is solved, and things look like becoming devilish flat here!"

And that is precisely my intention, thought Sir Richard. He had been careful to keep his views to himself, but privately he considered that Laurence and Corinna had been fishing in waters more deep and dangerous than they realised. It now became a matter of urgency to keep them out of serious trouble. The only remedy with Laurence was to remove him from the scene altogether and give him a fresh outlet for his energies. As far as Corinna was concerned, the remedy was not so simple; he could but try to appeal to her common sense. He did not relish the task.

He attempted it on the following morning, when he arrived to take up Laurence for the drive to Brighton. Lydia was occupied for the moment with domestic duties and Corinna was strolling idly in the garden. Telling the impatient Laurence that he wanted a quiet word with his sister, Sir Richard followed her there.

He went straight to the point, explaining his intentions with regard to Laurence.

"Oh, yes, that will be capital," she said in approval. "He needs occupation, and there's nothing for him now that Madeleine's affairs are in a way to being settled."

"I've good reason to believe," he went on, choosing his words carefully, "that in tracing Madeleine's cousin we've uncovered a particularly nasty hornet's nest, and that both of you would do well to avoid further involvement."

"You mean the smuggling?" she asked. "I expect you feel that it's your duty to inform on this man, but if you do so, poor Madeleine cannot return to France. You couldn't be so cruel, Richard!"

"No, I don't think I could. After she has gone, however, it won't be possible to evade the issue. In the meantime, I earnestly beg of you to have as little as possible to do with your friend."

"Not see Madeleine, when soon we'll be parted forever — or at least until this wretched war ends! No, I won't do it, and what is more, you have no right to ask it of me!"

"Only the right of a long-standing family friend who has your best interests at heart," he said quietly.

By now, her face was flushed and her eyes blazing. She was in no mood for reason.

"My best interests! I am vastly tired of both my family and you presuming to know what my interests are! Surely, I may be supposed to be the proper judge of that," she retorted in a voice charged with scorn. "I will *not* be dictated to, Sir Richard Beresford, by you or by anyone else! Have the goodness to leave me alone!"

To her astonishment instead of obeying this injunction, he caught her wrists in a firm grasp and pulled her towards him, his blue eyes unaccustomedly fierce.

"Leave you alone to put yourself into danger?" he demanded sternly. "Yes, you would be well served if I did. But allow me to tell you, Miss Haydon — since we are to be so formal! — that your tantrums don't impress me in the slightest, so you may as well cease playing them off on me."

She dragged her wrists loose from his hold and stamped her foot viciously.

"How — how *dare* you!"

"I can't imagine," he said coolly. "But I rather wish I had dared more in the past. I have been too easy with you, I fear."

"Too *easy*! Oh, you — you *odious monster*! Leave me at once — at once, I say!"

He bowed. "Very well. But I shall still be there, if you should need me."

"That will be never!" she flashed.

He gave a crooked smile. "Who knows?"

Then he turned on his heel and went back to the house, to leave immediately.

It was only to be expected that Lydia would take her brother-in-law's part. She knew very little of the situation, for Corinna and Laurence had so far kept most of their activities from her.

Now, however, Corinna could see no harm in telling her everything. Indeed, when she flounced into the parlour shortly after parting from Sir Richard and found her sister there, she could not refrain from giving vent to her feelings.

Lydia heard it all with many expressions of shocked surprise and dismay.

"Merciful heavens!" she exclaimed at the end. "It's a marvel that you and Laurie have not come to serious harm, such mad starts as the pair of you indulge in! Don't you think, Corinna, that it's high time you stopped behaving like a hoydenish schoolgirl and tried for a little more conduct? I do not at all wonder that Richard should be angry with you."

"What right has he to be angry with me? Even if Mama turns to him for guidance, *I* have no intention of doing so! He is not a relative of mine — if anyone has any right to meddle in my affairs, it would be my own brother, not your brother-in-law!"

"Laurie?" Lydia laughed. "Oh, yes, a fine one he would be to counsel you, I'll vow! Why, you are both fit for Bedlam!" Then, seeing the affronted look on her sister's face, her tone changed. "But seriously, my love, I most heartily endorse Richard's advice not to involve yourself further in the French girl's concerns. You have played your part in helping her to find her cousin, and now everything must be left to him."

"I realise that, of course, but what I refused to promise Richard was that I would not see her again during the short time she is to remain here. Madeleine is my friend, and one doesn't desert a friend because it happens to be expedient to do so."

Lydia sighed, recognising defeat. "Very well, I'll say no more on that head. But Richard is a friend, too, Corinna, and I do wish you didn't find it necessary always to mete out such Turkish treatment to the poor fellow."

"Poor fellow, indeed! He can give as good as he gets, I assure you!"

"Oh, yes, I believe he can, but he never does where you are concerned. He is too tolerant towards you by half."

"The very words he used himself to me not half an hour since," said Corinna scornfully. "Well, only let him try bullying me, that is all!"

Lydia looked at her consideringly. That sparkle in the eye — was it only defiance, or was there some other element, not so readily defined?

"I believe you would like that," she said shrewdly.

Her sister suddenly flushed and flounced out of the room.

It was late that same evening when Laurence returned in a jubilant mood.

"It's all worked out famously!" he told them. "Richard's fixed up with Colonel Wexham for me to go with the others on manoeuvres, but more than that, I'll have Cheveley with me! We looked in at their house in Rottingdean, and he'd come down from London expressly to join the local volunteers. His parents invited me to stay there until the force is ready to move, so I'll be off in the morning, lock, stock, and barrel! Dare say you'll be glad to be rid of me for a bit, Lyddy, if the truth's known."

"How could you possibly think so, and you such a restful creature! But tell me how you went on at Rottingdean — the ladies were quite well, I trust?"

"Oh, yes, they seemed in prime twig. Not that I saw much of them, for Cheveley and I had a deal to talk about. I believe they sent messages for you, but you must ask Richard about that, for he was chatting to Miss Cheveley for some time before we came away."

Was he indeed? thought Corinna. Well, doubtless he finds her company preferable to mine, for she would never forget herself so far as to quarrel with him. She would sit smiling up at him, tossing her black curls in a prodigiously fetching way, as she had done recently at the dinner party at Chyngton Manor. Why had they called at the Cheveleys' house at all? It must have been Richard's idea, for Laurence would scarcely think of it, not knowing then that his friend young Cheveley had come down from London.

It appeared that Richard was bent on seeking out Miss Frances Cheveley. Well, let him, and see if Corinna Haydon cared one jot! She noticed that he had not troubled himself to come into the house this evening, merely dropping Laurence off at the door.

He appeared only briefly on the following morning, too, for the purpose of conveying Laurence and his traps over to Rottingdean. Laurence was in high spirits and could not wait to set out for his new adventure.

CHAPTER TWENTY

During the days that followed the interview with her cousin, Madeleine felt at peace for the first time since leaving her native country. She had fulfilled her promise to the curé, yet matters had so arranged themselves that now she was free to follow the inclinations of her heart. Jacques had collected the letter which she had written to Monsieur Landier — a short letter, but one in which feeling fully compensated for brevity — and had promised an early delivery. Now she had but to wait in patience until the time came to make the crossing to France. She would be sad to leave her English friends who had been so good to her; but all else paled before the thought of being united with her beloved.

She retired to her room one night with happy thoughts such as these running through her mind. Yet, in spite of the labours of the day, she was not ready for sleep. Instead of undressing, she stood for a long time at her window, gazing down into the stableyard. It was a moonlit night, warm and sultry, and after a while she quietly raised the lower sash to stand leaning out, her elbows resting on the sill. Sunk deep in her reverie, she was startled by the sound of hooves approaching. She drew her head in from the window sharply as a horse and rider came into the yard. She could see that the beast was almost spent, and the rider covered in dust. Evidently this was one of Mr Grenville's midnight visitors, and he had ridden far.

It seemed that he was not expected, however, on this occasion, for Mr Grenville was not waiting to receive him. The rider slid wearily from his horse and looked apathetically about him. Tethering the animal, which showed little inclination to wander, he moved indecisively towards the house.

At this point, caution urged Madeleine to move farther back from the window. She was about to do so when the muted sound of another set of footsteps reached her ears. Curiosity kept her where she was, and she saw that Mr Grenville had now arrived to accost the visitor. She could not hear the words, but the lowered tone seemed challenging.

The stranger replied swiftly, a lengthy speech with a wealth of gesture which suggested one of her fellow countrymen to the watching girl. So far, she had distinguished nothing but a mumble, but now for a moment Grenville's angry tone brought his words quite clearly to her ears.

"Good God, there'll be all hell to pay over this! Why the devil did you come here? Clear out — I want no part in it!"

The other man's answer was inaudible, but there was no mistaking the menace in his attitude. For a few moments they argued, then Grenville appeared to submit. He led his visitor's horse into a stable, then reappeared to conduct the man himself away, presumably into the house.

Madeleine considered that she had seen enough. She recalled her cousin's advice; she must keep away from the strange comings and goings in this house, not seek to pry. She waited a while until she felt it was safe, then quietly shut the window and prepared herself for bed. Sleep was long in coming.

Soon after breakfast the next morning, she was summoned to Mrs Benton's presence. The lady seemed out of temper as she informed Madeleine peremptorily that she must leave the house at once.

"Leave, madame? But — but — do you then mean I am dismissed?" stammered Madeleine, taken aback.

"No such thing, girl. I am reasonably satisfied with your work and willing to keep you on, but you can no longer lodge under this roof. I warned you that it could be only a temporary arrangement. You must go at once, today."

"Today? But where am I to go, madame? I tried before to obtain a lodging in the village—"

"It's no concern of mine where you go," interrupted Mrs Benton crossly, "but go you must. The master commands it. Not but what," she went on, petulantly, forgetting her audience for a moment, "it is monstrously inconvenient for me not to have you at hand to assist me at night in retiring. However, my wishes and comfort are of small account, it seems."

She recollected herself suddenly and scowled at the troubled girl. "Doubtless one of the other maids can help you to find a lodging. *I* cannot be expected to trouble myself in the matter. The most I can do is to give you the rest of the day off so that you can settle your affairs. Be back sharp on six o'clock, though, to dress me for dinner. You understand, do you not, that you must have somewhere else to go for this very night, so that you may leave the house at the same time as the rest of the staff? I trust I make myself clear?"

Madeleine assented, going up to her room in a slightly bemused state. It was not such a blow as it would have been a few days ago, since Jacques had already announced his intention of finding her another lodging. She must let him know at once. They had made an arrangement whereby in an emergency she could leave a message for him with the landlord's wife at the Tiger Inn.

She set out for the village at once, and was soon asking at the back door for Mrs Warren, who was unknown to her.

Presently a thin, sharp-faced woman appeared, wearing an apron tied over a brown holland gown. She looked Madeleine up and down, then demanded to know her business.

"I've a message for Jack," said Madeleine. "It's very urgent. Do you think you can convey it to him at once?"

The woman nodded. She closed the door firmly, drawing her visitor into the adjacent washhouse, which was empty. "What's to tell?"

"I must see him without delay, before this evening. Tell him it's Madeleine — he will know where to find me."

The woman repeated the name to be sure she had it right, but otherwise displayed no curiosity. Evidently, thought Madeleine, she was quite accustomed to receiving messages for Jacques from unlikely sources; she and her husband were probably involved in the smuggling, too.

Madeleine thanked her and was about to leave, but the woman laid a detaining hand on her arm.

"Wait here," she instructed. "He'll come to you if he wants to see you, else I'll tell you to go. Mebbe a half hour, mebbe longer, no saying. Just wait."

Madeleine waited. It seemed a very long time standing immobile on the stone floor of the washhouse, about which a smell of damp and soapsuds lingered. There was nowhere to sit, so she leaned against the large copper with its wooden lid and the hole underneath where the fire was lit on washdays.

The door opened at last and he was there. He listened imperturbably while she explained, then nodded.

"Arrangements are already made, little cousin, so calm yourself. And your letter is on its way. I've found a lodging for you in a cottage on the outskirts of the village. Not that you'll be there much longer. I'll know more later, but I think I may have a passenger to take over to France in a few days' time. If so, you could come, too, though it would be wiser for you to dress as a boy. I can arrange for suitable garments."

"Dress as a boy — oh!" Madeleine's cheeks flushed. "But I don't care, not I, if only I may go quickly to France! And will you yourself be coming?"

"Of a surety, for this is a very important passenger, not to be trusted to others."

"You are very kind to me, Cousin Jacques. Tell me, what should I pay this good woman?"

"That is taken care of already. Now go. I will come to you at the cottage some time after dark during the next few nights in order to tell you of my plans," he said in parting. "Be ready to leave for France at a moment's notice."

That same afternoon, Corinna was hopefully awaiting a visit from Madeleine so that she could tell her friend of Laurence's departure for Brighton and also deliver his farewell messages. As she walked up and down in the shrubbery, she reflected sadly that they would have so little time now to be together before they were separated by a cruel war that turned friends into enemies.

She sighed, allowing her thoughts to drift. It had been prodigiously clever of Sir Richard to contrive such an irresistible scheme for removing Laurence from this neighbourhood. She had seen through it, of course, and guessed that he would have liked to do the same for her. What was it that he feared for them both when he had spoken of a nasty hornet's nest? It could not be only the smugglers, for Madeleine's cousin would see to it that no further violence occurred. Besides, Richard intended to put a stop to their activities as soon as Madeleine had left the country. All along she had sensed that there was something more in his mind, something which he saw as a serious threat to herself in particular.

Could it be that, like Laurie, Richard secretly believed that Fabian Grenville was working with the smugglers? He had played the suggestion down when Laurie made it, but that was only to be expected; any hint of support would at once have inflamed Laurie's curiosity. *That* would be a hornet's nest indeed, she reflected, with an involuntary shudder. If an investigation into the smuggling business should lead to the discovery that Grenville had a part in it, a scandal must ensue in which none of his neighbours would care to be involved. And Richard would consider that this would affect *her* more than anyone, for he was well aware that she had fallen in love with Mr Grenville last summer. Mama had made sure that he knew, she thought bitterly.

It must be nonsense, of course, to suppose that a gentleman of birth and breeding would stoop to deal in illegal traffic, and yet...

She recalled all the circumstances which supported it; the secret visitors to Eastdean Place, the visit there of Madeleine's cousin on the night Laurie was attacked. If all that were not evidence enough, why had a man-about-town such as Fabian Grenville suddenly decided to settle in a place he had always stigmatised as "a deadly boring hole," and to abandon his quest for an heiress? And finally, where was he finding the funds to lay out on all his house improvement schemes? Everyone in the neighbourhood had remarked that nowadays he seemed to have money to burn.

Her heart missed a beat as it suddenly occurred to her that perhaps she ought to warn Mr Grenville of Richard's intentions with regard to the smugglers. Without betraying Madeleine, she could not say that she suspected he was involved, of course; but the mere mention would suffice. She was surprised to discover any hesitation in herself about doing this; once, she would have rushed to tell him. Now — what precisely were her feelings now? That if he had embarked on such a course, he deserved to take the consequences? It was something very like that, she admitted.

It meant, as she had recently suspected more than once, that her period of enchantment with Fabian Grenville was gone forever. She could still on occasions react to his charm, as most females would to any personable man; but the former bittersweet ardour had vanished.

Even as this thought crossed her mind, it was accompanied by a strong mental image of Richard as he had looked in the dawn of that morning when they had landed at Cuckmere Haven. Other images followed, particularly those in which she had been sparring with him and had seemed momentarily to penetrate his guard. She lingered on these recollections, at the same time wondering why it was that she enjoyed trying to provoke him. Was it because she was always hoping that sometime his restraint would break down completely, and — and what? She suddenly blushed fiery red.

Resolutely pushing these thoughts aside, she decided not to wait for Madeleine any longer, but to go to their rendezvous at Eastdean Place with a note making an appointment for tomorrow. Corinna quickly dashed off the note, stowed it in her reticule, then donned a pretty straw bonnet with pink ribbons and set out.

She had to hold on to the bonnet once she had left the shelter of the village, for a light breeze was blowing in from the sea. She approached the now familiar side entrance down the lane with more confidence than previously, but suffered a sharp setback as she saw that this time the battered door was ajar. She and Laurence had always assumed from its state of neglect that no one ever used that entrance. They were evidently wrong.

She hesitated, half minded to turn back. But it seemed a pity to give up so easily, so instead she poked her head cautiously round the door. She looked anxiously about her, but could see no one. After a few moments, encouraged, she stepped inside among the trees.

A twig caught in her bonnet, pulling it off; the next moment the breeze had floated it away. She started in pursuit, heedless now of the noise she made. She had almost reached it when she was suddenly seized in a pair of rough arms and shaken as a terrier shakes a rat.

She let out a scream which was quickly stifled by her attacker.

"Who are you?" he demanded in a fierce voice with a slight French accent. "What are you doing here, *hein?*"

She shook her head, unable to answer because of the ruthless hand over her mouth. For once, she was frightened almost out of her wits, but instinctively she made some attempt to struggle.

Through her terror she heard the pounding of footsteps. A second man rushed towards them.

"Miss Haydon!" he exclaimed in accents of horror. "For God's sake! Release her at once!"

She recognised Grenville.

"A ladybird of yours?" demanded the other man, keeping a tight hold on Corinna but taking his hand from her mouth.

"The lady is a friend of mine," returned Grenville brusquely. "Release her, I say!"

"Only if you can guarantee her silence, *mon ami.* Otherwise, best let me deal with it." His tone was ominous.

"For God's sake, leave it to me, you fool! I know how to handle this — you return to the house. You should never have left it. Go, damn you, go!"

The man released Corinna abruptly, causing her to stagger. Grenville leapt forward to place a supporting arm about her, which at present she was too shaken to refuse.

"Be very sure you do," warned the other as he turned away. "One mistake, and you, too, will feel the consequences."

He disappeared among the trees, leaving Corinna still supported by Grenville. She was panting for breath, but gradually her wits were returning. She shook off Grenville's arm.

"You must allow me to assist you to the house, Miss Haydon," he said solicitously. "You need to rest and have a restorative after your unfortunate experience. Pray, at least take my arm."

"I w-won't go to your house," she stuttered, shivering slightly. "Leave me alone — I won't g-go!"

"But you must sit down — your limbs can scarce support you. There is an old summerhouse not far away. If you won't come to the house, let me guide you there to rest awhile."

She was still too overcome to object, so allowed him to take her arm and lead her to the summerhouse. On the way, they passed her bonnet lying in a clump of nettles and Grenville stooped to retrieve it. When they reached the hut, he pushed open the door for her, looking critically about him.

"Not as dirty as I feared," he remarked, leading her over to the bench and spreading his handkerchief for her to sit upon. "Can I fetch you anything, Miss Haydon? Smelling salts, a glass of wine?"

She shook her head. He saw that she needed an interval to recover herself and wisely remained silent. Presently she roused, turning an indignant look upon him.

"I suppose you have some explanation to offer as to why that person should show me violence?"

"I can only apologise most humbly, ma'am. He is — excitable — and no doubt was startled by you."

"Not half so much as I was startled by him. Is he a lunatic? You have some odd friends, I must say, Mr Grenville!"

"He's not precisely a friend—" He paused, turning over in his quick mind what he should say. "Perhaps he could better be described as — a business associate."

Her eyes widened. "It must be a strange business that brings you into contact with such a man. Can it be — is it possible that — Mr Grenville, are you in any way connected with the smuggling that goes on hereabouts?" she blurted out.

He started. "What gives you that notion?" he asked sharply.

She attempted a shrug, half frightened now at her temerity. "Only something my brother said when we heard neighbours speculating about your coming here to live and — and seeming to be affluent all at once. And then this ruffian—"

He had been listening to her stumbling explanation with a heavy frown on his brows, his mind working at lightning speed. He came to a decision.

"Miss Haydon, can I rely on your discretion? If I explain these matters, will you promise to keep what I tell you to yourself?"

So Laurie was right, she thought, with an inward apprehensive tremor.

"You can't expect me to make a blind promise," she said firmly. "If you confide in me, I must be free to decide for myself whether or not I can respect that confidence. There might be reasons—"

"So cautious?" he interrupted, with a wry smile. "That's not in your character as I know it. Nevertheless, I've decided to trust you with my secret, certain that when you know all, you'll perceive the necessity of silence. For this is a matter of *national* importance, not merely a personal issue."

"National importance!" she repeated, amazed. "I can't think what you mean!"

"That's not to be wondered at, for the truth must sound strange indeed."

He knew she was of a romantic disposition and saw that now her interest was keenly aroused.

"You say your brother suspected that I had some connection with the smuggling gang," he went on, fixing his expressive eyes on her with a serious look. "In a sense, that is true, but I have no part in their trade. They have another function which concerns me — they bring English spies out of France."

She gasped, but said nothing, hanging on his every word.

"A base was needed close to the coast at a point where the smugglers could land these agents, so that they might deliver their dispatches, then lie up for a time awaiting a return voyage."

"Oh!" She took a deep breath. "I begin to see."

He nodded. "Exactly. Someone in high places knew of the house I owned here, knew also" — he paused, then continued glibly — "of my particular circumstances. They approached me, offered the means to enable me to make the place habitable and to maintain the position of a country gentleman. I was to mingle with my neighbours in the normal way, in order to disarm suspicion. Can you wonder, Miss Haydon, that I agreed readily to the plan, knowing that by so doing I was rendering valuable assistance to my country in the emergency of war? What patriotic Englishman could have decided otherwise?"

She clasped her hands tightly together, carried away for the moment by his rhetoric.

"No, indeed! And to think that I so nearly misjudged you! Not that I could altogether credit my brother's wild fancies," she added, forgetting her earlier doubts.

"I trust he hasn't mentioned them to anyone but yourself?" he asked quickly.

"Oh, he did say something to Richard, but Richard laughed at him."

"Beresford? You're sure he didn't take it seriously?"

She shook her head in answer, but he could see she was troubled. In fact, she was wondering whether she ought not to divulge the whole story of Madeleine, and also Sir Richard's intention to put an end to the activities of the smugglers when the French girl had gone. Just in time she realised that those in authority must be fully aware of all that Mr Grenville had told her, and would therefore prevent any well-meant interference on Richard's part. She decided to say nothing.

"What is it?" he asked, for he had been watching her closely all the time. "There is something on your mind, I think. You'd best tell me."

"No, there is nothing. I was only thinking over what you had told me. It's so very strange, that I cannot take it all in at once! But I must go now," she finished, rising. "My sister will wonder where I am."

He jumped to his feet. "Of course. I'll drive you home."

She protested that this was unnecessary, but he would not give way; so she was soon seated beside him in his curricle heading for the village.

"One thing puzzles me," he said. "How did you come to be inside my grounds, for I suppose you must have been there when my confederate came upon you?"

"Oh, it was all the fault of this wretched article," she said ingenuously, touching the somewhat bedraggled bonnet which she had restored to her head. "I was walking along the lane beside your house and I came upon a door in the wall which was half open. Of course I should not have done, I know, but I fear I'm inquisitive by nature, so I just peeped round. And then a gust of wind took my bonnet, and I darted in after it, and that — that man seized me—"

She shuddered, hoping that he would be satisfied by this partially true explanation.

"I see. Do you often take a walk round my grounds?" There was a hint of doubt in his tone.

"Oh, I'm a great one for exploring the neighbourhood, as I think you know, sir!" she replied, forcing a laugh. "I was doing so when you met me the other day, if you remember."

He appeared to relax at this. "Yes, you were thinking of walking to Birling Gap on that occasion. If you will take my advice, ma'am, you won't go there. It isn't safe for you."

"Why not?" she asked quickly.

"It's the place used by the smugglers for landing contraband, and also for the more important business of which I've just told you. My word on it, I can't be responsible for what may befall you should you go there. These are dangerous men, Miss Haydon, and it's wisest to avoid their haunts."

"But what of you?" she asked solicitously. "You must be in constant danger yourself in such an enterprise!"

"Do you care?" He leaned towards her, placing his hand over hers.

She blushed and looked away as if confused; but inwardly she was thinking bitterly how contrary was life, which only offered the realisation of one's dearest hopes when they had ceased to matter.

"Please — don't—" she murmured weakly.

He withdrew his hand. "No, it's not the best moment to press you for an answer. Forgive me. But someday soon, my dear Miss Haydon, I shall ask that question again."

CHAPTER TWENTY-ONE

She was relieved that he refused to come in with her when they reached the house, excusing himself on the grounds of pressing affairs awaiting his attention.

She found Lydia awaiting her in the small parlour on the ground floor which they used during the day. She looked a trifle anxious.

"Oh, there you are at last! I wondered where on earth you'd gone. Madeleine is awaiting you in the shrubbery, by the way. I tried to persuade her to await you indoors, but she would not come. In view of what Richard says, perhaps it's as well. Oh, dear, Corinna, I do trust you are not getting involved in any more scrapes! What am I to do with you?"

Corinna made no answer, but hastened out to meet Madeleine. Her friend soon told her of all that had occurred that day, concluding with her removal to a cottage in the village.

"Where precisely is this cottage?" asked Corinna. "I must know how to find it, for I may need to visit you there at some time."

Madeleine gave her directions, but added that she thought it unlikely that Corinna would be visiting her there.

"You see, Jacques says he'll be taking me to France in a very few days. It seems there is an important passenger who must be conveyed with all speed."

Corinna wondered if the man who had attacked her earlier might not be this passenger, but she said nothing.

"I believe I know who it is," continued Madeleine. "There was a man — I think he was French — who arrived late last night, and is staying in the house. But secretly, *voyez-vous*, for I discovered it only by chance and none of the other servants knows he is there. What is more, Corinna, I suspect that is the reason why I was asked to leave so suddenly. It is most odd, *n'est-ce pas*, what goes on in that house? I asked Jacques if this visitor might be his passenger, but he refused to answer."

"You say the man was French?" asked Corinna, considering for a moment as Madeleine nodded. "Yes, *I* believe he was, but if so—" She broke off, puzzled. *English* spies, Mr Grenville had said, yet the man she had encountered was undoubtedly French. Would Frenchmen then be spying against their own country? She saw that Madeleine was eyeing her oddly.

"Do you know something of this man?" the girl asked suddenly.

Corinna nodded. "Yes, I do, but — forgive me, my dear, but I'm not at liberty to speak of it."

A hurt expression came into the French girl's face.

"So far, we have never had any secrets from each other, you and I, Corinna!"

"I know, and it's not my wish that there should be any now. But this isn't my secret, and I did in some sort promise to keep it. Please understand, please, my dear!"

Madeleine nodded, swallowing her chagrin, and they went on to speak of other things. Corinna told her of Laurence's departure and delivered his parting messages of goodwill.

"*Le bon* Laurie — how I shall miss him," said Madeleine sadly. "I shall miss you all, my dear, dear friends, and especially yourself, Corinna!"

Corinna put an arm about her. "We'll miss you, too, Madeleine. But recollect that you're going home to one who will amply console you!"

Madeleine blushed, her dark eyes shining.

Later that same evening, Sir Richard at last came to a decision to ride over to Friston House. He had been debating with himself about this all day; but whenever he recalled his most recent quarrel with Corinna, his jaw hardened and he told himself not to be a fool. It was plain that she considered him only as a tiresome mentor who sought to prevent her from acting as she wished. Plain, too, that in spite of all Grenville had done to arouse her disgust, she still chose to fancy herself in love with the fellow.

He had very little doubt that, as Lydia believed, Corinna was only indulging in a perverse clinging to an outgrown infatuation. That fact did little to improve the situation. While she persisted in fostering the illusion, she was unlikely to turn her thoughts elsewhere. Even if she did, he thought bitterly, it would certainly not be in his direction.

He asked himself when he had first come to love her, and the answer seemed to be always. From the days when she had been a little imp of mischief in a muslin dress more often torn and soiled than otherwise, until now, as a lovely young woman, she had held his heart in her careless hands.

He would have declared himself last year, knowing that she was supremely indifferent to all her other suitors and that he would have an influential advocate in her mother; but he had wanted more than complaisance, loving her as he did, so had waited for some sign of awakening love on her part. Then Grenville had arrived on the scene, and it had been too late.

This thought made him pull viciously at the rein, much to his horse's surprise; for those hands were invariably gentle, though firm. The animal showed its disapproval, and it was some moments before Sir Richard had soothed it again.

So what was to be done now? There were serious complications as far as Grenville was concerned; a reckoning must come before long, and she would be hurt just as much — though not as lastingly — as if her feelings for the man had been as deep as she supposed. Impossible to spare her that, for the issues were too grave, but most likely she would hate him thereafter.

It seemed, then, that he must renounce all thought of her. And of marriage? He did not think himself a natural bachelor. He was a home-loving man whose chief pleasures would always be found in the management of his house and estate and the society of his neighbours. It would be pleasant to have someone to share all this with him.

He was no coxcomb, but it had not escaped his notice that Frances Cheveley was not quite indifferent to him. He did not believe her to be in love, but a little encouragement on his side might well accomplish this. Should he offer for Miss Cheveley?

She was pretty, charming, agreeable, eligible... oh, my God! he thought with sudden revulsion, I am cataloguing her virtues as though running over the points of a horse I intended buying! What was this strange alchemy that made one woman matter above all others, in spite of her rivals' claims to as many virtues or charms?

He told himself that he must approach this matter in a rational spirit. He could offer Frances Cheveley only second best, but theirs might still be a marriage to bring comfort and security to both. He did not doubt that he could become very fond of her in time; for the rest, he would keep faith with her and try to make her happy. It was a compromise, but was not life made up of compromises?

By the time he reached this stage in his cogitations, he had arrived at Friston House. He stabled his horse and presented himself indoors.

"We're delighted to see you!" Lydia greeted him. "I only wish you'd come over earlier in time to dine with us, for it seems so quiet without Laurie. I never thought I'd have missed the wretched boy half so much! But I dare say he's better pleased to be with young Cheveley. How are they all at Rottingdean?"

"Very well, and they send all good wishes. Lady Cheveley hopes that you'll visit there again soon."

Corinna noticed a certain constraint in his manner as he replied, and wondered how far it might be due to Frances.

"It's our turn to ask them here," said Lydia.

"Oh, Richard repaid their original hospitality when he invited them to his house recently," said Corinna airily. "Such nonsense as it is, to entertain turn and turn about in strict rotation, Lyddy!"

"Well, one must observe the forms of social usage," replied Lydia. "And here is Bolton with the tea tray. You'll take tea, Richard, or would you prefer wine?"

"Tea will do very well, thank you. And how have you been passing your time?" he asked Corinna.

"I saw Madeleine today," she replied, a shade defiantly. "She's soon to leave for France, her cousin tells her. He has an important p—" she stumbled, recollecting herself in time — "that is to say, an important errand there, in a few days' time."

"Indeed?" He had noticed the hesitation and eyed her keenly. "I cannot suppose she'll be sorry for that."

"No. Another thing, Richard, she was sent away from the house this morning."

"Sent away? You mean dismissed?"

"No, but told that she could no longer stay there overnight, but must come in daily, like the others."

"That was very sudden, was it not?"

"Yes, well—"

215

She hesitated again, on the verge of repeating Madeleine's suppositions, but thinking better of it at the last moment. Really, it was very trying not to be able to be as frank with him as she had always been; but she must remember her promise to Fabian Grenville.

"Corinna," he accused, in a low tone, "I do believe you're keeping something from me."

"Oh, no, what nonsense!" She glanced at Lydia, busy with the teacups and not attending to their conversation. "Madeleine's cousin has found her somewhere else to lodge," she went on hurriedly. "A cottage almost at the end of the village, quite convenient for Eastdean Place. He says he will come there to let her know when he's ready for her to go, but she must dress in boys' clothes. Masquerading as a boy must be quite an adventure!"

"I should suppose the poor child has had enough of adventures," he said soberly, accepting a cup from Lydia's hands and passing it to Corinna.

"Do you mean your friend Madeleine?" asked Lydia, entering the conversation once more. "So I should think, and you, too, Corinna, for all you babble on so foolishly."

"Oh, pooh!" Corinna retorted, but she secretly acknowledged the justice of Lydia's remark. She had been talking wildly in the hope of diverting Richard's attention from herself. He was too shrewd by half, she thought, dismayed.

"I cannot pretend that I shall be other than relieved to see her go," he admitted.

"That's not a very kind thing to say!" exclaimed Corinna, though she knew quite well what he meant.

"Oh, of course Richard doesn't mean it personally," put in Lydia. "He likes Madeleine but he considers the situation to be vastly uncomfortable. Isn't that so, Richard?"

He nodded. "I know my duty is to take action against these smugglers, but until the girl is safely out of the country, my hands are tied. A word now to the authorities, and her escape route would be cut off. Yet there are reasons — urgent reasons — for stopping this traffic immediately." He frowned. "It's the devil of a coil."

Throughout this speech, Corinna's expression registered dismay. If only she could give Richard a hint as to what was going on at Eastdean Place! He would look very foolish when he discovered the truth.

At this stage, her thoughts broke off abruptly. Richard was a magistrate, and as such was kept informed of local matters touching the defence of the realm. Why, then, did he appear to have no knowledge of official protection for the smugglers who ferried British agents to and from France? Surely he would have been warned to turn a blind eye to the traffic?

Her head felt in a whirl. She sensed that Sir Richard was studying her intently, and rose to return her half-empty teacup to the tray in order to avoid his eye.

"Urgent reasons, you say, Richard, for stopping the smugglers' activities," repeated Lydia. "I collect there must be some new cause for concern?"

"Indeed there is. While I was with Wexham in Brighton, warning came through of a dangerous French spy on the run. Only a few days since, he'd killed a man and stolen some important defence papers. Precautions are being taken at the ports to prevent his leaving the country, but it struck me he might well use a less obvious way of escape, as we did ourselves. I suspect our friends operate chiefly from Birling Gap. It's not far from Brighton, and someone may be giving this man shelter until Fougeray can take him across the Channel."

Corinna could not control a gasp; fortunately, it was echoed by Lydia.

"How dreadful! No wonder you feel impelled to act! I collect you didn't inform the colonel of your suspicions, Richard? Of course, I suppose that would prevent poor Madeleine from returning to France, and most likely mean her cousin would suffer a dreadful penalty for his part in such doings!"

She broke off, too distressed to proceed.

His face hardened as he kept his eyes on Corinna.

"No, I did not tell him. I've decided to handle the business myself, for the present. Pray don't press me for details — I prefer to keep my own counsel. And now let us talk of pleasanter subjects."

"Oh, yes, but what if that man should be in this neighbourhood, as you seem to suspect?" persisted Lydia with a shudder. "I declare, I won't be able to sleep easy in my bed! He must be a desperado!"

"Yes, I believe he is," replied Sir Richard in a calm tone. "Since you feel so uneasy, Lydia, would you like me to stay here for the next few nights? I can easily do so."

"Oh, would you indeed? How vastly good of you, Richard! I suppose it *is* cowardly of me, but without Laurie, just two females in the house—?

"You're forgetting the servants," put in Corinna shakily.

"Well, there are sufficient able-bodied men about the house, it's true," admitted Lydia, "but one needs someone to take command in an emergency. Would you not feel easier yourself if Richard were here?"

"I'm not — certain — that there's anything to be alarmed over," replied Corinna slowly. "But if Richard does not object and it would set your mind at rest—"

"*Your* mind, I collect, does not require setting at rest?" Sir Richard asked swiftly.

"I think it's fuddled for lack of air! It's so close in this room! If you'll forgive me, I'll take a turn or two in the garden."

"Of all things!" exclaimed her sister in disgust. "Why, you've spent most of today out of doors as it is!"

Corinna made no answer, but quitted the room. After a moment, Sir Richard, too, rose.

"I'll ride home and collect my gear," he said to Lydia. "I shan't inflict my valet on you, by the way."

"No, for John's man will be only too pleased to have something to do. Are you sure, Richard, that this isn't putting you about too much? I feel ashamed — you're so very good."

"Nonsense. Didn't I promise John to keep an eye on you?" He nodded good-bye. "I'll be back presently."

He did not go straight round to the stables to collect his horse, however, but instead followed Corinna into the garden.

She was pacing up and down among the roses, evidently deep in thought. She looked up as he drew level with her, greeting him with an abstracted frown.

"Something is troubling you," he said quietly. "Will you not tell me what it is?"

She forced a laugh. "No, nothing, I assure you. At least — well, of course I'm upset at the thought of parting from Madeleine."

"I know that, but there's something more," he insisted. "I couldn't help but observe that you were in the grip of some strong emotion when I mentioned the French spy. Neither do I believe that it was any fear for your safety which caused your concern. I think you're in possession of some knowledge which you're keeping back from your sister and myself. This may be wise as far as Lydia's concerned, but surely, my dear

219

Corinna, you can confide in me." She started to protest, but he shook his head at her. "No, don't deny it — I've known you too long not to be aware when you're trying to keep a secret."

"If you persist in believing that, then why don't you let me alone and allow me to keep it?" she flashed at him.

He laid a hand gently on her arm. "I'll not quarrel with you, Corinna. There have been quarrels enough between us in the past. I dare say that was my fault."

"Oh, no!" She turned her face towards him, and he saw with surprise that there were tears in her eyes. "I've been a wretch to you at times, Richard — I freely admit it! But — but — just this once, leave me be, pray do! I don't rightly know what to think, or — or — what I should do, but I must find the answer for myself, believe me!"

He made no reply for a moment, looking down into her eyes with an expression which made her lip tremble. She turned her face away.

"I will do as you ask, my dear. But remember that" — his voice deepened — "I am yours to command in all things, should you choose to seek my aid."

He turned and walked slowly away towards the stables. Almost she ran after him to pour out her unquiet thoughts; but she controlled the impulse, and after a moment, returned to the house.

CHAPTER TWENTY-TWO

Madame Landier sighed, looking up for a moment from the white muslin cap she was trimming with lace. She stared into vacancy. She was a conscientious mother; and, like all such, there were occasions when she worried over one or another of her family. Now it was her only son, Patrice, who brought the shadow of anxiety to her eyes.

Since the girl Madeleine had left for England, he had not been in spirits. She had been the first female for whom he had shown any serious attachment; though naturally there had been the little flirtations one could only expect with a personable, light-hearted young man. Madame had known several months ago that there was someone, but he had not fully confided in her at that time. When Madeleine Fougeray had come to the house with the English people, however, she had seen at once how it was. She had taken to the girl, too, and would readily have welcomed her as a daughter. Patrice had told her everything then, and she realised how deep was his disappointment.

She put her work aside and rose to go into the kitchen to consult with the cook. One thing was certain, nothing could be allowed to interfere with that most important of French institutions, *le dîner*. Lately she had been ordering all Patrice's favourite dishes in the belief, shared by so many mothers, that food had great consolatory powers for her offspring.

Her efforts seemed to have missed their mark so far; this evening was no exception. She watched her son toy with each successive course, then refuse a marvellous confection decorated with strawberries and whipped cream which she had hoped would prove irresistible. She had begun to press him once again to partake of this, when she was interrupted by one of the servants, who came into the dining parlour to deliver a message to Patrice. She frowned at the intruder, and her husband looked shocked; but servants were not what they had been, and the man remained unabashed.

"There's a fellow asking to see you, monsieur," stated the messenger. "Urgently, he says."

"What manner of fellow?" demanded Patrice, half rising.

"A bargee, I think," replied the other with a shrug. "Says he can't wait, but he must see you in person."

Excusing himself to his parents, Patrice hurried from the room into the kitchen quarters of the house. A man stood just inside the back door, he was dressed in the stained and shabby garments of the bargemen.

Patrice went up to him. "I am Patrice Landier. What can I do for you?"

"It's what I can do for you," answered the other in a throaty voice. "I come from Pierre Bonnet, who has a farm on the coast. He sends you this" — he handed over an oilskin-wrapped packet — "and I was to give it to none other. Cost me a mort of trouble, bringing that here, I can tell you."

Landier turned the packet over in his hands thoughtfully for a moment before transferring it to his pocket.

"I'm obliged to you, and trust this may recompense you for that trouble," he said, offering a generous *pourboire*.

There appeared to be no doubt on this score, for the bargee pocketed his fee with alacrity and departed at once.

Landier hastened upstairs again, entered a small anteroom where he could be private, and proceeded to undo the packet with eager fingers.

There was a letter in a hand he did not know, but one that was undoubtedly feminine.

With suddenly bounding pulses, he broke the seal and read. He had mastered no more than half the contents when he uttered a cry of delight, then pressed the paper impulsively to his lips. It was a few minutes before he was again sufficiently calm to finish the letter; but after he had done so, there was no holding him. He rushed into the dining parlour, where his parents had just concluded their meal, and waved the letter excitedly in the air.

"You'll never guess!" he exclaimed in tones of exhilaration. "Something of the most wonderful! She is to return to me!"

"But, yes, I knew, my son," said Madame Landier, "from the first moment you entered the room. You must tell us all about it. But first, perhaps now you will eat your dessert."

After parting from Corinna in the garden of Friston House, Sir Richard had turned towards the stables to collect his horse; but halfway there, he changed his mind. Consulting his watch, he saw that it was already past nine o'clock, the hour at which the domestic staff of Grenville's house usually left the premises. He appeared satisfied by this reflection; instead of returning home at once, he took a leisurely route to the village.

Dusk was gathering, and the trees he passed were dark shadows. When he reached the village, no one was about and lights were appearing in some of the windows. He had no wish to draw attention to himself, so he trod quietly, keeping to grassy verges whenever possible until he came to the cottage where Corinna had told him Madeleine was lodging.

He tapped softly on the door. After an interval it was opened by an elderly woman. The door opened straight into the main downstairs room of the cottage; by the light of the lamp standing on the table, he saw that everything, including the woman herself, was neat and clean, though shabby.

"Good evening," he said. "I believe you have a girl called Madeleine lodging with you. I'd like a word with her, if you please."

The woman bobbed a curtsey, but her expression was wary.

"If you'll tell me your name, sir, I'll see," she said after a moment.

She did not ask him in, but partly closed the door after he had supplied the information. He could faintly hear her footsteps ascending the stairs which led out of the living room.

Presently she returned with Madeleine, who flung the door wide, inviting him to enter.

She greeted him shyly, for she had never been upon such easy terms with him as with Corinna and Laurence, and offered him an upright deal chair. Then she turned to address the woman in a low tone.

Presently the woman nodded and departed through a door beside the staircase.

"Is there any way in which I can serve you, monsieur?" said Madeleine. "There is nothing wrong with Corinna, I trust?" she added, as this unwelcome thought occurred to her.

"You may set your mind at rest on that score," he reassured her swiftly. "She's in the best of health."

"Ah, that is good. I was afraid, for a moment — since I could not think of any reason why you should visit me. But that will doubtless appear."

He nodded, turning over rapidly in his mind how best to approach the subject of this interview.

"Mademoiselle Fougeray," he said at last. "I have come here to seek some information which I believe Miss Haydon to possess, but which she will not confide to me. You see I am frank."

"Yes, monsieur, and I will be as frank with you," she answered, meeting his gaze levelly. "If Corinna does not choose to tell you of certain matters, do not ask me to betray her confidence."

"That's what I'd expect you to say, knowing you for a loyal friend. But might you not change your mind if you knew that the information Miss Haydon withholds could be a source of danger to her?"

"Danger?" She opened her eyes wide. "Yes, I realise there is danger in all those matters in which my cousin — alas! — is concerned. But danger to Corinna? That I do not see."

"I assure you that it is so, nevertheless. Perhaps you will permit me to ask you a few questions which concern only yourself, however, since you remain unconvinced."

She looked troubled. "*Mais oui*, monsieur, I will tell you anything I may," she said doubtfully.

"Good. I understand from Miss Haydon that you are to take passage for France shortly, under the escort of your cousin."

She nodded.

"Did he mention to you why he was making the crossing at this time of year, when smugglers don't usually operate?"

"Yes, he did," she acknowledged slowly. "But I'm not at all sure that I ought—"

"Mademoiselle, would you account me a trustworthy man in general?"

"But of a surety, monsieur! Did you not bring us safely out of France?"

"My part in that was negligible," he said diffidently. "Much more was due to Monsieur Landier." She blushed at the name. "However, I do think you've known me for long enough to believe me when I say I will do nothing to jeopardize your chances of a safe return to France. Neither do I intend any harm to your cousin, provided he's prepared to agree to certain terms which I intend to put to him."

"What do you mean, monsieur?"

"That is between the two of us, man to man. I wish to meet him, and I hope you will act as intermediary."

"Oh, I am not sure!" she exclaimed uneasily. "I don't know what I ought to do!"

"Do not be alarmed. What I intend is in your cousin's best interests, believe me. But will you not now answer my first question, mademoiselle?"

"He told me that he had an important passenger to convey to France within a few days," she replied reluctantly.

He nodded, satisfied. "Yes, I am tolerably certain that it was what Miss Haydon started to tell me, then drew back and would say no more."

"Why, yes!" exclaimed Madeleine impetuously. "So it was when she was talking to me this afternoon, monsieur, and I've never known Corinna to be at all guarded with me! I was telling her of my suspicions that this passenger might be a man — a Frenchman — who came secretly to Mr Grenville's house last night. And I also told her that it seems to me I was asked to leave so suddenly because of the need for secrecy. Then she said something that seemed strange—"

She broke off in dismay, realising too late that she had said too much.

"What did she say?"

She gave a Gallic shrug. "Ah, bah! Now I've already told you that, you may as well know the rest, for it does not help much. She admitted to knowing something of this man, but refused to say more. She spoke of having made a promise, but did not say to whom."

His eyebrows shot up at this, but for a while he was silent, evidently deep in thought.

"Mademoiselle, it is imperative that I should speak with your cousin," he said presently. "Could you summon him to you in case of urgent need?" She nodded doubtfully. "I urge you to do so, mademoiselle, for his own sake. Ask him to come here at this same hour tomorrow. You need say nothing of me, but I will be here."

"Unnecessary," said a voice from behind them.

They swung round sharply and Sir Richard came to his feet. The door through which the woman had vanished earlier was now open, and Jacques Fougeray stood on the threshold.

He shut the door and came forward into the room, one hand in his pocket, his attitude alert and defensive.

"You are the man who came from France with my cousin, I believe," he said, in level tones. "And you wish to see me?"

"My name is Beresford. Yes, there are urgent matters which I need to discuss with you."

"So. The nature of these matters, monsieur?"

"They concern a man whom you are about to convey to France."

The hand that had been in Fougeray's pocket was withdrawn, revealing a knife in its grasp. One quick movement brought him to Sir Richard's side.

"No!" screamed Madeleine. "No!"

Sir Richard caught Fougeray's wrist in an iron grip. For a moment the two men wrestled together, then the knife dropped with a clatter to the floor. Sir Richard kicked it some distance away.

"No need for that," he said brusquely, holding on to the other man. "Hear me first — it will pay you."

Fougeray wrenched himself free, regarded his opponent for a moment in silence, then shrugged.

"*D'accord.* I'll hear you, then we shall see." He turned to the trembling Madeleine and spoke soothingly. "Go to the woman, my good child, and do not concern yourself."

"But — but, Jacques, you will not — please, please do not harm Sir Richard! He is my friend, and I think perhaps yours, too, if you will let him be so!"

He grinned wryly. "I think your Sir Richard can have a care to himself, *petite*. But no, at this present I do not intend to harm him. Now go."

She obeyed, closing the door reluctantly upon them.

"And now be brief," recommended Jacques. "I may as well tell you that I overheard some of your conversation with my cousin. You spoke of a matter of business. Explain."

"I have a proposition to put to you, but first I'll tell you to your head that I'm well aware of the nature of your connection with a certain gentleman of property in these parts."

"*Vraiment?* You're a bold man, monsieur."

Jacques made a quick dart towards the knife, but Sir Richard put out a foot and tripped him. The Frenchman quickly recovered, snarling; but Sir Richard had already seized the knife, snapped it shut and thrust it into his own pocket.

"Fight if you must," he said, squaring up to the other. "But with fists, not a knife. No weapon for a French aristocrat, you must agree."

By way of answer, Jacques rushed upon him. He was a strong young man, but he found he had met his match. Sir Richard, like many another active English gentleman, was not without some expertise in the national sport of boxing.

"There's no need for this, you know," he said, warding off his opponent's blows, but making no attempt to score a hit himself. "Show sense, man — listen to me first!"

Jacques paid no heed, however, but fought on with unabated fury. At last Sir Richard, seeing no help for it, landed him a blow which rocked him off balance and sent him sprawling on the floor. He rose, panting.

"For God's sake, have done!" urged Sir Richard. "I intend you no harm — quite the contrary. Call a truce, and hear what I have to say."

Jacques glared belligerently at him for a moment, then shrugged and collapsed into a chair.

"Very well," he muttered sullenly.

Sir Richard sat down, tugging at his disordered cravat.

"Had you warned me of your intention to start a mill, I'd have removed this damn thing, and my coat, too," he said, breathing a trifle unevenly himself.

Jacques broke into a short laugh. "You're a cool customer, as I said before, monsieur! Well, what have you to say?"

"First, that I don't intend to take any action about my knowledge of your activities until your cousin, Mademoiselle de Fougeray, is out of this country. On that I give you my word."

Jacques studied him for a moment. "I think I can believe you," he said, at last. "And afterwards?"

"If you're wise, there will be no afterwards as far as you're concerned. I recommend strongly that you yourself should remain in France, never to cross the Channel again."

The other gave a derisive grunt. "And what do you suppose I should do in France? My lands are forfeit, and the only employment I am trained for is smuggling. Do you perhaps suggest that I should join Napoleon's navy and help him wage his war? Bah! That one is no better than the Revolutionaries who guillotined my relatives!"

"One cannot live in the past, my friend. True, your lands are irretrievably lost to you, but you may still return to France under your rightful title, as French law no longer persecutes aristocrats. Many emigrés have already returned, in fact."

Jacques flung out his hands. "An empty title! And I dare say plenty who will sneer at it! And how do you propose I shall get a living, monsieur? You don't answer that."

"On the contrary, that is the crux of my proposal. Would you agree that it's your capacity for organisation which has brought you success in your present trade?"

The young man nodded. "In part — perhaps the greater part," he admitted.

"Such a talent can equally be applied in other, more lawful, directions. Your cousin is to marry into a family with commercial interests, and I'm confident my friend Landier would gladly establish you in one such. As for your immediate needs" — he hesitated, then went on — "should you find yourself temporarily short of the ready, so to speak, I'll be pleased to fund you to any amount."

"*Diable!* And why should you do this for me?"

"Let us say, sporting instinct. In a sense, you've been forced by circumstances into this reprehensible trade. Besides, there's your cousin to consider — Miss Haydon is very attached to her."

Jacques gave him a quizzical look. "You are a strange man, I think. The pattern of an English gentleman of Quality, I might suppose, did I not know one quite otherwise at Eastdean Place. Very well, I accept your advice, but as to funds" — he drew himself up — "I thank you, but I have salted down sufficient to provide not only for my own needs, but also for a *dot* for my cousin Madeleine."

"There is a condition, however."

"Ah, now we come to it," said Jacques cynically.

"The passenger whom you're to smuggle out of the country is a French spy, as of course you know. I realise that this matters not at all to you, as you have no involvement with either side in this war."

"No. How could it be otherwise?"

"Precisely. My case is different, however. The man has stolen important defence papers which must not reach the enemy. I intend to prevent his departure."

"You said you would not inform the authorities."

"Neither shall I. That will come later, after you and Mademoiselle Madeleine are safe away. This is a matter for myself to handle. All I require of you is precise information as to when and where this man is to join you for the crossing."

Jacques whistled. "*Mon Dieu*, I said you were a cool customer! You're like to get your throat slit, but that is your affair. The time is half an hour before midnight tomorrow. We rendezvous at Birling Gap — you know it?" Sir Richard nodded. "There's a group of tumbledown cottages there — we meet in the end one. *Bonne chance*, my friend."

CHAPTER TWENTY-THREE

Corinna's uneasy frame of mind persisted through a somewhat restless night and the morning that followed. She scarcely knew how to face Sir Richard over the breakfast table, and was thankful to hear him announce to Lydia his intention of returning to Chyngton Manor for the remainder of the day.

After he had gone, she and Corinna set out to pay some morning calls. Lydia was fortunate in her neighbours, and so much enjoyed their company for the next few hours that she quite forgot her alarms of the previous day. She did notice, however, that her sister was not in spirits, and did her best to try and discover the cause.

"You're not in a fidget about that spy Richard told us of, surely, Corinna? It's not like you to pay much heed to alarms, and I must say you took the news far more calmly than I could, at the time. I feel better now, however, and think perhaps he may not be in this neighbourhood at all."

For a moment, Corinna was tempted to confide in her sister, but she at once rejected the notion. Lydia had been made nervous at the mere suggestion that a spy might be lurking in the neighbourhood, so how would she be likely to react were she to be told all that her sister knew? She would certainly insist on informing Richard, a step which Corinna could not yet bring herself to take.

If only she could see a way out of the tangle, she thought, and know for certain what she ought to do! Fabian Grenville's story had seemed so plausible while he was recounting it to her, but doubts had set in with Sir Richard's news of a dangerous French spy who might possibly be sheltering locally.

To add to this was the uncomfortable conviction that she could never entirely trust Mr Grenville. She did not know why she had changed, or when; but there was no doubt that at some moment the scales had fallen from her eyes to reveal him as untrustworthy, and herself as deluded. It was for this reason that she had avoided giving him an answer yesterday when he had asked her if she cared.

No, there was only one person to whom she might safely entrust all her doubts and fears, and that person was Madeleine. Mr Grenville's story would be safe enough with her, true or false, since the only person to whom she might reveal it would be her cousin Jacques, and he must know of it already.

Having reached this decision, she awaited Madeleine in the shrubbery throughout the afternoon with mounting impatience. By five o'clock, she realised it was hopeless. Her disappointment was intense. The thought of yet another day to endure of introspection and indecision was anathema to one of her impulsive, active disposition, yet what was to be done? She dare not again visit the summerhouse at Eastdean Place to leave a note for her friend; moreover, there was nothing to be gained by embarking on such a hazardous undertaking, as Madeleine would most likely visit her tomorrow, whether summoned or not.

She sighed and returned to the house with the intention of keeping Lydia company until it was time for their solitary dinner.

"Oh, there you are," said her sister, as she entered the parlour. "I was just about to send this out to you — it arrived by a servant not five minutes since."

She handed a sealed note to Corinna, who looked at it, recognised Madeleine's hand, then opened it eagerly. It contained only a few lines.

I could not come to you this afternoon, as madame kept me occupied. I leave for France tonight, and this may mean that I shall not see you before I go. There is but one chance, dearest Corinna — if you are able to meet me at the cottage where I lodge. I should be there by a quarter after nine this evening. Bring no attendant for safety's sake. If you cannot come, I wish you adieu, my dear friend, and pray we may meet again some day, when our countries are at peace.

She checked the exclamation which rose to her lips and read the message again. She needed time to think.

"What is it?" asked Lydia, with natural curiosity. "It's from Madeleine, is it not?"

Corinna was not practiced in the art of dissimulation but she recognised some need of it now.

"Yes," she answered, as carelessly as possible. "Explaining why she did not come this afternoon, and hoping to see me soon."

"Oh, is that all," said her sister, losing interest.

Corinna screwed the note up into a ball to indicate its lack of importance, but kept it in her hand as she sauntered from the room. Once in her own bedchamber, she smoothed the paper out, read it for a third time, then thrust it into a drawer of her dressing table.

There was no point at all in confiding its contents to Lydia; for she knew very well that her elder sister would refuse to countenance the assignation, and she herself was determined to keep it. She puzzled for a few moments over how to achieve this without Lydia's knowledge. Suddenly she recollected that

Lydia had been insisting a few hours ago that she, Corinna, should have an early night. The very thing! There was only one drawback to this scheme; even on an early night, she could scarcely retire before nine o'clock, or Lydia would be summoning medical aid! This must mean that she would arrive at the meeting with Madeleine at least a half hour later than her friend had suggested. But perhaps, after all, Corinna reflected, there was no real haste; was it not most likely that the smugglers would not move until after dark, which came very late at this time of year? No doubt Madeleine had suggested the earliest possible time in order to accommodate her friend, and not herself.

She made some little alteration in her dress, suited to dining without company, and returned to join her sister. When the meal was over they sat down at Lydia's suggestion to a game of backgammon; but Corinna's attention wandered so much that this brought small entertainment to either player.

"You're uncommon stupid tonight, my love," Lydia complained as she rose to put the board and pieces away. "I can't think what's amiss with you."

"Well, perhaps you're in the right of it when you keep saying I need an early night. Now I come to consider the matter, I believe I truly *am* tired. What, is it only ten minutes to nine?" — with a glance of feigned surprise at the clock, which she had been covertly studying on and off for the past hour — "I quite supposed it must have been after ten! I think I shall go up directly, Lyddy, if you don't object."

"Of course not, but will you not wait first to drink tea? It's a trifle early yet to ring for the tray, but still—"

"No, I won't take tea this evening, for I feel it may keep me awake."

Lydia stared. "You *must* be feeling out of sorts! When did anything ever keep you awake? However, do you go up and get a good night's rest. I dare say I shan't be long in following you myself."

"Pray don't look in on me when you do come upstairs, Lyddy, for it will surely disturb me," said Corinna on a sudden inspiration.

Lydia duly promised, and Corinna bade her good night without more ado. Quickly changing her present light sandals for the half boots more suited to a nocturnal pedestrian excursion, she selected a green hooded cloak to wear over her flimsy muslin gown. It proved not too difficult, if a trifle nerve-wracking, to creep down the back stairs and let herself out of the house unseen. Darkness was closing in earlier this evening, as the sky was clouded, with no glimmer from the moon to help her on her way. Fortunately, she had frequently walked this road to the village, although now the shadows wore a threatening aspect which made her start once or twice and look uneasily about her.

She reached Madeleine's cottage at last and knocked timidly on the door.

There was no answer. She could see a glimmer of light from behind the shutters of the window, so knew someone must be within.

She knocked a second time, more loudly. A few moments elapsed before the door was cautiously opened a crack.

A boy appeared behind it, clad in a rough suit of fustian. He stared at the visitor for a moment, then uttered a glad cry and opened the door wider to admit her.

"Corinna! You have come, after all! Oh, my dear, I am so glad!"

Corinna realised with amazement that the boy was none other than Madeleine.

The door was quickly shut and Corinna guided to a chair. No one else was in the room.

"I feared you could not come, since it's already ten o'clock, and I knew it would be difficult for you, at best. You may easily be driven back by the boy who is to take me to Birling Gap in a mule cart," Madeleine said. "I dare say you would prefer it to walking home in the dark unaccompanied? You have but to wait here until he returns from taking me. He's to come shortly at half past ten, and should be back well within the hour. What do you say?"

"I think perhaps I would prefer it, even though it means I shan't be home until close on midnight. But why is not your cousin himself coming to fetch you?"

"Because he had to arrange for a rowing boat to be in readiness at Birling Gap to take us out to the smuggling vessel. Jacques will meet me at the Gap just before eleven, and conduct me down the cliff path to the boat. There is to be another man to assist him with the rowing, and Jacques will leave me in his charge while he himself goes back up the cliff to collect his important passenger who will arrive later. He arranged it in this way so that the other passenger might not set eyes on me until we were all afloat. I think he doubted I would pass muster, even in my present disguise."

"It looks convincing enough to me," said Corinna, eyeing her friend critically. "I did not recognise you when you first came to the door! But, Madeleine, there is something I must tell you — indeed, I've been waiting anxiously to see you all day! It concerns this passenger your cousin is to take to France, and whom you suspected was the same man who arrived secretly at Mr Grenville's house."

Madeleine regarded her sharply. "You knew something of that one, but you would not tell me, Corinna. Have you now changed your mind?"

Corinna said that she had, and proceeded to tell the whole story as briefly as possible.

"You perceive my quandary," she concluded. "This man whom Mr Grenville declares is a spy for my country may well be quite otherwise, judging by what I learned from Sir Richard. This could mean that Mr Grenville himself has been taken in, or that—"

"That he was lying to you," Madeleine finished for her.

"Yes, and that would make him—" she broke off, unwilling to put it into words. "But ought I to have told Sir Richard?" she continued unhappily. "If important defence papers are to be out of the country, some action *must* be taken, and yet I cannot be sure — oh, Madeleine, what ought I to do?"

Madeleine considered for a moment.

"This I can tell you; Sir Richard knows you were keeping something back, for he came to question me about it yesterday evening."

Corinna started. "Richard came here to see *you?*"

"I, too, was surprised. He urged me to divulge anything you might have confided to me of the matter, for he feared it could bring you into danger. Of course, I knew nothing, and told him I would not have betrayed your confidence in any case. But I did mention to him my own suspicions. He then insisted on talking to my cousin. I was afraid to involve Jacques, but while I was hesitating, my cousin himself arrived here, and they met."

"What did he want with your cousin?"

"I cannot say, for Jacques sent me from the room. They fought at first, but afterwards all seemed well. What I do think, though, Corinna, is that Sir Richard and Jacques have come to

238

some agreement, perhaps made some plan," she added shrewdly. "Jacques would tell me nothing beyond that Sir Richard will not jeopardise our escape, and that he — Jacques — will remain in France with me. For that I am profoundly grateful to your Sir Richard, for I think he must have persuaded Jacques to it."

Corinna could say nothing for a moment. She was quite overcome by what she had just heard; but a feeling of relief gradually crept over her. If Madeleine's cousin had shared his knowledge of these illicit dealings with Sir Richard, then perhaps she had no further need for anxiety.

Madeleine drew a borrowed fob watch from her pocket, consulted it, then uttered a distressed exclamation.

"He's ten minutes late! And Jacques said I must be there by eleven sharp! What shall I do, Corinna, if he does not come?"

Corinna could not imagine, but she did her best to allay her friend's fears.

"Be sure the boy will arrive in a few minutes," she said soothingly. "I tell you what, my dear, why should I not accompany you in the cart, instead of waiting here alone? In that way we could be together until the actual moment of your departure. And there's still so much I wish to say to you!"

They had scarcely agreed on this when they heard the rumble of wheels outside, followed by a knock on the door. Madeleine opened it at once, to see with heartfelt relief a boy looking very much like herself, only a trifle dirtier, standing on the doorstep.

She scolded him in a low voice for his dilatoriness while she handed him her small carpetbag and made haste to climb with Corinna into the cart. They moved off at once, the mule plodding along at little more than a walking pace.

By now, it was fully dark, with the sky still overcast and no stars to be seen. A small lantern was fixed in the cart so that the two passengers, uncomfortably crouched on the floor together, could faintly see each other's faces.

"This reminds me of our voyage from France," said Corinna, with a nervous low-pitched laugh. "How short a time we've known each other, Madeleine, yet it seems like a lifetime! And now it may be years before we can meet again, without even the pleasure of keeping up a correspondence. But I will *not* be gloomy," she continued resolutely, "for you are to marry the man you love, and live in your own country — and with your cousin there, too, safe from the dangers he must have faced eventually, had he remained here to follow that abominable trade. And you say this was by Richard's contriving?"

"I am almost certain of it, by what Jacques hinted. He is one to keep his own counsel, my cousin, but that is understandable, *n'est-ce pas*? Your Sir Richard is a gentleman to be relied upon in all things, I think."

"I don't know why you keep referring to him as *my* Sir Richard," objected Corinna.

"Because he *is* yours, oh, but completely, *chérie*! Do not pretend that you are ignorant of it."

"I can't think what you mean." Madeleine saw by the faint light from the lantern that her friend's face was flushed. "He is a good friend of all my family."

"Friendship, bah! He loves you to distraction — I can tell you, *moi*, for I know what it is to love! And I think perhaps you are not totally indifferent to him, in spite of fancying yourself in love with that Mr Grenville, who is not fitted to clean Sir Richard's boots," declared Madeleine roundly.

Corinna was silent for a moment. Her friend wondered if she had gone too far, but did not relent. Since they were to part at the end of this short journey, she felt she must make some push to assure Corinna's future happiness; of one thing she was convinced, it certainly did not lie with the villainous Grenville.

"I may as well tell you all *that* is long since past," said Corinna, breaking the silence. "If I admit the truth, indeed, I think it was no more than a passing fancy. But as to Richard — oh, I don't know, my dear! I fear you may be mistaken about his feelings towards me — we do nothing but quarrel when we're together, though I freely admit that's my fault, not his. I must have long since given him a disgust of me! And then there is Miss Cheveley, you know. She's so agreeable, not at all like myself — and he's been visiting her home frequently of late."

"Bah! It is you he loves," stated Madeleine firmly. "As for you, Corinna, I think you should ask yourself just why it is you take a perverse pleasure in quarrelling with him. But all that will arrange itself, my dear, and someday — alas, perhaps a long time off! — I may learn that you've found happiness together."

They clung together wordlessly for a moment, scarcely noticing when the cart came to a standstill. A dark figure loomed suddenly over them.

"You are late."

Madeleine recognised her cousin's voice, and detached herself from her friend's embrace. He stared angrily at Corinna.

"What madness is this? Why have you brought Miss Haydon here?"

"I am to blame," said Corinna. "I went to bid good-bye to Madeleine not long before the cart arrived for her, and I thought I might as well come, too, since I'm to return home in it."

"You are too venturesome, mademoiselle," he said severely, helping Madeleine down. "You must return home at once."

He lifted his cousin's baggage out of the cart and was about to turn away when Corinna stretched out her arm to him.

"Help me down, please. I won't stay a moment, I promise, but I want to watch her go—"

He looked as though he would refuse, then shrugged, and helped her to the ground.

"If you must, though it's too dark for you to see us for more than a few yards down the cliff. But pay attention, and don't linger here. You, boy, help the lady back into the cart as soon as I've gone, and then drive her smartly to Friston House. Understood?"

The lad nodded, and Jacques pressed some money into his hand. Then he turned to Madeleine, who was clasped in Corinna's arms. At this final moment of parting, they could find no words to say.

"Come, little one," said Jacques gently. "We must go at once, and so must your friend, else she'll be in grave danger. Goodbye, mademoiselle. Thank you for all you have done for my cousin. Perchance you two may meet again — who knows?"

Madeleine released Corinna and took her cousin's arm.

"God bless you, my dear, dear friend," she said in a broken voice.

"Safe journey, my love — be happy."

Corinna's tones were no steadier than Madeleine's.

She moved to the edge of the cliff, watching as the others began their descent; but tears dimmed her straining eyes and the surrounding darkness soon swallowed up the shadowy forms.

Still she stood there, staring down the dark cliff to the grey luminosity of the sea at its foot, pounding remorselessly against the pebbly beach.

That sea would divide them now, perhaps forever.

CHAPTER TWENTY-FOUR

At about the same time that Corinna was attempting to steal from the house to meet Madeleine, Sir Richard had surreptitiously entered the grounds of Eastdean Place.

He had learnt enough from Jacques Fougeray last night to confirm his suspicions of Grenville's real activities, and to convince him that the man being harboured by Grenville was the wanted French spy. Since the proper authorities could not be alerted until Madeleine was safe away, it was Sir Richard's intention to carry out the arrest himself. Fougeray had promised assistance, having no political involvement with either country, but feeling that he owed some return to Sir Richard. They had laid plans to take the spy at the rendezvous at Birling Gap, when he would be alone.

It was another purpose which had brought Sir Richard here at this hour. Even more important than the capture of the spy was the recovery of the important documents he had stolen. If all went well later, this should be achieved, for the man would be carrying them with him. But this was to hazard all on one throw of the dice, which was not Sir Richard's way. It was reasonable to suppose that the spy would have concealed the papers somewhere in his room until the moment of departure. Sir Richard intended to effect an entry and search that room.

He was not himself familiar with Grenville's house and grounds, but he had learnt a good deal in this way from Laurence while the latter had been keeping watch there. After circling the house stealthily, paying particular attention to the servants' quarters on the ground floor at the back, his patience was rewarded by the discovery of a window left slightly open at the top, in a room near the kitchens.

He quietly eased the window down sufficiently to admit his by no means slight form, finding a foothold on a shelf inside. His boot squelched in some slippery substance on a dish which clattered as he stepped on it. Removing the shutter from a dark lantern he was carrying, he saw that the substance was a blancmange, now a shapeless mess. He grimaced, prudently clearing a space on which to plant the other foot before stepping down on to the floor. Evidently this was the larder.

He pushed open the door, emerging into an unlit passage which he soon discovered led to the kitchens in one direction and the servants' back staircase in the other.

He stood at the foot of the staircase, listening for a moment. Hearing nothing, he allowed himself a brief survey of the stairs before closing the shutter over his lantern and ascending in the dark to the second landing. The passage here was lit, so greater caution was needed. Madeleine had told him that the spy's bedchamber was situated on this floor, the first door on the right opposite the backstairs. He located it easily, but halted on the top stair before crossing to it.

It was as well he did so, for just as he was about to dart towards it, he heard voices approaching from a bend in the passage farther along. Quickly he retreated halfway down the staircase, lying flat against the banister railings, trusting to the darkness for concealment. He set down the lantern on a lower stair and drew a pistol from his pocket.

The voices came nearer until they materialised into two men who halted outside the spy's room. One was Grenville, the other a short, thickset man with a French accent. They had evidently been arguing, for Grenville's voice was querulous.

"No, damned if I'll come down to the Gap with you — where's the point? Everything's fixed right and tight, and my part's done — I want no more of it, I can tell you!"

"You'll come, *mon vieux*," replied the other in a threatening tone. "If anything goes wrong, I want you there to answer for it."

"What the devil d' you mean? This fellow Jack's arrangements never go wrong — he's fixed up scores of crossings. Don't mind telling you I'm sick to death of the business — wish I'd never been fool enough to get involved!"

"But you are involved and don't you forget it. We go together to this Birling Gap, and we'll get there earlier than arranged, too. We'll set out at, say, a quarter to eleven since it will be wiser to go on foot."

Grenville was still protesting as the Frenchman opened the door of the room and pushed him inside.

As it closed behind them, Sir Richard cursed his luck. This alteration in timing could well throw out the plans he and Fougeray had made. If this precious pair set out at a quarter to eleven, they would reach the Gap not more than ten minutes past the hour. And Fougeray had arranged for Madeleine to be there at eleven o'clock, so that he could have her safely stowed away in the boat before trouble started. Now it looked as if Fougeray would have to hustle to get the girl away and return in time to assist at the spy's arrest. The worst of it was, he knew nothing of the change in time.

It looked as though the Frenchman's chances of escape were somewhat higher than they had bargained for; which made it more than ever advisable to lay hands on those papers at once. The devil of it was, he thought, the two might remain in the spy's room until they were ready to set out, thus depriving him of any chance to search it.

But then the door of the spy's room opened and both men emerged.

"Time for a glass of brandy before we go," he heard the Frenchman say. "Devilish cold out at sea — a man needs something to warm him."

They moved briskly off by the way they had come. Sir Richard waited until they were out of sight round the bend in the passage; then moved quietly, pistol in one hand and the lantern in the other, up the stairs and into the room opposite.

It was, as he had expected, unlit, so he had recourse to his lantern. He surveyed the room. All traces of occupation had been removed apart from a small travelling bag which stood on a chair near the door, as if ready to be snatched up when its owner was leaving the house. This looked the most promising place to start.

He opened the bag, which was unlocked, and went carefully through the contents. There was very little, and nothing unexpected. Disappointed, he removed everything carefully on to the floor, then examined the actual lining of the bag. After a few moments, he gave a satisfied grunt. He had discovered a false bottom to the bag.

He lifted the lid, disclosing inside a number of small documents.

He took these out with an exhilaration which quickly evaporated as he subjected them to a quick scrutiny. The defence papers were not among them.

Nevertheless, they were of some value. Even the superficial scanning he was able to give to them showed that they contained information for the French agent's use which would prove of interest to the English authorities. He folded them to a size convenient for stowing away in his pockets. That done, he repacked the bag exactly as he had found it.

He was opening the door to step out into the passage when he heard footsteps approaching. He closed the door quickly, looking around the room for somewhere to hide in case anyone should enter. Seeing another door in the opposite wall, he darted across, pulled it open, and found himself in a small closet. Once inside, he darkened his lantern, but had not quite enough time to close the door completely before someone bearing a candlestick entered the room.

Peering cautiously round the crack in his door, Sir Richard saw that the man was neither Grenville nor the spy, and guessed that it must be Thomson, the valet. Evidently he had been sent to collect the bag, for he did not linger, but at once took it up and went out of the room.

This indicated that the others were about to move. He must be off, too, if he were to arrive ahead of them. He emerged from his hiding place and crossed to the door, ready to open it when he had given Thomson sufficient time to move away.

To his dismay, he heard voices outside. He was ready to dive for cover again when he realised that they were going past the door, not about to enter. A moment later, a few creaks warned him that someone was using the back staircase. Taking a risk of being seen, he silently turned the doorknob and opened the door a fraction so that he could peer round it.

Three figures were descending the stairs, their backs towards him. Their way was lit by the candle carried in the valet's hand. Sir Richard swore softly as he closed the door. They were evidently leaving by the back door; which was his intended exit, and, indeed, the only one to which he could be sure of finding his way from here. There was nothing else for it but to allow a short interval for them to get away, and then to follow with all speed. He would need to watch out for Thomson, as it was certain that the valet would remain in the house.

Doubtless his function now was to lock the rear door after his master had left.

He fumed at the delay, but too much was at stake to risk a confrontation yet. He would wait five minutes and then follow.

This he did. He managed to negotiate the first flight of stairs without too much difficulty in the dark, but was obliged to throw caution to the winds and use his lantern to locate the second. He had just found it and was about to descend, when Thomson, bearing his candle, appeared at the foot.

Sir Richard drew out his pistol.

"Not a sound," he commanded, "if you value your life! Stand still."

The valet obeyed, the candle wavering in his trembling hand.

Sir Richard rapidly descended, the pistol pointing unerringly at his victim, until they stood face to face. The valet's was now an unhealthy pallor.

"Have your master and the other man gone?" he asked. Then, as the valet nodded: "You're certain they've left the house? Speak, man!"

Thomson moistened his lips. "Yes — I — I — shut the door after them but — but a few minutes since—"

"I'm sorry about this," said Sir Richard, as if apologising for a social solecism, "but it does seem the best way if you're not to make yourself a nuisance."

He suddenly pocketed his pistol and lashed out at Thomson's chin with all the strength of a punishing right.

The valet went down like a log, the candlestick falling from his hand and extinguishing itself.

Sir Richard stepped round him, dashed to the rear door, and let himself out.

He began to run.

Corinna was recalled to a sense of her surroundings by the boy with the mule cart jerking impatiently at her arm.

"Miss, miss, come away, do! Jack said not to stay, an' I must get back to the farm, miss, an' I've to tak' ye to Friston first, so I reckon we'd best get started — come along, miss, won't ye?"

She yielded at last to these entreaties, giving one last, lingering look down the cliff before turning to move towards the cart. The boy put out his arms to help her climb up, then paused suddenly, his ears alert.

"Someone's a comin', miss," he informed her in a whisper. "Du'nno who it be, but reckon I won't stay to see. Up wi' ye, then!"

She heard for herself the steady tramp of approaching feet and felt a sudden surge of panic. Could this be the mysterious passenger arriving earlier than expected? Like her companion, she had no desire to discover. Quickly she scrambled up into the cart and almost fell back on to the floor as the lad urged his mule forward.

"Halt! Who goes there?"

The challenge rang out sharply before they had covered more than a few yards. The boy ignored it, frenziedly whipping his beast to greater effort.

Two figures emerged from the gloom. Suddenly a pistol shot rang out, whistling past the boy's ear. Even as he pulled up the cart in panic, one of the figures ran forward to snatch him from his perch and fling him savagely to the ground. He lay there with the breath driven from his body, too terrified to move a limb.

Corinna, cowering down in the cart, uttered a piercing scream as the same man pounced upon her. By the light of the lantern, she saw with alarm that he was the assailant of yesterday.

He dragged her roughly from the cart and pulled back the hood of her cloak to see her face.

"*Diable!*" he exclaimed. "It's your doxy, Grenville!"

The second man rushed towards them, and, trembling, Corinna recognised Fabian Grenville. He pulled her from the Frenchman's grasp.

"For God's sake, what are you doing here, ma'am, alone and at this hour?"

She stared wordlessly into his pale, strained face. Shaken though she was, she realised she could attempt no explanation without betraying Madeleine.

"Hell and the devil, what's to do?" he burst out, as she remained silent. "We'd best put her back in the cart and let the lad take her out of this!"

The spy stepped back a few paces.

"Stand aside, Grenville!" he ordered. "She's meddled enough — we'll see an end of the bitch!"

Terrified, Corinna saw that he held a pistol levelled straight at her heart. All at once, she found her voice and screamed at full pitch.

"No!" shouted Grenville. "For God's sake, no!"

He stepped in front of her.

At the same moment, another figure came hurtling out of the shadows, pistol in hand.

"Halt in the name of the law!"

Half fainting now, Corinna knew it was Richard's voice.

Several things happened together, too swiftly for her to follow in her dazed state.

The spy fired. Grenville, hit, collapsed at her feet. She heard the bark of a second shot, saw the spy spin round towards his opponent, then drop in his tracks, the pistol falling from his hand.

A rush of feet coming up the cliff, and then Jacques Fougeray dashed forward to the cart, a knife glinting in his hand.

"Take a look at 'em, Fougeray," said Sir Richard coolly. "Be with you in a moment."

He went quickly to Corinna, who was staring down petrified at the inert form of Grenville. He placed a strong arm about her, looking anxiously into her face.

"Are you hurt, my dearest? Have you any injury? Tell me, for pity's sake, my love!"

To his immense relief, she managed to shake her head.

"N-no," she said, clinging to him. "I'm unharmed — but Mr Grenville—"

She stared in horror again at that motionless form, and shuddered. Sir Richard's arm tightened about her and she clung to him, shaking from head to foot.

Fougeray, who had gone first to the spy and found that life was extinct, now came to stoop over the other casualty.

"That one's finished," he said briefly. "I've left it to you to search him." After a moment, he straightened up. "This man, too — shot clean through the heart."

Corinna uttered a low moan, and Sir Richard felt her body sagging against him. He lifted her in his arms and placed her gently in the cart. Then he removed his coat to make a pillow for her head.

"Swooned, has she?" asked Fougeray. "Just as well, perhaps. I dare say she'll recover after a good night's rest. Is there anything more I can do to assist, my friend? It did not go quite as planned, but the end's the same."

Sir Richard turned from his anxious contemplation of the prostrate Corinna.

"No, nothing more — the rest is for me to settle. You go now, Fougeray, and my thanks."

"What about you, my lad?" asked Fougeray, as the farm boy, having plucked up his courage after his assailant had been shot, crept back to the cart. "You're all right, eh?"

The boy nodded.

"I'll square accounts with him," said Sir Richard. "I could wish for a more comfortable vehicle in which to convey Miss Haydon home, but it will serve." He held out his hand. "Go now, Fougeray — safe voyage for you both, and a fair future. My regards to mademoiselle."

The Frenchman clasped his hand warmly.

"My good wishes for you, too, *mon ami*. *Adieu* — or it may perhaps be *au revoir* — who knows?"

CHAPTER TWENTY-FIVE

A fortnight later Corinna and Lydia were sitting with their Mama and two younger sisters in the drawing room of their home at Tunbridge Wells. No scene could have been more peacefully domestic, and for once Corinna had no complaint to make about this. She felt, indeed, that she had thoroughly satisfied her appetite for change and adventure, and would now ask for nothing more than a quiet life.

She and Lydia had come to Tunbridge Wells a few days after the violent events at Birling Gap. She shuddered still whenever she recalled that night; but mercifully the soothingly familiar routine of life amidst her family banished for the most part these unpleasant memories. It had been at Sir Richard's suggestion that Lydia had taken her sister home. She had agreed wholeheartedly, especially as Mrs Haydon's recent letters had complained that they were all missing Corinna.

They had seen little of Sir Richard since he had brought Corinna back to Friston House on that fateful night. He had stayed only long enough to place her in Lydia's care, saying that he had much still to do before he could think of sleep, so he would return to his own home for what remained of the night.

He had called briefly on the following day, obviously still much occupied with the aftermath of yesterday's violence, and inquired after Corinna's health. He did not see her, for at Lydia's insistence she was indulging in a protracted lie-in to recuperate after her ordeal. He stayed only long enough to satisfy himself that she had taken no lasting harm, and to recommend an early removal to Tunbridge Wells.

The two sisters had put their heads together in order to present Mama with a carefully expurgated account of the death of Fabian Grenville. They had told her that he had foolishly been involved in some illicit dealings with the local smugglers, and one of them had shot him. Naturally, she was very much shocked, and in the first few days after hearing this dreadful news, she had persisted in exclaiming over it repeatedly in horrified accents.

It was Lydia who succeeded in putting an end to this by saying roundly that the less Corinna heard of the matter, the better.

"Oh, to be sure, of course! How very thoughtless of me, my love! Poor child, do you think she is dreadfully cut up? Of course, you and I both know quite well that she wasn't *truly* in love with him, but I dare say she feels badly, all the same. We must think of some plan to divert her mind. Perhaps I could give an evening party with some dancing — not a *ball*, of course, but just an informal affair. The younger girls would love that, too, wouldn't they? I could invite some of her admirers — it may be that she will turn to one or other of them, now that there is positively no hope of—" She broke off, slightly embarrassed at what she had been about to say. "Well, at any rate," she concluded, "I will certainly avoid all mention of *his* name for the future! I'm grateful, my dear, that you did just give me a hint, for I fear I *do* tend to run on at times."

Lydia was tolerably certain that, although the shock of Grenville's death had naturally somewhat subdued her sister's spirits, she was not grieving for him as the only man she could ever love. For some time now — in fact, ever since Corinna's return from France — Lydia had noticed a change of attitude.

On several occasions lately she had tried to invite her sister's confidence, so far without success.

The two of them were shopping in the Pantiles parade one morning, a pleasant colonnaded walk lined with trees, when they saw a familiar figure strolling towards them. Corinna, losing her clutch on a bandbox she was carrying, started impetuously forward.

"Richard, oh, *Richard!*" she exclaimed, extending both her arms, an eager expression on her face.

He took her hands in his, smiling down at her with his blue eyes alight.

"You've dropped your parcel," he said, releasing her after a moment and stooping to retrieve the bandbox. "How d'you do, Lydia? Have you had news of John yet?"

Lydia took his outstretched hand, noticing with surprise as she did so that Corinna was actually blushing.

"Oh, yes, a letter came yesterday, forwarded from home. I have it with me, in my reticule, and I'll read it to you — that is, parts of it," she amended, blushing herself.

"Then I suggest we sit down on that bench," he went on, indicating a vacant seat outside one of the shops. "Did you bring the carriage, or did you walk across the common?"

"We brought the carriage, of course. I am not near so addicted to walking as Corinna, recollect! It's to take us up in half an hour, so there's time enough for you to hear John's letter."

They seated themselves in the shade of the colonnade, and Lydia gave her husband's news. Stripped of its more personal content, the letter was not a lengthy one. John's ship was at present taking part in the blockade of the French Channel ports, but might sail for the Mediterranean eventually. He was not only in the best of health, but obviously glad to be in action again; although some of the sentences which Lydia refrained from reading may have ameliorated this impression.

Sir Richard listened, questioned, and commented, then said that he had himself already written to his brother, but so far received no reply.

"Oh, but there's a message for you!" cried Lydia. "As there is for all my family, too. He says — 'Give my best to old Richard, and I hope to see him spliced by my first leave.' There! But he doesn't say to whom," she added with a mischievous grin.

"Hm," commented Sir Richard dismissively. "And now perhaps you will want to hear my news."

He was taken aback by the startled look which Corinna turned suddenly upon him.

"It is merely," he said, in mild surprise, "an account of what followed upon the scenes of violence in which you were unfortunately involved, Corinna. But if you'd prefer me to be silent" — he studied her face intently — "pray say so at once."

"No, no," she insisted. "I thought perhaps you were about to speak of — but no matter for that! Lyddy and I are curious to know what happened afterwards, and it's better you should tell us while we're alone, for we've kept most of it from Mama. Except, of course," she added, in a weaker tone, "the one fact which *had* to be told."

"Grenville's death?" he asked gently.

She nodded.

"Very wise, if I may say so. Have you seen any of the notices in the newspapers? They were likewise discreet. For security reasons, the powers that be kept the full facts from the journalists, so there was no widespread scandal."

"What happened to the local smugglers?" asked Corinna. "Have they been apprehended?"

He shook his head. "There was no way of tracing them for certain. The one man taken into custody was Thomson, the valet, as there was evidence enough that he was involved. The smuggling fraternity in our neighbourhood are wisely lying very low. Dragoons have been riding by night through the village and the surrounding area, and a Revenue cutter is keeping watch off Birling Gap. There'll be no more ferrying of spies in those parts, and all smuggling will stop for many a long day."

"But did Madeleine and her cousin get safe away? You haven't heard that they were caught?"

Her voice trembled.

"I am confident that they succeeded in escaping," he reassured her. "I was so closely concerned with the authorities in this affair that I should most certainly have been informed had they been captured. But I've heard nothing, and it's a fortnight since. Rest assured, my dear girl, that your little friend is now safely in France."

She breathed a deep sigh. "Please God it may be so!"

"But how did Grenville first become involved in that dreadful business?" demanded Lydia, who had so far been listening silently while she stowed her precious letter away in her reticule. "And when did you first suspect him, Richard, for one sees now that you did?"

"It happened quite by chance. While we were in Paris, I visited Perrin's gaming rooms one evening, chiefly to keep an eye on young Laurie. Grenville was there, and I happened to overhear a conversation in the cloakroom between him and another man, a Frenchman whom he seemed not to know at all. The Frenchman evidently knew a deal about Grenville, however — that he was short of money and that he owned a house on the coast of Sussex. He hinted that there were easier ways of getting into funds than" — he hesitated, then continued — "than those which Grenville had been unsuccessfully pursuing lately, and told him that Napoleon paid well. That was all I heard, but it was enough to give me food for thought. My friend at the embassy had told me that Boney's agents used the gaming houses for their intrigues, but at that time I could not quite see why they should be interested in Grenville."

"Oh!" exclaimed Corinna. "But later, of course, when we were back in England, and — he — had settled in the house, and appeared to have plenty of money at his disposal—"

"Exactly so. Especially when reports came to me from your little French friend of mysterious late-night visitors, and Laurence discovered a connection with the smugglers. I began to put two and two together, and a vastly unpleasant sum it made."

"You don't know — I never told anyone this, except Madeleine — but he tried to pretend to me that he was giving shelter to *English* agents. You see, I went to the summerhouse at Eastdean Place to leave a message for Madeleine, and that dreadful man was there — the spy, I mean. He attacked me, and then Mr Grenville came and sent him off. That was when he told me this — this untruth. At the time, I didn't know what to believe."

"Did that occur before I brought you news of the French spy?" asked Sir Richard.

She nodded. "Yes, you told us that same evening. I wanted to confide in you, but I felt bound by a promise I had made to him. I was so uncertain what I ought to do — so miserable!" she burst out.

"I guessed you were keeping something back. But never mind that now. It's all over, and we may forget about it. I only brought the subject up because I thought you would forget the more readily if you knew what had happened subsequently. I may be wrong in that — I don't know."

"See, here is our carriage," interrupted Lydia. "Will you drive back with us, Richard, or is your own vehicle at hand?"

"Why, no, I went first to your house and left my curricle there. But surely it's a shame to sit in a carriage in such perfect weather for walking? Why do we not load it with your parcels and stroll back together across the common?"

Corinna agreed enthusiastically; and Lydia was about to fall in good-naturedly with the plan when something in Sir Richard's expression caused her to change her mind.

"You two may walk, by all means, but as for myself, I declare I'm fagged to death with trailing around the shops! I'll see you at home later, in time for nuncheon."

Having helped her into the carriage with her own and Corinna's purchases on the seat beside her, he turned to offer Corinna his arm.

They walked along more or less in silence until they had left the busy streets for a tree-shaded path through the common, quiet save for the twittering birds.

"There's something I must ask you, Corinna," he began almost abruptly. "I don't wish to wound you, God knows, but I must have an answer. It is this — how deeply do you grieve for Grenville? Is it at all possible that a little time may heal your loss?"

He was startled by the sudden flash of anger in her golden eyes.

"How stupid you all are!" she flung at him. "You, Mama, Lydia — you all persist in thinking that I am — was, I should say — as infatuated with him as I was foolish enough to be last year! Of course I am grieved, as anyone of feeling must be at the sudden death of an acquaintance — more especially when there is violence connected with it! Such shocks, though mercifully rare, are not easily overcome."

She paused and he nodded, waiting to see if she would have anything to add to this.

"But as for a more — intense — personal grief, a sense of irreparable loss, that I certainly do *not* feel," she continued. Then, almost defiantly: "Does that answer your question?"

"Indeed it does," he said woodenly.

They walked along in silence for another few minutes, meeting no one on their way, while she glanced covertly at his inscrutable profile.

"If you must know," she said in a milder tone, "I have realised for some time that it was all a silly girl's nonsense, and that the man I'd been attracted to was only a figure of my fancy, vastly different from the reality."

"When did you discover that?"

She noticed he was still looking straight ahead, keeping his face in profile. She pondered for a moment.

"It's difficult to say. When we were in Paris, I think. But there's a regrettable streak of obstinacy in my disposition" — she gave a little laugh — "and I don't flatter myself that you haven't noticed it! At first I wouldn't admit my mistake, even to myself. Later, however, I caught myself out in several ways. You remember when Laurie first suggested that — he" — evidently she found it difficult to speak the name — "might be involved with the smugglers?"

He nodded, but did not interrupt.

"Well, I was quite ready to credit that, which shows I had no illusions about his character. Yet twelve months ago, had anyone *dared* to breathe a single word against him—! And then, you know, when he was paying me attentions, quite particular in the end, I assure you—"

She saw a muscle move in his cheek, but still he said nothing. He silence began to pique her, but she tried to ignore this, intent now on unburdening herself.

"I only half believed anything he said — less than half! — whether it was on that subject or when he tried to convince me that he was working in British espionage. It was then that I freely admitted to myself that I no longer cared at all for him, or even *liked* him — and that I'd been deluding myself all along."

She stole another look at him. Surely he must say something *now*? If there had been any substance in Madeleine's assertion that he loved her, Corinna, and not Frances Cheveley — if he had meant anything at all by his endearments as he supported her in his arms on the cliff that night — then surely he would speak?

Suddenly she knew how very much she loved him, with the mature love of a woman and not the green sickness of a young girl. And she wanted him to declare himself hers — wanted it desperately, so that frustrated longing boiled up within her, exploding at last in anger.

She wrenched her arm from his and turned on him with the familiar golden fire in her eyes.

"Have you nothing to say — nothing? I tell you all the innermost secrets of my heart, while you stand there like a wooden image, with never a word of — of understanding or sympathy? You're an odious, unfeeling creature, Richard Beresford, and I never want to set eyes on you again!"

His control snapped suddenly. He turned towards her, clasping her in a strong, almost rough, embrace.

"By God, Corinna, I can take no more! Is *this* answer enough for you?"

He kissed her with all the pent-up ardour of past years.

She yielded in ecstasy, tightening her arms about him.

"Oh, Richard, Richard, that's what I've wanted you to do all along, whenever we've quarrelled!"

He drew a little apart from her.

"Do you mean to say," he asked incredulously, "that *you've* fallen in love with *me*? I've loved you since you were a saucy little chit in the schoolroom — but that you should reciprocate, never entered my wildest dreams."

"But it's true," she insisted, nestling close to him once more. "I do love you, and, what's more, I think it's been going on for a very long time. Oh, Richard, how happy I am! I'll never want to quarrel with you again, I promise!"

He kissed her once more, this time lightly, and smiled.

"We'll see about that," he said cautiously. "But if by any chance you should happen to forget that somewhat rash promise, my dearest, at least I'll know how to put an end to our tiff, won't I?"

She chuckled delightedly. Then hearing someone approaching along the path, she moved reluctantly out of his arms to walk demurely enough at his side, even though her bonnet *was* slightly askew.

A NOTE TO THE READER

It's wonderful to see my mother's books available again and being enjoyed by what must surely be a new audience from that which read them when they were first published. My brother and I can well remember our mum, Alice, writing away on her novels in the room we called the library at home when we were teenagers. She generally laid aside her pen — there were no computers in those days, of course — when we returned from school but we knew she had used our absence during the day to polish off a few chapters.

One of the things I well remember from those days is the care that she took in ensuring the historical accuracy of the background of her books. I am sure many of you have read novels where you are drawn out of the story by inaccuracies in historical facts, details of costume or other anachronisms. I suppose it would be impossible to claim that there are no such errors in our mother's books; what is undoubted is that she took great care to check matters.

The result was, and is, that the books still have an appeal to a modern audience, for authenticity is appreciated by most readers, even if subconsciously. The periods in which they set vary: the earliest is *The Georgian Rake*, which must be around the middle of the 18th century; and some are true Regency romances. But Mum was not content with just a love story; there is always an element of mystery in her books. Indeed, this came to the fore in her later writings, which are historical detective novels.

There's a great deal more I could say about her writings but it would be merely repeating what you can read on her website at **www.alicechetwyndley.co.uk**. To outward appearances, our mother was an average housewife of the time — for it was usual enough for women to remain at home in those days — but she possessed a powerful imagination that enabled her to dream up stories that appealed to many readers at the time — and still do, thanks to their recent republication.

If you have enjoyed her novels, we would be very grateful if you could leave a review on **Amazon** or **Goodreads** so that others may also be tempted to lose themselves in their pages.

Richard Ley, 2018.

Sapere Books is an exciting new publisher of brilliant fiction and popular history.

To find out more about our latest releases and our monthly bargain books visit our website:
saperebooks.com